The Library
of
Indiana Classics

The Christmas Story.

How
Dear
To My
Heart

by EMILY KIMBROUGH

DRAWINGS BY HELEN E. HOKINSON

INDIANA UNIVERSITY PRESS
Bloomington and Indianapolis
in cooperation with the
Delaware County Historical Alliance

First Midland Book Edition 1991

The Library of Indiana Classics is available in a special
clothbound library-quality edition and in a paperback edition.

Manufactured in the United States of America

Library of Congress Cataloging-in-Publicatiion Data
Kimbrough, Emily, date.
  How dear to my heart / by Emily Kimbrough ; drawings by Helen E.
Hokinson. — 1st Midland book ed.
    p. cm. — (The Library of Indiana Classics)
  ISBN 0-253-33120-X (cloth). — ISBN 0-253-20685-5 (paper)
  1. Kimbrough, Emily, date —Biography—Youth. 2. Authors,
American—20th century—Biography—Youth. 3. Muncie (Ind.)—Social
life and customs. 4. Indiana—Biography. I. Title. II. Series.
PS3521.I457Z464 1991
818'.5403—dc20
[B]   91-10238

1 2 3 4 5   95 94 93 92 91

To Charles Mayberry Kimbrough

Of Muncie, Indiana,

And His Son Hal

Who Is My Father

Introduction

Emily Kimbrough was born on October 23, 1898, at 715 East Washington Street, Muncie, Indiana. She was the first child of Hal Curry Kimbrough and his wife, Charlotte ("Lottie") Wiles Kimbrough, formerly of Indianapolis. The Wiles family was well known in Indianapolis, where they lived beside the Benjamin Harrisons. There are some delightful anecdotes of the feisty Wiles family in the pages that follow.

Hal Kimbrough was the oldest of three sons born to Charles Mayberry Kimbrough and Margaret Curry Kimbrough. The C. M. Kimbrough family live in a grand home at 615 East Washington Street, just a block west from Miss Kimbrough's birthplace. Emily wrote extensively about her beloved grandparents and their home, which she called the "Big House." Charles M. Kimbrough was the president of the Indiana Bridge Company. All three sons, Hal, Frank, and Lloyd, were at various times president of the Indiana Bridge Company and were all active in the civic life of Muncie.

The Kimbrough family was highly involved in the cultural, social, and political aspects of Muncie. Charles M. Kimbrough was a state senator and widely known for his political and civic activities. The arts were especially important to the Kimbroughs, and they were significant in the development of early associations for art, music, and theatre. The love of the arts was implanted early in the life of Emily Kimbrough, and she remained a staunch supporter of all forms of art throughout her life.

When Emily was eleven years old, her immediate family—including her new brother, Charles, born in Muncie in December of 1904—moved to Chicago. Some of the friends she made at this time were to become lifelong associates. *The Innocents from Indiana*, published in 1950, is the story of the family's move to Chicago and Emily's not-too-easy adjustment to life in a big city after her childhood in Muncie, Indiana.

A liberal arts graduate of Bryn Mawr College with the class of 1921, Emily Kimbrough became the editor of *Fashions of the Hour*, a publication of Marshall Field and Company in Chicago, and worked there until 1928. Later she became the fashion editor and eventually the managing editor of *Ladies Home Journal*, and resided in the Philadelphia area. Her writing—appearing in virtually every leading magazine in the country—addressed a great range of topics. She was in demand as a speaker, and she travelled extensively. *It Gives Me Great Pleasure*, published in 1948, is a delightful recounting of her experiences while on lecture tours.

After graduating from Bryn Mawr, Emily Kimbrough and her long-time friend Cornelia Otis Skinner travelled to Europe. The numerous entertaining adventures of these young ladies provided material for *Our Hearts Were Young and Gay*, co-authored by Cornelia and Emily in 1942. The book became an immediate bestseller, and the movie version of the book appeared shortly thereafter. War-time audiences loved the light-hearted movie, and the demand for more writing of this type produced a series of sixteen books authored by Emily Kimbrough.

Virtually all of Miss Kimbrough's books became bestsellers during the post-World War II era. Her writing style was clean and crisp, and her delightful sense of humor was surpassed only by her ability as a storyteller. Her last book was published in 1976, and her last published writing was the introduction to *A Suite of Poems* by her childhood friend in Muncie, Elisabeth Ball.

Miss Kimbrough was married in 1928 to John Wrench, an Englishman. The couple had twin daughters, Alis and Margaret. Alis McCurdy is a judge of Olympic figure-skating and a referee of world-class tennis. She lives in California. Margaret Kuhn presently lives in Connecticut and is the former coach of the Danish figure-skating team. Both daughters are witty and share their mother's interest in living life as intensely as possible.

New York City was the home of Emily Kimbrough, although she spent summers at her beautiful oceanside home in Watch Hill, Rhode Island. An energetic individual, Miss Kimbrough entertained constantly. She believed that one must contribute to life rather than take from it. Her zest for living and her appreciation of the arts had a profound impact on her niece Linda Kimbrough, a Chicago-based actress, and on her nephew Charles Kimbrough, currently starring in the television series "Murphy Brown."

Miss Kimbrough maintained an active lifestyle until her death at her home in New York on February 10, 1989.

How Dear To My Heart was Emily's third book. It is the story of her early childhood in Muncie in the early years of this century. Her nephew Charles Kimbrough, in an interview in 1989, stated, "A good part of her always remained 'the little girl from Muncie.' "[1] Emily expressed great fondness for Muncie in interviews. "It was a great advantage to a child in a small town. . . . There was a sense of familiarity among people, a sense that you're part of the community. In Muncie there was a sense of being encompassed. I daresay there were small towns in this country where the meanness that Sinclair Lewis wrote about in 'Main Street' existed. But as a child I was only aware of the warmth."[2] "I wanted to write about the foibles of human beings, the absurdities and the poignancy. I want people to say 'That's just the sort of thing that happens to me.' "[3] She expressed the feeling of never wanting to grow away from her roots.

The reprinting of *How Dear To My Heart* by Indiana University Press in cooperation with the Delaware County Historical Alliance was made possible in part by those who contributed to the Emily Kimbrough Memorial Fund at the time of her death. It is with gratitude that we recognize the significance of those who honor Miss Kimbrough in a way that she would have chosen.

We invite you to revel in the nostalgic tales of a bygone era and to join in the remembrances of one who became dear to the hearts of millions throughout the world.

Harold L. Caldwell
Authorized Biographer
Muncie, Indiana
November 10, 1990

---

1. *Muncie Star*, August 6, 1989, attributed to Charles Kimbrough.
2. *St. Louis Post-Dispatch*, December 1, 1985, attributed to Emily Kimbrough.
3. *Muncie Star*, May 1, 1970, attributed to Emily Kimbrough.

Foreword

In these pages I shall not write an autobiography. I shall try only to write something about a happy childhood in America. A childhood that was happy in great part, I think, because it was spent in a little town, where I was not a stranger to anyone. And so I am setting down these things, partly out of a debt of affection to the town, and partly because I would like to say over, for those of us who remember them, some of the things which we shall never see nor hear again. The lamp on the newel post lighted with a wax taper held high in the Winter dusk. The gas fire which burned against an asbestos shield in my grandfather's den. The used carbon from the street corner lamps that made good chalk for marking hopscotch squares. The street cry of fresh lye hominy and horseradish. And the squeak of wagon wheels on the snow.

I shall not, I know, be accurate, because I shall not even try to verify my memories. This is no historic chronicle of a period. It is only an effort to say aloud some of the things which the smell of burning leaves in the Fall brings back to my mind every year.

How
Dear
To My
Heart

Chapter One

Grandmother Kimbrough called our house one evening about six o'clock. I was washing my hands for supper and I heard Mother answer, because the telephone was in the back hall just across from the bathroom door. It hung so high on the wall that, stretching up to reach the mouthpiece, she always sounded a little breathless. Whenever I talked into it, I had to stand on a chair. All children did. There was a calendar hanging in our kitchen that showed a little girl with yellow curls, and wearing only a pair of panties. She was standing on a chair, and saying into the telephone, so the printing underneath read,

"Is 'oo there, Santa Claus?"

I listened to Mother's conversation, of course, and in a minute or two it was well evident to me that something was going on. I heard her say,

"We'll come right up; Hal's home. Don't worry, Mother."

And she hung up.

I whisked out the side door and hid behind the syringa bushes.

Grandfather's house was in the next block. I don't suppose in that flat Indiana landscape there was sufficient difference in elevation to be discernible to the naked eye, but it always seemed to me that Grandfather's house was on the top of a hill. Certainly it was higher than our house and bigger. In fact, it was known in the family as the big house. My Uncle Frank, Daddy's younger brother, and Aunt Helen lived a

1

block beyond us and over one, on Main Street. Uncle Lloyd, Daddy's youngest brother, and Aunt Huda lived next door to Uncle Frank. We always talked about going to Uncle Frank's, or Uncle Lloyd's, but never to Grandfather's. We always said the big house. I thought it was necessarily bigger than ours, because grandparents lived in it. I thought when you were very little you lived in a little house, but when you got bigger your family moved. By the time you were grown up and had children, your parents, being grand-parents, moved into a big house. My best friend, Betty Ball, lived in a big house herself. I explained that to myself, and to her, by the assurance that she must be adopted, and that her foster parents had real grandchildren somewhere. The peo-ple she called Mother and Father must actually be *grand-parents,* with real grandchildren somewhere, or they wouldn't live in a big house. It haunted Betty, and annoyed her mother considerably. She was my mother's closest friend, and exactly her age. But it satisfied my sense of justice and the fitness of things.

Mother and Daddy came out the front door, and hurried up the street. I let them get a little ahead of me, and then scuttled after them. It was early Spring, but chilly. Mother had snatched her golf cape off the hat-rack in the vestibule, and was hooking it at the throat as they passed me. I had not stopped to put on any kind of a coat lest I be caught, but I was too excited to feel cold. I knew something was up, and I knew that if I *were* caught I would be given a sharp·spank in the rear and sent home. This made the suspense almost unbearable. I passed the Ross's house safely—they were our next door neighbors—and then the Vatets'. After that there was a bad.stretch, because there was a vacant field with no protecting shrubbery—nothing to hide behind until clear across Vine Street where Lydia Rich's house stood on the corner.

When Mother and Daddy reached the corner, they saw my two uncles and aunts hurrying along Vine Street, and waited for them. By the time they had all met and started off together, they were so busy talking that it was safe for me to pass the field and cross the street behind them. I was not allowed to cross the street alone, so that if I had been discovered then, I could expect the application of Daddy's bedroom slipper, but not one of them looked back. And by the time we had passed the Richs' and reached the big house itself, I was at their heels like a puppy. They stopped so abruptly in fact, that I very nearly walked up the back of Mother's legs before I could stop myself. She turned around, saw me, and all she said was,

"Out of the way, dear," and pushed me a little, nowhere in particular.

I knew then that whatever had stopped them must be awful, and I raced around in front of them with my heart pounding. I thought it must be something dead on the sidewalk, so I put my hands over my eyes and then looked down between them, but I couldn't see anything. I took my hands away and still I couldn't see anything. I looked back at the family, all of them, and they were staring into the street. There, against the curb, right at the carriage block, was a great, black *thing*. It had a top, with straps at the corners to tie it down. There was a front seat and a back seat. Far in front of the front seat were shining brass lamps. I could not imagine what the contraption was for, unless it was some kind of a couch to go in the Turkish corner of the library, except that it had big wheels.

Grandmother Kimbrough stood on the carriage block, with her back to the *thing*.

Barely five feet two, never weighing more than ninety-six pounds, she was as quick and sharp as a dragon-fly. Her dark eyes were flashing from one member of the family to another.

She pushed up her hair off her forehead in a nervous gesture, that soft brown hair which was a constant exasperation to her.

"Why can't it turn gray, the pesky thing?" I heard her demand frequently. "Every respectable woman my age has gray hair. People will think I touch it up."

She folded her arms tight across her chest, a Napoleon on the carriage block I would remember her.

"Your father," she said grimly, "has bought an auto*mo*bile."

Grandfather was standing at the head of the *thing*. He looked very handsome, I thought, and not excited. I had *never* seen him look excited, nor even worried. Once I had heard him say to Uncle Frank, "If you're worrying about that, Frank, then I'll *stop* worrying. One is enough."

People frequently told me that my grandfather was a very distinguished looking man. He said, when I repeated it to him, that it meant he had a very large nose. He had brown eyes, too, very dark brown, a broad forehead, and more respectable hair than Grandmother's. It *had* turned gray, with white on top, like a blackboard that has recently been wiped over lightly with the chalk eraser. His mustache matched. He was not remarkably tall, but his shoulders were broad and straight, like a soldier's. That, I thought, was because he had been in the Civil War when he was eighteen and had been taught to march. When we walked down town, he spoke to everybody we saw.

"Hello, Mr. C. M.," or just "C. M.," people would call back, even from across the street.

He waved at that moment to me, and I waved back just a little, so as not to be noticed. He smiled at all of us and then looked at Grandmother, and then turned back and smiled at us again. I knew he was feeling exactly the way I was— pleased and scared.

Everybody started talking at once. Aunt Huda said you

"Your father," she said grimly, *"has bought an automobile."*

could get coats with bonnets and veils to match. They kept
the dust off, and were the latest style. She was going to write
to her sister Bertha in New York and ask her to send her an
outfit. Aunt Helen was talking to Grandmother, telling her
not to be upset, that it would be lovely. She had heard they
were very safe, and she knew that Father Kimbrough would
be careful. The boys—that is, my father and my two uncles, but
I called them that because everyone else did—started over to
the automobile itself. They were talking about machinery.
Grandfather called out,

"Mr. Lockhart, I would like you to meet my sons, Hal and
Frank and Lloyd."

I had not seen that there was somebody on the couch; but
a man climbed down from it, and was introduced to us. He
had driven the automobile from the factory and was going
to stay for two weeks to teach Grandfather, and see that it
was all right. He led the boys to the front and opened it up.
They were all talking at once, and pretty soon they lay down
on their backs and wiggled underneath. Grandmother was
saying to the daughters-in-law—I always called them that,
too, because everyone else did——

"It was that play we saw in Indianapolis, *The Man from
Home,* that did it. Your father got it in his mind the moment
he saw that same auto*mo*bile on the stage."

Grandfather interrupted.

"A Haynes, made in Kokomo. A good *Indiana* product, and
you are not to worry, Margaret."

And then, of course, it had to happen. Mother saw me
again and recognized me. She didn't scold, which was astonishing, but she fussed. She took off her golf cape and wrapped
it around me—I was always being enveloped in that plaid-
lined, woolen garment, with the hood jerked down so that
I couldn't see—and Daddy carried me home over his shoulder. He turned me over to Zoe for my supper and to go to

bed, and that was the last of the excitement I saw. As I left, Grandfather was asking if anyone would like to take a drive, and Grandmother was the only one declining. I missed, too, what happened the next day, but both grandparents told it so many times during the later years of motoring, that I learned every word and gesture. A different version from each of them, of course.

Early in the morning my grandfather rode out to his factory in the machine, the trained expert, Mr. Lockhart, at the wheel. Some time later, about ten o'clock, he telephoned my grandmother and asked if she had been to market. She said that Noah, who was the hired man, was just bringing around Prince. Well, Grandfather told her, if she would care to drive down town in the new auto instead, he and Mr. Lockhart would come for her in about twenty minutes. A mental conflict must have rocked her. There was the danger of the infernal machine, the fact that the night before she had declared she would never set foot in it and Grandfather could go back with it to Kokomo, the knowledge that it was the first one in the town, and the recollection of Aunt Huda saying that it was the most stylish thing you could have, everyone in the East was getting one, her sister Bertha had told her so.

When Grandfather arrived about half an hour later, Prince was back in the barn, and Grandmother was standing on the carriage block. At the sight of him, however, she jumped off and backed away, because *he* was at the wheel and the mechanic from Kokomo was sitting beside him.

"Charles," Grandmother said, "I will not put my foot in this carriage, with you driving. Why, you don't know anything about the crazy thing."

Grandfather told her that he had been driving that morning for two hours, and that Mr. Lockhart considered him extremely apt. Furthermore, he did, after all, build bridges and

might therefore be supposed to know something about machinery. The steering contrivance was not unlike driving a
horse, once you accustomed yourself to minor differences.
But if Grandmother were nervous she had better have Prince
brought around again.

Grandmother climbed into the back seat and sat down.

"I will die with you," she said with obscure menace, "and
you will always be sorry."

She bounced herself down on the black leather cushion with
all the vehemence of her ninety-six pounds and slammed
the door, thwarting Mr. Lockhart, who had come round to
perform that little courtesy.

Mr. Lockhart reported to Grandfather that she was safely
aboard, and Grandfather recited aloud the steps toward putting the machine in motion. The left foot down, the right
hand over and back, the right hand then on the steering
wheel throttle. And with that a roar convulsed the machine
so that it sprang into the air, and stopped dead. Mr. Lockhart got out, went around in front, released an iron bar
from a leather loop, ground it a few times and the engine
roared again. Grandmother was already out and on her way
back to the house. But Mr. Lockhart coaxed her in again.
Grandfather called out that he knew exactly the cause of the
mishap. It was not the fault of the engine but of his own mis-
judgment of the allotment of gasoline. The machine moved
ahead once more, in jumps, but it kept going. Grandmother
grabbed the carriage strap nearest her. They turned the corner on Monroe Street, and she held on with both hands.

A great many people saw them go up Main Street, and
witnessed the unusual behavior of Mr. Meeks, the butter and
egg man. He was a sturdy man with a round face that was
almost as red in the Winter as in the Summer. His hands were
red, too, with cracks running up and down across them on
both sides. He was a farmer and worked hard but he loved

to tell jokes and to laugh, slapping his big red hand down as
if he were spanking himself when he was especially tickled.
Once a week he brought in butter and eggs to regular cus-
tomers. When the automobile with Grandfather driving it
passed him, he was just getting out of his buggy at the house
next to Mr. Bernard's little store. The horse went up over the
sidewalk into the yard and one of the shafts of the buggy
got stuck between the fence palings. Grandfather called out
that he was distressed but couldn't stop. People who didn't
see it could scarcely believe what Mr. Meeks did. He turned
around in the yard and shook his fist after Grandfather.
Grandmother had her eyes closed in such angry determination that she didn't see it.

Of course Grandmother knew every inch of the way by
heart. A railroad track ran along the first cross street beyond
Mr. Bernard's little store. This was a branch line of the Penn-
sylvania Railroad and carried only freight but it did cut right
across the town and people always drew in their horses to
look up and down before they crossed the track. Grandfather
didn't draw in the machine. He was concerned about Mr.
Meeks' horse being stuck in the fence and not quite sure,
furthermore, of the process of stopping, so he just bumped
over the tracks without even slowing down. It jarred Grandmother but she kept her eyes closed. Fortunately there wasn't
a freight train coming.

The stores began on the other side of the railroad track.
They were low frame buildings, most of them, sometimes
with a cement front and a big window to make the store look
more stylish. The street was wide but from the railroad track
on there were no trees. All the way into the center of town
it was bare—dusty and hot in Summer, muddy at other sea-
sons. There were hitching posts along the curb on either side
and generally some horses and buggies or wagons waiting.
Grandfather passed them safely. The Kirby House, a hotel,

stood on the corner a few blocks beyond the railroad tracks. The building was higher than any near it. Mostly men hung around this hotel and in the Summer they sat in a row on wooden armchairs out in front on the sidewalk. There was a cuspidor between every two chairs and the men tilted their chairs back against the front wall of the hotel and watched the people go by. Grandfather passed the hotel and the men cheered. Even if Grandmother's eyes had been open she would have looked away. Walking down town, she would have taken the other side of the street.

There were saloons in that block, too. One of the saloons was made to look like a log cabin and had sawdust under the swinging door. I never could see far enough inside to know how it looked there, though I always squatted down and tried to. There were two drug stores on that side of the street also, and a boys' clothing store with life-sized wax figures in the window. Mr. Hummel's bakery was on that side, too. Walking along, you could get in one block a warm sugar and cinnamon smell from the bakery, a sharp tingling odor from the drug stores, and a sour, musty smell from the saloons. I consider it not only the preferable side of the street, but one of the most interesting stretches in the whole town. The other side of the street had the best market in town—the Sterling Cash Grocery. Above it was the best club in town, too—the Commercial Club. That was where the children's dancing classes were held and most of the grown-up dances, too. People gave parties there. If you were a member, you could watch parades from its front windows.

The next corner, at Main and Walnut Streets was the busiest intersection in town. On Saturdays a policeman stood there all day. So many farmers came into town that the wagons and buggies were always getting snarled up. The policeman had to tell them when they could go. The buggy wheels were always getting caught, too, in the trolley track on Main Street, especially where it turned into Walnut. The policeman had to help pull them out. The dry-goods stores were on Walnut Street—Vatet's and McNaughton's. There were several buildings more than two stories high. It was the heart of what we called "down town," or "up street."

Grandfather came all the way up Main Street with no trouble; none of the horses along the curb shied; he didn't get caught in the trolley track nor have any difficulty about the trolley. The trolley wasn't even in sight. He was very pleased when he got to the corner of Main and Walnut. He even took one hand off the steering wheel to wave at the policeman, whose mouth dropped wide open at the sight of this vehicle. That pleased Grandfather, too. So he turned around and said loudly and cheerfully, "Where do you wish to go, Margaret?"

His voice was so loud and so close that it *made* her open her eyes, and when she saw that his face was turned toward *her*, and not out toward the *road*, she screamed at him,

"Mr. Topps's, Mr. Topps's!"

The shrillness of her tone and her agitation must, in turn, have startled him, for he jumped perceptibly as he turned his head back to the front again. And in the passage he caught sight of Mr. Topps's butcher shop. With a sweep that would have brought around the mighty *Oceanic*, "Greyhound of the Seas," he swung the wheel, and the machine responded. Up over the curb they went, across the sidewalk, and, cleaving a sharp, broad wake, straight through Mr. Topps's plate glass window to the very dot of their destination, the meat counter itself. There, shuddering, the carriage stopped.

Mr. Topps stood on the other side of the counter about two feet away from the front lamps, his cleaver upheld in his right hand, his eyes staring, his teeth bared in an unnatural grin. There *had* been two or three other people in the shop when the conveyance approached the window, but the sight of Mr. Topps's face had caused them to turn and see what was coming upon them. So they too were now on the far side of the counter with him.

When the clatter of falling glass stopped, Grandfather spoke out of the awesome silence.

"This, Margaret," he announced, "is where you said you wanted to come."

Mr. Lockhart went back to the factory about two weeks later, assuring the family that Grandfather and the automobile were now completely to be trusted with one another. Grandfather celebrated the occasion by inviting the County Commissioners to ride out with him, and inspect the site for a new bridge. I was allowed to go, too, though Grandmother thought it was terrible to allow a *child* to ride in the automobile. I sat up in front between Grandfather and Mr. McCormick. I wasn't in the least scared, but I was very excited.

The Commissioners were tickled with the invitation, too; nobody but the expert mechanic had ridden with Grandfather since his excursion into Mr. Topps's. They dressed themselves up, Grandfather said, as if they were going out to the cemetery to hear the Decoration Day speeches, instead of over to Selma to look at a creek. He himself wore a long tan linen coat over his suit; Grandmother had bought it in Indianapolis at L. S. Ayers' and told him it was called a duster. He wore a cap with a visor, pulled well down, to shade his eyes, and he also wore a muffler around his neck under angry protest. But Grandmother said rushing the way he did, stirring up a wind, would give him an attack of quinsy.

The road we drove along was dirt, of course, pointing straight to the far horizon. On either side, the fields were black with fresh-turned soil opened to the sun by the first Spring plowing. I knew that the oak leaves must be the size of squirrels' ears, because that is when the farmers say it is time to plant corn, but I didn't see any oak leaves. The throttle was up to thirteen miles an hour. The warm wind rushing through the automobile made my eyes water so that I couldn't see much of anything. But Grandfather did point out a big willow tree with leaves, he said, like a fine spray that had dropped down on it. And I made out a patch of Spring Beauties underneath—like left-over snow.

But *nobody* got to see—as we Hoosiers say—the bridge site, because a farmer shot at us with buckshot, and his little boy threw stones. Their team had been scared by an automobile the week before, we found out. The plow had been broken, and one of the horses had gone lame. So the little boy was on the lookout, in case it came back. Of course he could hear us coming from quite a long way off—see us as well. They had plenty of time to load and get a good aim.

Two of the Commissioners were hit with the stones, and big bumps raised up on their heads, but the buckshot missed us. Grandfather made nothing of the incident, beyond an anxiety that the machine might have been dented, and he was incredulous when the two Commissioners said they would like to return home. He agreed, of course, but when he turned the automobile around, we went down the road bank and into a brook, because he hadn't backed before.

A friendly farmer, with a team, pulled us out, and he was the one who told us why we'd been shot at. It was after dark when we got home. I had fallen asleep until Grandfather stopped to get out and light the acetylene carriage lamps, and then I climbed out, too, to watch him open the glass doors of the lamps, and light the burners with a match. They hummed and sputtered and sent off a musty smell, which he said came from the brass cylinder fuel tank attached to the running board. After that I was wide awake, and saw each of the Commissioners get out at his house, carrying his shoes

and socks, which were wet from pushing the machine out of
the brook. Grandfather wasn't wet; he had had to stay at the
wheel to steer, and he was very apologetic about everything.
He had wanted so much, he said, for them to have a pleasant
outing, and to look over the bridge site.

Well, Mr. McCormick said, to tell him the truth, they had
been out the week before in a hired carriage from Loan
Franklin's, and had seen the bridge site. This time they had
only gone to have a ride in a machine, and, by golly, they
had certainly had it.

That was not by any means, however, the only time the
automobile was stoned. For a long time after that it was
likely to happen whenever Grandfather drove out into the
country. And inasmuch as fifteen minutes of driving in Muncie in any direction would bring you to the country, the
chances were that anytime you went for a ride you were apt
to be pelted. Grandfather always used to warn the guests of
this probability, and to assure them that there was nothing
personal in the attack.

"It is the machine which they are throwing at," he would
say, "so do not be disturbed by it."

I don't know that all the guests felt as interested in the
motive as Grandfather did, yet he never lacked for guests.
And the machine was, at least, not shot at again. I doubt if
Grandfather would have stopped even if it had been. I think
an automobile was the only possession that he ever really
cared about. No automobile that he owned later became, for
that matter, a convenience, a means to an end. It was an end
in itself, a beautiful, shining creation that moved for him—
once he understood it—and with every roll of the wheels
brought him further into unknown country, which the most
familiar lanes became from the driver's seat.

He always pointed out sights to the other occupants, as if
they could not possibly have seen them themselves, and yet

he never took his own eyes off the road ahead, lest he miss something coming. It was startling, at first, to see his right or left arm shoot back or out the side of the car while he called,

"View," or "Tanager," or "Nice pair of horses," or "Good corn there."

But we grew accustomed to it and learned to follow the direction in which his hand was pointing, not where he was looking.

Grandmother Kimbrough was not one of the passengers for a long time after her baptism at Mr. Topps's, though all the rest of the family went whenever they had a chance. Grandfather was hurt by Grandmother's prejudice, so he seldom mentioned it. They had always done everything together, and it was inconceivable to him that she should not share this joy as she had all the others. The boys were itching to share the joy of driving, but he did not allow them to drive for a long time, although they knew a good deal more about the engine than he did. It was *his*, and he liked to sit behind the wheel, pull on his black leather gantlets, which came almost to his elbows, squeeze the big black rubber bulb that blew the horn, and then boom out in front of our house.

"Is there anybody here who would like to take a little drive?"

And *everybody* would come out on the porch to wave and say they would be there in just a minute, as soon as they got their wraps. We all had automobile clothes in no time, and we would bustle into them—dusters and bonnets with veils. Sometimes Mother just tied a veil over her regular hat, but it was a special veil that was gathered into a big hard button in the front, and was heavy, because she was afraid the wind would bring on her neuralgia.

All the boys had motoring caps, too, for that day when

they would be allowed to drive. I had a special arrangement of veils, wound around under my eyes and down and around my neck, because the dust from the roads made me sneeze so badly. Later I had a kind of helmet, which came from New York, with a ventilator in front and a pipeline going into it. But it made me break out in such bad prickly heat that Mother finally let me stop wearing it. It didn't really keep out all the dust anyway. Nothing could do that. But Grandfather always called out if there was something coming toward us on the road, and we all covered our faces, until he said,

"Coast's clear."

It was the Fourth of July picnic that broke down Grandmother's resistance. The daughters-in-law had the idea for it during dinner one Sunday noon at the big house. We could get an early start in the morning, they said, and maybe go ten or twelve miles, eat our picnic and then come home in the afternoon. We ought to get back easily by supper time and be ready for the fireworks afterwards that the neighborhood always had at the big house. The boys were pleased with the idea, but Grandfather said he didn't know. He kept looking down at Grandmother at the other end—we were still at the table. I was holding my breath, praying as hard as I could, and saying at the same time eeny, meeny, miney, mo, on my fingers under the table—to see if we *would* go or not. Mother said she would make the Thousand Island dressing, and bring it in a Mason jar. It was her specialty, and she was proud of it. Everyone said that would be lovely, and we could keep the lettuce in a moist towel and mix the salad at the picnic. Then Grandmother spoke.

"You'd better make the coffee too, Lottie," she said. (That was my mother.) "Yours is the best; we can heat it when we get there. You other girls can bring some cake and some fruit,

maybe. Your sponge cake is always nice, Helen. But I'll bring
the rest of the dinner."

There wasn't a sound for a minute. The sun through the
colored glass windows above the sideboard made little red
and blue flickering patterns on the embroidered centerpiece,
and everybody seemed to be watching them. I stopped saying my prayers, and counting eeny, meeny, miney, mo, and
holding my breath, and looked at Grandfather. He had caught
my mother's eye and was grinning at her from ear to ear,
with his eyes all puckered up almost as if he were going to
cry.

Then everybody began to talk at once. But not a mention
about Grandmother riding in the automobile for the first
time after that terrible other trip of hers. They just said how
wonderful it would be to have one of her real picnic meals
—fried chicken they hoped. She didn't know why *not*, she
told them sharply, and sandwiches, and some deviled eggs.
Erna could bake an apple pie, too, just as well as not—Father
and the boys always liked that cold. If we went past the
Claypool farm we might telephone ahead and ask them to
pull some corn fresh, and we could stop and pick it up on
our way. We could roast it, but then that might be awfully
hot in the middle of the day.

That started a discussion of which way we would go. Aunt
Huda said she thought it would be nice to go out towards
Winchester. There were pretty places for picnicking along
the way. Uncle Lloyd said the only picnicking places there
were too near town where they used to go with the horses.
If you drove as far as ten miles in that direction it wouldn't
be anything. Uncle Frank said he thought the way to Indianapolis was as good as any. Aunt Helen said she could see
that road any time she went over on the Interurban. She
wanted something new. And Uncle Frank told her the only

new thing he didn't want was a road he didn't know about.
Mother said she thought it would be lovely to try to find
some water, whatever direction it was in. But they all told
her you couldn't go round and round just looking for water;
you had to aim for something in particular. Grandfather said
suppose they all let me decide. It was a very breathless moment for me, but I managed to say,

"Let's go to Hartford City."

I had been there once to see my cousins, Inez and Mac,
and remembered how I had liked the sidewalk in front of
their house; it was wooden and narrow and off the ground
so that it was like a bridge. They all said that was as good a
direction as any to go, though we couldn't possibly get to
Hartford City—at least not there and back in the same day.

"Do you know"—Uncle Lloyd's voice to me was shocked—
"that Hartford City is *eighteen* miles away?"

Chapter Two

We started on the Fourth about nine o'clock in the morning.
Grandmother said that Grandfather had been out since seven,
fiddling over the machine, and polishing the monogram. The
monogram was a brass CMK in scroll letters, tacked across
the radiator, and almost covering it. The boys had given it to
them both in June, for an anniversary present. Grandmother's
acknowledgment of the gift had been polite, but certainly
not hearty.

I had been out at half-past seven at our own house, but
very briefly. Daddy had agreed to buy some firecrackers for
me—my very first. Before that I had only seen the ones in the
evening at the big house. All the other children had some
of their own, and I wanted them, too. So Daddy and I took
the package out at half-past seven. He lighted a piece of
punk and gave it to me. Then he put one bunch down on the
ground, and held my hand, leaned over with it, and touched
the string that stuck out. The whole thing shot off with a
bang, and jumped into the air. I was back in the house
with the screen door shut behind me before the last one went
off. I was dizzy with rage, yelling at the top of my lungs,

"I didn't ask for noisy ones!"

And I got sent to my room until time to go to the picnic,
for having a bad temper and not counting ten to keep it
down.

By the time Mother and I started, everybody else was up
at the big house. The food was all packed, which was exactly

what I wanted to see done, and they were ready to get in. They had on their dusters, bonnets, veils, and caps. Mrs. Hageman called out from her porch across the street that we all looked very stylish. Grandmother called back that we would be home in plenty of time for the fireworks, and to be sure to come over. She said of course they would, and that Mr. Hageman had some fine, big sky-rockets to bring. Grandmother told Mother privately that they were dangerous, tricky things, and she wouldn't have one around herself. But she waved to Mrs. Hageman and said that would be lovely. Mrs. Little was on her front porch, too, pinching dead leaves off her vines. She was Mr. Hageman's sister, and lived on the corner opposite the Richs'. She called that we had a lovely day for our excursion and God speed to us; she was quite a literary person.

We sailed off down Washington Street with flags flying, the veils from the motor bonnets and my butterfly net, which was hanging outside. I was making a butterfly collection with Betty Ball and wanted to get some more specimens if I could, but there was no place for me to hold the net in the car. I was wedged in the front seat between Grandfather and Uncle Lloyd. We were all of us in rather a tight squeeze. Daddy and Uncle Frank sat in the back seat, with Grandmother between them. Aunt Huda and Aunt Helen sat on little stools. Grandfather had them made at the factory. Mother started out sitting somewhere between the two little stools, but later she shifted and sat on Daddy's lap. Next to Grandmother and me she was the lightest—she weighed ninety-eight pounds, and was always squeezed in after the other places were taken, but didn't mind a bit, she said.

It was a hot day, the kind of heat that made my hair curl up wet across my forehead, and my shirt and panty-waist stick to my skin. The kind of heat that made the air shimmer, and the sounds in it seem especially loud—the chatter of a grasshopper or the deep rasp of a bumble bee. You could not hear those sounds, of course, above the noise of the automobile, but that was the kind of an Indian Summer day it was.

Every few minutes Grandfather would point violently behind him with his right hand, and call out,

"There's the old Semple place, Mother," or "That must be the farm Anna Goddard bought."

Sometimes he would fling his left arm across my face and call out,

"Butterfly, Emily."

But either I didn't see it, or it wasn't the kind I wanted. They were mostly clouded sulphurs—the little, pale yellow ones that always dance up and down in the dust and in the bands of heat. I don't know how Grandfather saw the things he pointed out, because he never moved his head to the right or left, but one arm and then the other was going almost constantly, like a swimmer's. Grandmother was being very brave and having a good time, although she was scared, but this signaling annoyed her.

"I can see for myself," she told him, "except when your arm is in the way. And I know the Meeks' place as well as you do. I've come out here for thirty years to get chickens. And without so much noise and dust," she added under her breath.

But I heard her and so did Grandfather. I saw him grin.

Pretty soon, however, we were further than we had ever gone with the horses in so short a time, and Grandmother began to be excited.

"Goodness," she said, "this is beautiful country. I hadn't any idea it was such beautiful country."

She didn't mean beautiful country of hills and valleys or mountain streams, of course. She meant fertile, rich country, heavy with corn as far as you could see. "Corn knee high by

the Fourth of July," we pray for and boast of. And it *was*
knee high that year. Country Gentleman sweet corn, and
Golden Dent feed corn, motionless and glistening in the silent heat.

Sometimes the fields were interrupted by a little patch of
woods—the trees well apart from one another and with no
underbrush below. That is the way they are in Indiana. The
sight of one of these with its shade made the boys begin to
think of eating.

We didn't know that we were starting that day a refrain
which would echo down through all the years of motoring,
when Mother said she wished we could find a brook—there
must be one a little farther along—and Grandmother said
that she didn't like one grove of trees, because it was too
close to the road. If people passed by they could see exactly
what we were eating, and Aunt Huda said that she wanted
a brook, too, like Mother. Aunt Helen was with the boys. It
made very little difference to her what she was looking at
when she was eating, except that she would just as lief
there weren't any cows. Grandfather was very impatient with
the idea of dinner. The engine was running along like a
bird, he said; it seemed a shame to stop it. Besides, when we
stopped we wouldn't have the breeze that the machine was
making for us. Just skimming along like this at eighteen miles
an hour was his idea of a picnic. Everybody said,

"That's right, Father," and "Certainly, we are all loving it,
Father."

Except Uncle Lloyd. He always spoke right up, and he
was special with Grandmother Kimbrough—the other boys
all laughed about it—because he was the youngest. He just
said quietly that he'd hate to think of that beautiful dinner
Grandmother had put up for us going to waste. That settled
Grandfather. He banged his hand down on the steering
wheel.

"Of course we'll stop. I want a piece of that chicken right now, Mother."

And then he slapped the wheel again.

"But we'll let Emily decide where. She told us where to come in the first place."

Mother called out from the back seat,

"Oh, Father, don't."

But the rest of them said,

"Oh, let him, Lottie; it doesn't hurt her."

Grandfather leaned his ear down to me and said,

"Where do you want to eat, Emily? We'll stop there."

"Aren't we going to Hartford City?" I asked him. "That's where I said to go, to Cousin Inez and Mac's with the wooden sidewalk outside."

"That's just where we'll go," Grandfather declared with solemnity. "By jiminy, we'll drive all the way to Hartford City."

There was bedlam all around. The daughters-in-law said they would love to see Inez and Mac, but they didn't think that was the idea of a picnic. Grandmother said Grandfather oughtn't to do that without telling her. If she had known we were going to Hartford City, she would have brought the mustard pickle recipe Inez wanted. The boys were delighted. Would you ever have believed, they kept asking, that you could get into a contraption and drive to Hartford City in the morning, and get there for dinner? And they didn't like sitting on the ground for picnics anyway. The food was fine, but grass was terrible and your knees got stiff. They wouldn't even listen to the daughters-in-law, they were so excited about what the machine could do. And while the argument was still going on we actually came into the town of Hartford City. We turned up the right street, and stopped outside Cousin Inez's own door. The wooden sidewalk was outside just the way it had been before we owned an automobile, up on little planks off the ground like a bridge.

Grandfather put his right hand down outside the car and squeezed the big rubber bulb over and over again. It made a deep doleful sound, something like a bullfrog. Inez and Mac came running out on the porch—everybody on the street came out on their porches, too—but Inez was so surprised that she got dizzy, and had to sit down for a minute, in a rocking chair, before she could come down the steps.

She was very pretty, with blue eyes and dark hair worn in a pompadour. She had the most catching laugh of anybody I knew. She laughed a great deal and I loved to hear it. It was low and full. Mac laughed a good deal, too, but more of a chuckle than a laugh came out. He was short and very fat. They had been married only two years. I had been the ring bearer at their wedding, carrying the ring in a basket of ferns and pink roses. Mother had fastened the ring to the handle of the basket with a piece of darning cotton so that it wouldn't get lost down in the basket. She tied it so tight, too, that the best man couldn't get it off. The minister finally held the basket up in the air, so that he could see it better, and jerked and jerked. The ring came away, but the darning cotton came, too. Inez wore it that way at first, with the long black thread attached. She was superstitious about taking off her wedding ring.

Neither she nor Mac had ever seen an automobile before we drove up. Mac kept walking round and round it just saying, over and over,

"Well, sir, what do you think of that? Well, sir."

Everybody was talking at once. You could hardly hear anything that made sense. But Inez hugged me and said it was wonderful for me to bring the picnic there.

After a while we all went into the house. The boys carried the things for the picnic. Inez put the big coffee pot on the stove right away, and all the daughters-in-law helped her set the table. Grandmother unpacked the basket in the kitchen, and mixed up the salad in a bowl with Mother's Thousand Island dressing. The men all sat out on the porch and looked at the machine until Mother sent me out to tell them everything was ready. We ate at the dining room table, but ate with our fingers because it was a picnic. And there were two kinds of cake, because Inez had happened to bake an angel food the day before. Angel food cake was her specialty.

As soon as dinner was over we had to pack up and start right back, though they all said they were too full to move; but we had to, because everybody would expect us for the fireworks that night. Nobody could get over it that we were in Hartford City for dinner, and were going to be back in Muncie for supper. They all kept saying that it didn't seem right somehow; it sort of scared you. Cousin Mac told Grandfather,

"Well, Uncle Charles, I guess nothing will stop you now. One of these days you'll be driving right down to New York City."

Grandfather was so pleased that he let Uncle Lloyd crank.

It was the best start we had made. When Grandfather wouldn't let anyone help, he had to run back from cranking to switch a button over from the magneto to "spark," and pull down the throttle. But sitting in the seat, he could do that the minute the engine caught from Uncle Lloyd's cranking. The magneto was the only part of the whole automobile that I hated. It made a noise like scraping your nail on a blackboard, and I always put my tongue between my teeth until we were on "spark."

We waved and called back to Inez and Mac until they were out of sight, standing on the wooden sidewalk in front of the house, and then Grandfather began pointing out the sights again that we had just passed on the way in, first with

his left hand and then with his right. He showed me a butterfly that I did want for my collection, but no one would let
me go after it because the engine might stall if we stopped,
and we didn't want anything to hold us back.

We came back over the same road, because the boys
thought it was better not to take any chances on a new one,
and Grandfather pushed the throttle up to pretty nearly
twenty-three miles an hour. He said it was safe on a familiar
road. Grandmother begged him not to, but the others talked
her out of being nervous. They all loved it, they said. I was
quite scared myself because the wind made such a noise.
I shut my eyes to slits, which made the scenery exciting and
not so scary.

We were coming along lickety-split and not very far from
Muncie, when Grandfather saw some cows. They were crossing the road quite far ahead, going from the pasture over to
the barn. He didn't want to slow down too much, he said,
for fear he might stall the engine, and he wanted to give
them warning anyway. So he put his hand down the side and
squeezed the bulb as hard as he could, over and over.

Grandmother called from the back seat,

"Father, don't blow it so long. You'll deafen all of us."

He muttered to us,

"I have to blow. My throttle's stuck. I can't slow her down."

And then the cows started to run, up the road and down
the road, and back into the pasture, and some streaking
across to the barn. The little boy who was driving them was
scared at the noise and the stampede. He was taking them
home to be milked, so he started running up and down after
them, yelling, and trying to coax them. But no one could
hear his voice over the horn and the engine. Grandfather was
wild, too.

"Holy smoke!" he kept saying.

But he didn't dare stop altogether by turning off the engine, because he didn't know whether he could start again. And the more the horn blew, and the closer we came to them, the worse off the cows were. The boys said,

"Keep on going, Father; keep on going, Father."

I don't think he shut his eyes, and maybe the boys didn't, but certainly the rest of us did. The last I saw we were going into the cows. When I opened my eyes again, we were past them. They were still running, and the horn was still blowing.

"That was a close shave," Daddy yelled.

Grandfather nodded his head proudly. By this time we were coming into the lower end of Walnut Street, making more noise than the whole fire department. Everybody along the sidewalks jumped into the doorways. There were lots of people, too, the way there always are on a holiday, but they scattered.

Grandmother's voice was so high you could hear it above the horn. She was so mortified, she said, she wished she were dead. If anyone persuaded her to set foot in this dratted carriage again, she would know she was crazy. Look at Mrs. George Maring over there, staring at us as if we were a lot of hoodlums. That's what we were too, skiting over to Hartford City and back in a day.

I don't suppose we could hear all of it, but we heard most of it.

We turned the corner on Madison Street, came up Washington, got to the front of the house, and Grandfather stopped the engine. He stopped blowing the horn, too. All his passengers got out, wriggled and stamped a little to get the stiffness out of their muscles, and said it had been a wonderful day; they would never forget it. They thanked Grandfather Kimbrough for the beautiful trip. Then we all scattered to go home and change our clothes for the fireworks. Mother thought I ought not to come back—that I had had enough for one day. But Grandfather said I had slept a long time after dinner, coming back from Hartford City, leaning up against him. It wasn't as if the Fourth of July came every day, and there shouldn't be anything tiring in just spinning along in the comfortable machine, the way we did. I wasn't really worried. Mother nearly always did what he asked, and in a minute she said, well perhaps it would be all right; I could take a longer nap the next day.

I wasn't a bit sleepy, but I was too excited to eat much supper. We all had to take baths—we were so dirty from the dust. Mother said her teeth felt gritty, and Daddy washed his hair. I got dressed up in a white dimity dress with a Dresden sash and a hair-ribbon to match, and then I climbed up and down from the ground to our porch in the spaces between the cement blocks of the foundation, until Mother and Daddy came out.

When we reached the big house we saw a great many people there. Grandmother and Grandfather were standing on the front steps, shaking hands with them all, and they were dressed up, too. Aunt Helen and Uncle Frank were standing behind them, and Uncle Lloyd and Aunt Huda. Aunt Helen looked beautiful in a white embroidered dress. Her eyes were very dark brown, wide apart and big. Her hair was dark brown, too, and she wore it parted in the middle, and smoothed down on either side to a knot at the back—not in a pompadour like nearly everybody else. She and Uncle Frank had been married for only six months.

Mother and Daddy spoke to everybody there, but I ran up on the porch where the other children were. It was a rule that we had to stay up there, to be out of the way and where we wouldn't get hurt.

When everybody seemed to have arrived, Grandmother and Grandfather sat down in chairs at the head of the steps, where they could see everything and keep any of the children from sliding past them. Some of the people sat on the

stone blocks on either side of the steps, or on chairs on the
lawn. Daddy, Uncle Lloyd, and Uncle Frank went down to
the big bundle of fireworks by the wall—not a very high
wall—next to the sidewalk. They took out the pinwheels first,
and nailed them on the trees in front. People were chattering while they waited, and Grandfather's big voice cut
through them without effort:

"Great Scott! Wait until I get my automobile out of the
way. Don't set off one of those things until I get my machine
fixed. It might catch fire."

Uncle Lloyd asked if he couldn't do it, but Grandfather
said no, he would rather tend to it himself. He had to go
back into the house to get his duster on, so he wouldn't get
dirty; but when he came down to crank the machine, he
tucked the duster up around his waist out of his way, as he
always did. The engine started right up, the throttle didn't
stick at all, and he drove back to the barn without any trouble.

By the time he came back to the porch, the pinwheels
were ready and the boys set them off. They were wonderful,
whirling round and round in the still, hot night, lighting up
people's faces and dresses and hands, and making everything
seem much blacker when they stopped. The boys asked what
we would like next and most people wanted Roman candles.
So they shot them off, standing close together—no one else
was allowed to be near there—and sending them out away
from the house. The lightning-bugs were glowing off and on
all around, and the Roman candles' showers would light up
their black bodies. Then it would be dark, and their thin
glow would come on again. There were flower pots that were
pretty, set along the wall, where they sizzled up in bright
patterns. And there was red fire, which didn't do anything
special but burn red and light up all the people very clearly.
We children loved that. It was fun to see peoples' faces coming out of the darkness, and being lighted all of a sudden,

looking just the way they always did. You could say, "I see Mrs. Rich," "I see Mrs. Franklin," "I see Mrs. Little." If they had been strange, of course, the excitement of discovery would have been no fun.

Finally, we got to the sky-rockets. They were always kept for the last, because they were the most important. Grandfather had had a stand built for them out at the factory. It was a sort of slanting trough on legs, and the boys pointed it away from the house, as they had headed the Roman candles. They set it down in the ground quite firmly, and it took a little time. We children were allowed to come down off the porch while they were doing this, if we didn't go near the fireworks. So we raced to the corner and played tag under the overhanging street lamp, where the June bugs and moths thumped against the globe, other bugs crawled over its surface, and the carbon lamp inside hissed and sputtered.

"You're it! You're it!" we shrilled, darting out of the rim of light into the shadow and back, squealing and shrieking, until the boys made their voices heard and told us to come, everything was ready.

We climbed, panting and jostling, onto the porch, skirted around Grandmother and Grandfather, and sat at the far end in the swing and on the railing. We were a little uneasy about the rockets; they went up so suddenly. The Roman candles always gave a warning "putt" or two. The first rocket sprang from the trough, and we all jumped. The grown people down below squealed. But it was beautiful when the shower fell like gold sleet out of the sky, after the flaming rush had reached its peak. They went off, one after the other then—twelve, twenty, I don't know how many—until Uncle Lloyd said,

"This is the last one. This one will sing *Good Night, Ladies,* as it goes."

Someone started the song *Good Night, Ladies,* and every-

Then he called out: "This is the brightest and best of them all."

body took it up until the whole party was singing it softly
—the children's voices high and thin, the men's and women's
dividing into parts, and Grandfather's bass holding them all
on its solid fullness. I think it must have made a sweet sound
in the close, dark night. And Uncle Lloyd waited to light the
rocket until we had sung the song through twice, joining his
tenor to the other boys'. Then he called out—the singing
stopped—"This is the brightest and best of them all," and
touched his taper to the wick.

Up it leaped with its hiss of speed, faltered a moment, and
then plunged straight across the street, through the open
front door, and down the hall of the Hagemans' house.

Nobody could believe what had happened, but the boys
were the first to get across the street, everyone else close behind them, calling back to get the fire department. I suppose
somebody did telephone, because it wasn't very long before
we heard the alarm bell. It was funny, too, to hear the bell
and not have to ask where the fire was. The bell always
rang the number of the district, like three rings, a pause, and
then two. Grown-ups would say,

"Hush, children, I want to hear where the fire is."

But if they didn't hear soon enough they would go to the
telephone and ask Central where it was. If they did hear,
they would look at a card that hung beside the telephone
and read,

Ring	District
3–2	Plum to Elm
4–1	Washington to Adams

And so on down the list.

But no one on Washington Street had to read the card that
night. The fire engines themselves came clanging and chattering up its length, the horses thumping along, breathing

hard, the coach dog, that belonged to the Fire Chief, stretched out between the wheels of the Chief's cart, running his fastest.

By that time there wasn't very much for them to do. The boys had stamped out the sparks along the hall rug. The rocket itself had died out at the foot of the stairs. It was a wonder, somebody said, it didn't go right on up and out the attic. There was not very much damage done, beyond the rug and the woodwork scorched. It ended the party, however, and everybody left, including the fire department. Grandmother and Grandfather and the rest of the family were the last to go. They wanted to be sure that everything was all right. Just as they started down the steps, Grandfather shook hands with Mr. Hageman and said,

"When I think of how near my automobile came to being in the path of that rocket! It might have caught the full brunt. Nothing short of providential that I got the machine out of the way, and gave the thing a clean sweep across here."

Chapter Three

Grandfather wanted everyone to ride in the automobile. He liked especially to take a passenger who had never ridden before. He could point out then and explain every feature of the carriage, and every detail of its mechanical operation. Some people understood it better than others. I don't suppose Chris *heard* it the time he rode.

Chris was a Norwegian who came once a week to Grandmother's and once a week to each of the daughters-in-law to clean. He was not more than five feet tall, broad, heavy-set and with thick gray hair. He must have been proud of his hair, because wherever he went he always brushed it with every brush he found in the house—until we learned to lock up all the brushes the day Chris was coming. He couldn't speak English very well, but then he never spoke much anyway. He looked just as I imagined a gnome would look—small, wrinkled, and brown. He lived in a little one-room shack miles out of town, but always came to our house long before anyone was up. He brought with him a paper package of food which he would always add to the dinner he was given at the house. He always carried a package home, too. Nobody could ever guess what was in that package, because there never seemed to be anything missing from the house where he was working. Yet he carried something away with him, always.

The only other man we ever had to do work like that was named Orville Harrold. He went to New York to become an opera singer—after that we had only Chris.

One late afternoon, just as Chris was starting home with his mysterious little package under his arm, Grandfather Kimbrough drove up in front of the house, blew the horn, and called out, "Is there anybody here who would like to go for a little drive?"

I ran out, but I was the only one at home. Mother had gone down to meet Daddy at the Electric Light Plant to walk home with him. When Grandfather saw Chris he said he would take him home. Chris grinned all over his face when he understood what Grandfather wanted. He climbed into the back seat. I don't know how Grandfather knew where his shack was; it was the only time I ever saw it. But it was a good thing he did, because the moment the engine started, Chris's mouth flew wide open, his eyes shut tight, he reached out both hands, grabbed the carriage straps at either side— but never budged from the middle himself. And that was how he rode all the way out. Grandfather had to shake him when we stopped at his shack before Chris would open his eyes, and unclench his hands from around the straps. I don't believe he liked it very much. And I think he must have told Erna enough in his broken English to make her not like it either, because she would never get in. Erna was Grandmother's hired girl. I was sorry about Erna's being scared, but not as upset as about Zoe's not going.

Zoe was more my family to me than all the other members identified by family titles. A family was what you belonged to, I understood, and I belonged to Zoe.

She was, I suppose, my nurse, except that in Indiana—at least in Muncie—nobody had a nurse. That would have been stuck-up and Eastern. So Zoe was our extra hired girl. I do not know how it was before she came. She was, for me, the beginning.

Mother and Daddy used to laugh about the maids they had when they were first married. They were country girls, in from the farm. Mother, coming from Indianapolis, which was really a city, wasn't used to them. The first one put a place for herself at the table. Mother didn't know what it was for, until the meal began and the girl came in and sat down. After Mother got over her surprise, she said she tried hard to find topics of conversation that would be congenial to the three of them. She suggested the next day that the girl would be happier in the kitchen, and that she and Mr. Kimbrough had a great deal of business to talk about which wouldn't be interesting to her. After that, she said, she and Daddy had to find business to talk about, which was difficult, too.

Amelia wasn't like that. She was German, and didn't want to sit in the dining room. She taught me to talk, Mother said, only it was in German instead of English—and Grandfather was put out about it, too. It was, nevertheless, a very sound foundation because it brought me into excellent standing at Mr. Hummel's bakery. We were there, Amelia and I, nearly every afternoon in the course of an outing. And from the moment I was able to say in German, cakes and cookies, the bakery output was at my disposal—hot, buttery, and sweet, fresh from the oven. We sat in the back room where the family lived, and ate the sweet things. Amelia and the Hummels had coffee, too, but I was not included—though I knew the word for it.

Amelia went back to Germany to be married. Her successors made no impression on me, because Zoe filled my world. She was extra, too.

Mother persuaded Grandfather to allow her to hire a girl to take me out in the afternoon. Daddy was behind her in the idea, but they wouldn't have dreamed of doing anything without Grandfather's permission. Daddy, of course, did the supporting but Grandfather made the decisions. And he was unhappy about this one. He didn't ordinarily care what people thought—but he didn't want Mother to be looked upon as unnatural for not wanting to take care of her own child.

Mother told him that she loved taking care of her baby, but she loved to read, too, and to go down to meet Daddy and wait for him if he were late at the Plant, and walk back with him. She didn't believe people would think those things were unnatural. Grandfather agreed with that—Grandmother prodding him all the time, Mother knew, saying that Lottie was such a little thing anyway, and the baby was too fat for her to be lifting all day.

Mother's first substitute was a colored girl, who took me out in the afternoon, gave me my supper, and put me to bed. But her life with us was short, my parents told me, and ended abruptly.

Mother and Daddy, out walking one day, encountered Mrs. Leo Ganter. They were pushing me in my sled, Mother remembered. The sled was really a baby carriage, except that it had runners instead of wheels, a high handle in the back, and in the front a curving dashboard—like the one on a sleigh. Mrs. Ganter stopped to speak to them, and then looked down at me.

"Why," she said, "this is the child that spends every afternoon in my kitchen with our Mary. Some friend of Mary's leaves her there while she goes up the block to do Mrs. Smith's cleaning for her. We're all so devoted to the baby, but we never could find out whose it was."

After that my nursemaid resumed her daily cleaning at Mrs. Smith's uninterrupted—and Mother the natural care of her own child.

I was four years old when Zoe came. She was colored by nature, Mother said, like leaves—a tawny, golden shade—not so yellow as seed corn on the stalk, nor tan like wheat stacked in the sheaves; not nearly so brown as a pussy-willow bud in the Spring, nor as an oak leaf in the Fall. And this was the way I learned about the shades of a color. Zoe's was new to me. I had never been especially aware of a colored person before. I loved her color because I loved everything about her. We made games of it and it tickled Zoe.

"Come on, honey," she would say, "let's go walkin' and match Zoe's color."

And we would go down by the river bank, out to the country. She walked slowly, but lightly, and I darted ahead and around her, bringing back, like a retriever, my find of an acorn, a hickory nut, straw from a haystack, an oak leaf turned brown. And I would put them eagerly and earnestly against her hand or face when she sat down to rest—matching Zoe's color, and learning how much more beautiful a color becomes through awareness of its delicate variations.

She was tall, even a little taller than my Father. When I first saw a picture of the Caryatids, I thought at once of the way Zoe held herself. Perhaps her carriage, too, was a heritage of burdens borne on the head.

"Try to walk the way Zoe does," Grandmother Wiles would say, and with a painful smack place a book on my head.

"Show her, Zoe. You move from your hips, don't you? It's so smooth, like water flowing."

And Zoe would laugh like a child, her head thrown back. She didn't know how she moved, she said. Gettin' from one place to another was enough, without worryin' how to do it. But she would humor Grandmother by making me walk behind her with the book on my head—up and down my room, and she chuckling all the time.

There was never such a lap as hers for climbing into—easy to reach, and with lots of room when you got there. Her strong arms and big gentle hands would make a barricade to hold you in safely. There and the playhouse in the apple tree were the best places in the world to be.

Not so good a story teller as my Grandmother Wiles, she was a better singer. Rocking back and forth out on the porch, sometimes, or in front of the fire in my bedroom, always just before bedtime, hedging me in on her lap, she would sing of golden slippers, sweet chariots, and journeys home.

I generally behaved myself for her; she saw to that with a firmness that brooked no argument. A pouting child, she said, she would not tolerate.

"Pull in your lower lip," was her order. "You got it out there to ride me to town on?"

Crybabies, too, she said, could stay away from her.

"I can't pay mind to somebody bubbling like a pot on the stove. Hush yourself, and Zoe will fix it."

Mother and Daddy were young and gay. They went out a great deal, when Daddy was not working too hard—picnics, hay rides, sleigh rides, skating parties at Petty's rink, dancing parties at the Commercial Club, or in Mr. A. L. Johnson's Ballroom. Later, when I was older, Mother was·my companion, my rare delight, though she was never my solace. There was too much untempered quicksilver in her veins. Zoe was my solace. And in the Summer when Grandfather bought his first automobile, she was my companion, too, everywhere except in the machine. She would not set foot there, though I begged and begged her.

There was one time when I would not set foot in it either, one time in every day. That was when Mr. Hinkley came. Mr. Hinkley's coming was almost the next best thing to Christmas. Perhaps that was because he came more often. I liked quantity. Zoe knew how important the daily occasion was.

Mr. Hinkley and his wife had no children. They lived on a farm outside of town, and that Summer they made use of it for children. Every day all through the Summer, Mrs. Hinkley made a big freezer of rich, yellow vanilla ice cream from her own farm cream. They wouldn't even sell it to grown-ups, and Mr. Hinkley brought it into town himself every afternoon—and every afternoon, from the first warm day of June until August, when we went to Walloon Lake, my ritual was the same.

In the mornings I might do a number of things. I could stand on the step of the ice wagon and fill both hands with chips. I always ran with them into the house, all my muscles puckering with the cold, to get a clean, thin wash rag; because, sucked through a wash rag, the taste of ice was wonderful. Nearly every day, too, I rode on the back step of the vegetable wagon with the canvas cover, all the way to the big house.

On Saturday mornings all of us in the block would meet at the corner of Vine and Washington, to wait for the street lamp man. He always changed the carbon then, lowering the big arc light carefully. The minute he opened the globe, we would swarm around him, begging for the used carbon. It made the best chalk for hop-scotch, or for any kind of marking. We tried to follow him to all four corners of the block, which took a long time. Some of us were always called home before we could get half-way around. The music teacher was coming, and we had to get our hands washed and do a little practicing.

Sometimes all the neighborhood children played in my back yard—in the swing, up in the tree house, or running in and out of the spray from the hose, which we hung over a limb of the apple tree. We often had a lemonade stand, too, down at the corner—one cent a glass.

The neighborhood took in more than the block, and the children in it were of all ages. Besides the Riches and the Franklins, there were the Heaths and the White boys, Evelyn Hageman, where the sky-rocket went, Luella Morrison, Matilda Over, Marian Miltenberger, Louise Carey, Maurine

Doran. Maurine was very pretty. She moved away and everybody missed her, but she used to come back to visit. And
then she got married to a soldier named Wayne Clark. Later
there was a rule that everybody in the Army had to be called
by his first name. Wayne was his middle name, so then we
all had to learn to call him Mark—Mark Clark.

All of us would meet . . . to wait for the street lampman.

Lots of times we were all at Bennet Heaths' or the White boys'. Theirs was a good back yard, because they were always building things in it. Once they had made a house, and we had two clubs there. The boys had one of their own, called The Boys' Club, but we all had one, too, called The Anti-Gum and Literary Society. All the meetings were in the house they built, until they decided to dig a cellar under it, and the whole thing collapsed.

They built a toboggan, too, and we could slide on it as much as we wanted. It wouldn't collapse, because the boys got Lorene Slinger to slide down before they tried it. She lived out of our neighborhood—we had to go over to Adams Street to get her—but she was fatter than anyone in ours. We weren't exclusive about our neighborhood—Lorene *could* have come anytime. The only person we kept out for a while was Lydia Rich, after she persuaded us to eat elephant ears. They were weeds that looked like the ears of elephants. They grew in the lot across the street from her house, and she told us they tasted better than anything she ever ate. We picked a leaf, divided it, and each took a bite—about a dozen of us, and at exactly the same moment each of the twelve of us gave a scream of pain and fright, and ran for home. Our mouths were wide open. We were yelling and trying to get air at the same time. The taste of the weed was like pepper and ammonia mixed, and we nearly strangled. That was why we kept Lydia out for a while.

At twelve o'clock our mothers would come to find us, or call from their front porches. We would scatter for dinner. In the afternoons, all the older ones of the bunch would go to the Owl Drug Store for sodas. Once in a while Zoe would take some of us younger ones. We sat by ourselves. At home in the block we would have played together. Here, they scarcely noticed us, although we would all sit close together in the back of the store at the ice cream parlor tables. Both tables and chairs were of thin wood, with twisted metal legs and backs. Overhead a revolving fan with long blades hung from the ceiling. It ruffled constantly a pile of sheet music stacked on the candy counter. The music was free—popular songs and ballads, with the words "Bromo Seltzer" on the cover. Each song had printed across the top, "Try this on your piano," and those of the bunch who could play the piano always did take some pieces home to try. They used that sign as a slang expression, too. If one of the boys hit another, not in a real fight, but just teasing, he would say, "Try *this* on your piano." Or if one of the group offered another a piece of candy, the thing to say was, "Try this on your piano," varied by, "Try this on your pianola."

The Owl had pretty good candy, as well as the best sodas. Not chocolates, but hoarhound, jaw-breakers and candy kisses. At least those were my favorites. Although the soda fountain, the chairs and tables, and the candy counter were in the back of the store, the smell of hoarhound penetrated, at least in Summer, to the front where the medicine was sold. In Winter, essence of wintergreen oil rose above all the other smells, probably because so much of it was sold to be rubbed on the chest for colds. Oil of cloves, too, sold for toothaches, made a lovely aroma. With an all-season base from sharp disinfectants, the whole establishment provoked intoxicating sniffs from the front door to the back counter.

After Mr. Hinkley started coming that Summer, however, only the very oldest ones went to the Owl.

Zoe would get me up from my nap, take me into the bathroom, and give me a sponge bath with cool water—squeezing the wash rag on my chest, until the cold drops of water ran into my navel, making me gasp. I could dress myself by putting on my panty waist backwards, so that it buttoned up the front. H and W, the tabs on it said, in red letters, and they were the first I learned. After I had buttoned my panties to it, there was nothing more except my dress. In the Summer that was all I had to wear, and it was a source of never-ending surprise and pleasure to me. Sandals, of course, sometimes with socks, sometimes without, a thin dress on top—dotted swiss, mostly—and nobody cared if my panties showed right through. Then my hair was brushed back tight, and the curls wound around Zoe's fingers, though no matter how tight back it was brushed there was always some left that lay wet and sticky across my forehead. Then I was ready. Zoe would give me a saucer and spoon, and a nickel, telling me to sit still and not get all dirtied up, but wait for Mr. Hinkley.

She would open the screen door and watch me go down the porch steps. She would always pick, too, a dark red bloom from the sweet-smelling shrub beside the steps, and tie it into a corner of the handkerchief pinned on the front of my dress.

With the saucer and spoon in one hand—the spoon pressed down under my thumb to keep it from slipping—a nickel embedded deep in my clenched left hand, already moist again from the heat, I would sit waiting on the steps to the sidewalk, my skirt pulled out from under me, so as not to muss it. The waiting itself was part of the happiness which the occasion always brought. Up and down the street I could see the other children sitting waiting, just like me, but we didn't call to each other. We were listening for the sound of Mr. Hinkley coming. The shrub in my handkerchief was a sweet and heavy perfume, when I sniffed down toward it on my chest. I could hear flies against the screen, and bees mumbling in the rambler roses. I could hear the screen door open, and Zoe straightening the porch furniture and lowering the straw curtain against the afternoon sun, straightening the matting on the floor, and always stopping to pick off some dead leaves on the trellis up the porch.

"Hear him comin' yet?"

"Hear him comin' yet?" she would ask.

And I would shake my head, not wanting to break the silence lest I miss the first sound—not wanting to break through, either, the hazy mantle that wrapped me in heat and smell, and a dreamy sense of the cool stone under me, and the little drops of sweat across my forehead.

When I heard the first far-off sound of a bell tinkling, I always pretended it wasn't so—lest I be mistaken and disappointed. The second or third time I was sure. I would break through the haze now—leaning forward to look up toward the big house, the direction from which the sound was coming. Slowly, inevitably, the sound would come into view—the bell Mr. Hinkley was ringing. Leaning forward in his buggy, looking out from side to side, ringing his bell and calling,

"Ice cream for the children. Any children who want ice cream today?"

If only he needn't have stopped before he got to me; but there were children all along the way, all of them wanting ice cream and he had ice cream for all of them.

On the day of our Fourth of July picnic, I missed him, of course, and the next day was Sunday. He didn't come that day. We children on Washington Street wouldn't have been allowed to buy any if he had come. All our families were Presbyterians. But on Monday afternoon, I sat watching for him. Two whole days had been lost. I was sucking hard on a honeysuckle stem. I had pulled it out with my teeth, from the vine up on the front porch.

I sat watching him come. He stopped at the Richs'—Lydia, Mary, Edward were holding up their saucers—even Lenore, though she was almost grown-up.

Grandfather came suddenly around the corner of Vine Street, driving the automobile. He pulled up in front of our house—he always reared back when he stopped, and braced his feet with all his might, as if he were reining in a team of Percherons. He started to squeeze the bulb of the horn, then he saw me.

"Want to come for a ride?" he called.

I shook my head.

He caught sight of Zoe behind me on the porch.

"Zoe"—he wanted a passenger very much, I knew—"let me show you how remarkable this automobile is."

Zoe's voice came over my head, declining with fervor the invitation. It would take, she implied, something near death to get her into that contraption.

Grandfather drove off in a series of explosions and jack-rabbit lunges. Zoe's steps faded across the porch, and the screen door slammed behind her.

I was alone again, and the only sound above the bees was the clop-clop of Mr. Hinkley's horse, across the street.

I went down the steps very carefully, so that I was at the curb exactly as he said "Whoa." That was part of the ritual I had made. Mr. Hinkley looked down and smiled at me. His smile was so strong, it pushed his eyes almost shut.

"What would you like today? We have peach, strawberry, raspberry."

That was his ritual. Mrs. Hinkley made only vanilla.

Then it was mine to think very hard, staring at the horse, looking so funny with his ears sticking up through a straw hat on his head. He was covered, too, with a tasseled and fringed net, to keep off the flies.

"Chocolate," I said at last.

He slapped his hand on his knee, and told me I was a caution.

He lifted the lid of the freezer, and put it upside down on the seat beside him. He held my saucer and spoon in his left hand, and took up the big steaming ladle in his right. Of all the sounds for which I listened on those murmuring, hot Indiana afternoons, this was the one that brought the sharpest delight—the sluice of the ladle down into the rich, luscious cream below. Then it was back at the surface again, brimming and spilling over the thick, soft treasure. And now all of it heaped up, was on my saucer, the spoon buried in it. Licking that off was the first pleasure, before the eating began. I pried out the sticky nickel from the palm of my hand, and held it up to him.

"Thank you, Mr. Hinkley," I said. He would take the ice cream back if you didn't say thank you.

He put the nickel in a deep chamois bag with a metal

clasp. He replaced the lid on the freezer, gathered up the reins, and moved off down the street, and around the corner, waving back until he was out of sight. I watched him go around the corner, before I went to the steps. He wanted you to do that. He didn't like you to be greedy.

Every foot back to my top step was undertaken with apprehension. I might slip, or tilt the saucer, or stumble, or dislodge the spoon. The passage was fraught with potential mishaps, each of which I *had* experienced. I reached the step safely, turned around slowly, and sat down. Now was the golden moment. I squashed the spoon down slowly, letting it fill up over the sides, and lifted it to my mouth.

A shadow passed across us, the ice cream and me. A hand reached down for the spoon. It was not the kind of hand I had ever seen before; it had wide cracks packed with dirt all over it, sores in big red blotches, and nails torn down below the quick; it was covered with dirt and gave off a loathsome smell.

I must have stared at it for a little time, because a voice said, "Come on, little girl, look up here."

He stood swaying on the sidewalk below me, his face on a level with mine, and the stench from it made a vomit come suddenly into my throat. He had sores on his face, too, and a beard—short, stiff, with particles of food or something stuck in it. His mouth was slobbery, the rims of his eyes were red as a peeled blister, and wet, too. He lurched forward at me.

"Come on, little girl. You come with me. Want some candy?"

He bent over, unsteady but quick, jerked my saucer of ice cream out of my hands, and pressed it against his face. It ran underneath the saucer faster than he could lick it, over his sore, bristled chin, down his neck, making trickles in the dirt.

If I could have vomited. If I could have run, or screamed.

But I couldn't move, not even my arms. I was locked fast with terror.

My ice cream—my moment of pure gold in every Summer day—spilling down with slobber and filth over a man who wanted to take me away with him.

He threw the empty saucer down on the grass, wiped the back of his hand, with the sores, over his mouth, put that same hand around my arm, and squeezed it like a lemon. And in all the pain, I could not make a sound come.

"Take your hand off that child! Get away from her! You dare come 'round her!"

Zoe was there, coming through the screen door, swiftly across the porch, calling as she came, threatening, her deep voice cracking with the volume and the fury hurled into it.

The hand let my arm go, the smell, the filth and the shadow went away from me, the figure lurching, stumbling, running, half-falling and righting itself down the street. I sat as I had sat when I lifted my spoon to my mouth. My hands would not move, nor my legs, not even my head. I could hear Zoe when she came. I could feel her warmth and her strength when she lifted me up, but I could not tell her anything.

She called to Frieda, the hired girl, as we came into the house, to get Dr. Cowing on the telephone, and Mother at the big house. All the time she was moving back to my room with me in her arms.

I think I was not far away from dying that day—if not being able to breathe or move, and if shock, fright, and horror *can* bring you to death—and I think I was so close to it that Dr. Cowing needed to hurry. I don't know how we came to the rocking chair—there were moments when the struggle for breath was the only thing I knew. But I was lying against her arm and stiff across her lap, and she was singing.

It wasn't a kind of singing that I had ever heard—more of

a talking, in a singsong, now low, now a little higher, and the feel of a drum in it, pounding, pounding, pounding. There were words, but I didn't know them. They came again and again, weaving in and out of the drum in her voice, the beat insisting in urgent monotony that I listen, and I did.

I think I heard that day a chant and a prayer to a source of help far older than my Presbyterian God. I think it was as though Zoe, in her need for someone she loved, groped and fumbled her way back, back through her own people to a litany she had heard long years ago by word of mouth, passed down by how many mouths, through how many generations.

On and on, over and over, the words came, and my breath came, too, a little deeper, a little steadier, and I could hear more clearly. My head turned at last, and I could look up at Zoe. Her eyes were closed. She was straining forward, chanting, chanting. And then I was asleep—my arms and legs soft and curved again into her lap, the sound of her voice and the drum-beat fading out of my ears. They would never fade out of my memory. Though I could not reproduce them, I would hear them always.

I woke at supper time. I was in my own bed. Grandmother and Grandfather were there, too, but Mother was on the bed, sitting close to me. I felt fine. I jumped up and threw my arms around Mother. Daddy came into the room talking in a little more than a whisper.

"Well, they got him—down at the Big Four, trying to sneak out of town on a freight. He's locked up."

I knew whom they meant. I began to remember what had happened. My legs shook with a queer feeling.

And that was the time, the very moment, when Zoe said, "Mr. Kimbrough, you were askin' if someone would like to take a drive in your automobile. Well, I would—thank you— if you'd care to take me and Emily."

But she had said she would never set her foot in one! No one spoke for a long moment. Then Mother said she would go, too.

Zoe wouldn't put on a duster, nor a veil—said if she needed to jump, she didn't want to be bound.

All the rest of the family waved us off.

It was Mother who leaned across me, put her hand on Zoe's knee, and said, "I think I can match Zoe's color today, Emily." She'd heard our game, and she was smiling, with her eyes wet. "I'd match it exactly—with pure gold."

Grandfather's arm shot back across us.

"That's good corn over there, Zoe," he said in a husky voice.

Chapter Four

Even after Grandfather bought the automobile, he didn't always ride in it. He reserved it for special occasions. The horses were for every day. Maud was the general family horse. Grandmother used to drive her in the phaeton and always went out to get Grandfather at the Bridge Works every afternoon. I often went, too.

The factory was three miles out of town, away from the business section. It was not a pretty drive. The only way to get there was through a poor section of town, past tumble-down houses, not much more than shacks. All of them were gray; not painted gray but the gray of neglect and poverty. Out near the factories the houses of the factory workers were clean and neat, with pretty flower beds in Summer. Those we passed in the poor section belonged, Grandfather said, to the workers who liked to be near town, foreigners for the most part. They generally got drunk in the saloons every Saturday night. Saturday was pay day. Daddy would be telephoned by the police to get them out of jail. He would take them home.

A pretty drive was to go down town and then turn north to the river. The Big Four tracks and depot were to the south. The Walnut Street bridge over White River was one Grandfather had built. Beyond it was Minnetrista Boulevard where all the Ball brothers lived in big houses facing the river. Mc-Cullough Park was on that side of the sluggish yellow stream, too. The Ball Brothers' Glass Factory was across the road from the Bridge Works and was much bigger. The factories, Grandmother said, were what made the town so dirty. You couldn't, she insisted, leave your lace curtains up a month at a time.

But the Bridge Company factory itself looked clean, with a neat high iron fence all around it, and a light tan brick building in the front, with a closely cropped lawn. More fuss made over it, Grandmother said, than over the one at the big house—and a gravelled driveway on one side. That was the office building. The real factory part, the plant, was in the back, behind the yard where the steel girders and smaller parts lay in orderly sections. Overhead a monster crane traveled the length of the yard, carrying the steel into the plant. It was called a Gantry Crane, and—though I would not have hurt Grandfather's feelings by telling him so—it was more fun to ride in than the automobile. I sat then, in a little cab high up in the air and watched the driver scoop up, in the giant tongs, long strips of steel, just as if they were jackstraws. We would carry them, swaying and swinging below us, all the way to the plant, and lower them just where the men inside wanted them.

On the opposite side of the office building, from the steel yard, the men had vegetable gardens. Those who lived near by worked there in the evenings, except, of course, in Winter. We would often see the families there. Many of these were foreigners, too. Grandmother and I would watch them from the carriage, while we waited for Grandfather to come out. The men going home from work would pass us on their way to the gates. Some would stop to talk to Grandmother. She almost always said to me that she wished she could get up enough courage to ask them what they'd brought in their dinner pails. She didn't believe there was anything she was so curious about. She would know, she said, if she could find *that* out, just what kind of wives they had—at any rate what kind of housekeepers they were, and she would certainly like to know. She did so like anything to do with housekeeping. But she was too shy ever to ask. She said they would think she was interfering.

Noah, the hired man, drove Grandmother to market. Noah was tall, spare of figure and speech. He wore faded blue overalls most of the time. He also wore, the year round, the kind of hat which the horses wore in Summer as a protection against the flies. It could not have been his own. It was probably Maud's or Prince's—straw, with a peaked crown and holes on either side for the ears to come through. His concession to the formality of driving Grandmother was a suit coat on top of the overalls. He conceded no change in his head covering. Noah "chewed," which, in Indiana, means that he chewed tobacco, and always spat before he spoke—both infrequently.

One day when Grandfather came out of his office, Noah was there instead of Grandmother. And he said,

"While we was waiting, I've been feeding grass to your insect."

From that moment on Grandfather had a strong dislike for Maud. I never knew anyone less influenced usually by what other people thought. But he said Noah was right—Maud did look more like an insect than a horse. Grandmother always felt that it was Noah who set him thinking about a machine.

Prince was a little bit more stylish, but not much. He had a silver tube in the side of his throat—I do not know why. The family said he had once been a race horse. Why that should have given him a silver tube I never understood, any more than how my Presbyterian Grandfather ever became possessed of a race horse. The only thing of which I am sure is that on frosty mornings Prince's tube made his breath whistle in and out, with puffs of steam, like a peanut wagon.

I could drive Maud sitting by myself, with just somebody

beside me. But I wasn't allowed to touch Dave, not even to hold the end of the reins, the way I could always do with Prince or Maud if people didn't want to be bothered with letting me really drive. Dave was Uncle Lloyd's horse. Uncle Lloyd rode him most of the time, though he could be driven to a very light, little cart that held just two people. Uncle Lloyd was at Harvard then, but Grandmother used to say that at vacation he was on Dave or driving him before anybody else would have had time to get up from the depot. Uncle Lloyd was blond—not such a towhead as Frank when the boys were little, she said, but his hair was very yellow. He wore it parted in the middle and slicked down, though it curled a little on either side of the part in front. He had blue eyes and very pink cheeks. I always loved the clothes he wore, and yet I cannot name any of them, except a full black cape which he wore in the evenings, when he was especially dressed up and I saw him a few times, bow ties in the daytime, and bright yellow gloves when he was driving Dave. The bright yellow gloves are what I remember best. Holding the reins and the whip and raising one hand to wave, he spattered by like the wind, the little cakes of mud flying out from under the wheels. He taught me very early to say Dave was a pacer. Sometimes he took me out with him, but usually he drove alone, or with a lady.

All the boys rode, though I don't think Uncle Frank liked it as much as Daddy and Uncle Lloyd did. Daddy said they started riding when they were very little. Some Indians came into town with a carload of wild ponies to sell, and Grandfather bought three of them at two dollars apiece. They had never been broken but the Indian rode each one of them about an hour—with a halter on but no saddle—and said they would be all right. So Grandfather told him to take them on up to the house, and put them in the barn.

When he came home for dinner that noon, he told the

boys what he had bought for them and said they could go
out and try them. He would not have time because he had
to get back to the factory. Almost anything scared Grandmother usually, but this time she wasn't nervous. Grandfather said they were ponies and she thought it meant little
Shetlands—the kind she saw in the dog and pony shows—not
much bigger than a Saint Bernard. So she sent the boys on
out and went upstairs to take a rest.

Daddy said he was so excited when he got out to the barn
he thought he would choke. The other two boys let him stand
in front of them at the door and count,

> "Eeny, meeny, miney, mo,
> Cracka, feeny, finey, fo,
> Oppa, dooja, popa, dooja,
> Ick, bin, ban, do,"

to decide who was to have the pony which was in the first
stall, in the second and in the third, before they saw them,
so there wouldn't be any fighting about their looks. Then
they rushed pell-mell over to the stalls they had drawn and
every pony let fly with his back legs, exactly at the same
moment, Daddy said, with a kick that should have landed
them all into kingdom come, but just happened not to touch
them. Every time, however, that they would try to get in
the stalls, the kicks came exactly the same way at the same
time—and the boys were a little discouraged.

It was Uncle Lloyd who suggested that they try dropping
down on the ponies' backs from the hay-loft. Maybe they
wouldn't mind if the new owners didn't come up from behind. Grandfather had bought the boys some saddles from
a batch that came in from the West to Mr. Wachtel's store.
Mr. Wachtel didn't know what to do with them. Nobody in
those days, Daddy said, rode horseback with a saddle. Even
the doctor drove a carriage. The only time Daddy and the

other boys ever rode horseback was morning and evening, taking Grandfather's cows back and forth from their pasture outside of town. And, of course, although they always rode at those times and raced around the pasture, they wouldn't have used saddles. But Grandfather was buying some other things from Mr. Wachtel so he took the saddles along, too. He probably had it in his mind that some day he would get ponies for the boys, and it was just as well to have the saddles on hand when he could get them so cheap. But you couldn't put them on these ponies—not that first day, anyway.

Uncle Lloyd dropped down first onto his pony. He was the baby but he was always the ringleader, Daddy said, and not afraid of anything. The other two weren't exactly afraid, but just a little uncertain. Uncle Lloyd landed square on top of his pony and the animal, of course, began carrying on. But Uncle Lloyd held tight and grunted out to one of the other boys to get the pony untied. Daddy managed to do that— the Indian had left the halter on—and the last he saw, Uncle Lloyd was still on, but the pony was lying close to the ground, stretched out with the speed he was making. And then they were out of sight. It never occurred to Daddy to be worried. It just looked better fun than he had thought. He tore up the ladder as fast as he could lick it to the hay-loft, and dropped down on the back of his own pony. He yelled to Uncle Frank to untie him. Then he was lifted in the air, he said, with a rush that took the breath out of him and made his eyes sting. When he could see again they were passing Mrs. Bradbury's house. Someone was standing just inside the gate, but he had no time to see who it was. He thought he heard a scream, but between the noise of the wind in his ears and the gallop he couldn't be sure.

It was a wonderful day. Uncle Frank got his own pony untied by throwing down some extra food into the feed box, leaning out from the partition of the next stall, and untying very slowly while the pony was eating and didn't notice; then racing back to the loft and dropping down before the pony had a chance to discover it was loose. The scheme worked and they were down the road hell-bent for election like the others. No unit ever met up with either of the other two, but somehow, by late afternoon, they were all back in the barn again. They were none of them very sure about where they had gone—they hadn't been able to see well enough—but they were yelling so loudly when they came into the house, over which pony was the fastest and the strongest, that they didn't hear any of the uproar which the sound of their voices caused. When they came through from the back of the house and stepped into the front room, they realized suddenly that what looked like half the town was there, and was shouting at *them*.

Grandmother was on the horsehair sofa by the front windows, but she sat up when they came in. The boys couldn't make out at first what they were all talking about. Finally they got it through their heads that first Mrs. Bradbury and then everybody all over town—even up in the West End— had seen one of the boys skim past and had known he'd be dead in no time at all, so had hurried to tell Grandmother. She had not been worried when the first two or three arrived. They were just ponies the boys were riding, she explained, that Charles had bought from an Indian who was in town. But the women kept shrilling that if those were ponies they were the biggest they ever saw. They might be *little* horses, but they were certainly horses, and evil beasts. By the time the same story had arrived, told by seven or eight women from all over town, Grandmother was ready to die of fright. She walked up and down; she even *ran* up and down the block, calling the boys. But finally the women persuaded her to come in and lie down on the sofa under the windows, where she could hear them if they came back—or if anybody came to bring news of their getting killed.

Doctor Bowles was out in the country somewhere on a case. They couldn't reach him. Grandfather was at the factory, and the women were too nervous to hitch up a horse and go after him. So they just milled around all afternoon, Daddy said, moaning and going to the corner to look, and telling awful stories about people who had been killed.

Grandfather came home soon after the boys did, and the women scattered because he was cross with them for scaring Grandmother. Boys couldn't be sissies, he said; you had to give them a little breadth, and you mustn't be scared. A boy on a pony was the most natural thing in the world. That was all very well, the women told him, but he hadn't seen them. They didn't protest very much, however; Grandfather was always a man of considerable authority.

Grandmother got up and came to supper, but didn't want to talk about the ponies. The boys went upstairs and got cleaned up and when they came down asked if they could talk about it after supper. Grandfather said they could and even went out with them to the barn. Daddy said the ponies were probably exhausted by then. At any rate they were as quiet as could be, munching away in their stalls. They even let Grandfather go in where they were. Not one of them kicked. He said they were fine little animals and he thought the boys would get a lot of pleasure out of them. But they were not to frighten their mother again. They said,

"No, sir."

From that moment they lived with, and on, their ponies. They may have been anything but Saint Bernards, but the boys treated them as if they were. They led the animals when they weren't riding, fed them anything they could sneak out of the house, even tried their best to take them up to their rooms—until Grandmother stopped that. And eventually they got saddles onto them.

Grandmother was still agitated after what her friends had reported seeing on the first day, but Grandfather scoffed at it. A lot of women, he said, with not enough to do, working up a tall tale. Out of what? Three little boys riding on ponies.

He himself hadn't seen any of them ride until about three weeks after he had bought the animals. He was in town one day from the factory, for a Bank Meeting. It was in the Fall and there had been a week of rain. If you stepped into the street the mud was up to your ankles. The wagon ruts were so deep that they were like little ditches with water running through them. The board sidewalks were oozing. Grandfather was coming along Walnut Street from the Bank. He had on gaiters, but he was picking his way carefully to keep from going down over the tops of them, when Daddy rounded the corner on his pony. Daddy said it was always a bad corner, more slippery for some reason, than anywhere else, and also bad because something was there that his pony never liked. No matter how nice he was the minute before, he always shied at that spot, and then streaked past. Usually Daddy was ready for it, but on this particular day the mud was so deep and so slippery that when the pony shied, it skidded and slid on its belly. Daddy went off, skidded on his belly, and landed in a big puddle. They both got up together and shook themselves. The pony didn't bolt. Daddy ran and jumped on its back and they were off again, lickety-split, up Walnut Street, the mud and water streaming out behind them like a curtain. Daddy never even saw Grandfather, but heard afterward that he had had to go in and sit down on one of the revolving stools at the counter in Mr. Vatet's dry goods store before he could go on home. That night after supper he called the boys into his den and had a talk with them. He said he wanted them to enjoy their steeds, but hoped they were not being injudicious in handling them. The boys said, no, sir, they were not. Grandfather said, very well, but to remember that an excess in anything could bring about a misadventure. The boys said, yes, sir, they would remember. He never referred to the matter again except to ask from time to time how the ponies were doing. And when the boys answered, "Fine, sir," he was satisfied.

But years later Daddy found out that they had caused the town more palpitation daily than a three-alarm fire.

The ponies, he said, never became what you might call gentle, and yet in their own way they were biddable; they just didn't like to go slow. Neither, for that matter, did the boys.

When Uncle Frank and Uncle Lloyd were sent East to boarding school, the ponies were sold. Daddy's was sold, too, but that was because of Daddy's illness.

He used to say sometimes that Tom Sawyer and Huck Finn may have gone to their own funerals, but at least he heard the music for his.

It was the Spring when he was seventeen. He caught a chill one day from getting caught in the rain and not changing into dry clothes when he came home. And though Grandmother got out the tub and made him sit in it for a long time, steaming and with a mustard plaster on, the trouble, she said, had already started. He was very, very ill, growing steadily worse, until one day about three weeks later they thought he was going to die. The doctor said that he wouldn't last the night. Late in the afternoon Nell Wilson came up to the house to arrange for the music at the funeral and she played over some of the pieces that Grandmother said were Hal's favorites. Daddy heard them from upstairs, and didn't really care much at the time, though he knew they were having a rehearsal. He said it did give him a sort of a queer feeling.

Instead of dying that night, however, he got better and was finally well again. But Grandmother said they ought to send him out West, he looked so gaunt and thin with his clothes hanging on him. His eyes were way back in his head, and he had no color at all. That was just the kind of person, she insisted, that consumption was waiting for, and if they didn't get him away he would be down with it. Dr. Bowles agreed with her, and Grandfather felt it would be a fine developing experience for him, anyway. So they sent Daddy to a ranch which his Uncle Rob, Grandmother's brother, had in Colorado.

He rode out there every day and nearly all day. He did start to cough, and sometimes had quite bad attacks when he came in from riding. Uncle Rob was concerned; but Daddy put on weight so fast they thought it couldn't be consumption. When he came home he looked fine, but on account of his coughing out there, Grandmother didn't want to run the risk of his being sent away to school. In fact, she didn't want him to go to school at all. She said stooping over to study would compress his chest. Dr. Bowles seemed to think it would be just as wise for him not to be too cooped up. So Grandfather had him sworn in as a deputy county clerk where the hours would be light, and yet where he could study and learn some law, which ought to be a pretty good education. Muncie was the County Seat of Delaware County, so it was very handy to have him set up in a little office in the court house, right in the middle of town.

Daddy learned quite a good deal of law, he said, and worked so hard that he had very little time for anything outside. He saw his friends in the evenings, but Grandmother and Grandfather didn't approve of cards or dancing, so he

didn't go around with the fast crowd that skited all over
town in their buggies. But he had girls. When he came home
at night, Grandmother said she could always tell whom he
had gone to see and how the girl had treated him. He always
sat down at the piano, with his hat on the back of his head,
and played hymns when he came home, no matter how late
it was. He knew about music and could play other things,
but he always took to hymns when he had been out to see a
girl. And Grandmother knew, lying in bed upstairs, what
hymns went with what girls. *Jerusalem the Golden* was a
good evening. *From Greenland's Icy Mountains* was not
such a good one. And then he met Mother and bought a
horse.

He had not had a horse after he came back from Uncle
Rob's ranch. He had driven a little, but he got the horses
from Loan Franklin's livery stable. He didn't have time to
ride any more. For picnics or sleigh rides out in the country,
he could always hire a horse or go with some of the rest of
the crowd. But just at the time he met Mother he saw a
horse, a beauty; a thoroughbred somebody had brought up
from Kentucky. Lady was her name and he bought her.

Mother lived in Indianapolis, fifty miles away, and he
courted her a long time, riding over on the Interurban to see
her. When he couldn't get away he rode his beautiful horse,
Lady, up and down the country roads. He loved her more
than anything else he had ever owned. She followed him like
a dog; she did tricks. One of the things he taught her was to
high-step in time to music. Out in the back road, up and
down by the hour, he would walk in front of her, whistling,
singing, beating time, making music, and teaching Lady to
step high to the beat. She would rock her body from side to
side in perfect time and nod her head to him.

Finally Mother, after a decent interval of maidenly deco-
rum, said yes, she would marry Hal Kimbrough.

The wedding was in Indianapolis, and they went down to New York on their wedding trip. They heard *Siegfried* one afternoon, at the Metropolitan Opera House, and *Lohengrin* that night; three other operas on the following three nights and wished there had been more. They also saw *The Bells of Normandie*. They had never been able to hear enough music, even in Indianapolis, and they soaked it in, Daddy said. He said, too, that it was certainly a far cry from his evening programs of hymns.

When they came home they lived at the big house while our little house was being built in the next block. Daddy was not the clerk of the Court, any longer. Grandfather felt he had had enough education and it was time for him to go to work. So he went out to the Bridge Works, into the shop. Grandmother taught Mother to cook, and loved having a daughter in the house at last. Grandfather had loaned Daddy the money to build our little house but charged him one per cent more interest than the bank would have charged, because he had no collateral. That was part of the training, he said, toward becoming a man.

The young couple used to walk up the street every evening to see how much work had been done. And every morning Daddy got up early and rode Lady before he started off to work. He never took her out to the factory, because he said there wasn't a place suitable to put her in for the day.

Once a young man who had been a beau of Mother's in Indianapolis came through Muncie and stopped off to see her. She went down to the Big Four Station to meet him, and when they were walking home she showed off a little about her husband—how good-looking he was, and how stylish. On their way to the big house, Uncle Frank passed them riding his horse. He pulled up and spoke and Mother introduced him. But that, she said, was only Daddy's younger brother. A little farther on Uncle Lloyd drove by behind David. He was spinning along, his bright yellow gloves gleaming, going too fast to stop but saluting with his whip. And Mother explained to her erstwhile beau that that was Daddy's youngest brother. Both of the boys were home from the East on vacation. Daddy was in the factory with his father. And just then Daddy came along, pedaling his bicycle wearily, his face streaked with grease. His overalls were filthy; so were his hands on the handlebars from which his dinner pail was swinging. This, Mother said, half laughing and half in tears, was the oldest of the boys—and her husband—who really had the best horse in town. Daddy walked beside them, pushing his wheel.

The little house was barely finished in time for my arrival. Grandmother and Grandfather were spending the Winter in Mexico when they heard the news of a baby in the offing. Somehow Mother and Daddy got a little behind in their letters and Grandfather became anxious, so he sent off a telegram demanding to know if everything were all right. And Daddy wired back,

"Lottie not very well but very happy. Both send love, Hal."

Grandfather was in a blasting fury. He took apart the telegraph system and the government of Mexico for such garbling of a message, until Grandmother came back to the hotel from a little shopping tour with her friend, Mrs. George Maring. She saw the message and jerked Grandfather's coat tails until she could make him listen to her that the message was not in the least garbled. It made perfectly good sense and simply meant that Lottie was going to have a baby. Such a possibility had, evidently, not occurred to him. But he strode off to the railway office at once, telling Grandmother to pack up. And within twenty-four hours they were on their way home. Grandmother told him that it was non-sense for them to rush off so. The baby could not possibly be due for a long time. He pointed out that the telegram did not state the date. Since she, obviously, could not refute this, there was nothing for her to do but to come along, as she said, to keep him quiet. They *were* somewhat premature, as far as their arrival home in April was concerned, because my birthday was not until the 23rd of October. However, Grandmother said that it had been only an excuse to get home, anyway. She knew that Grandfather had been restless for the Bridge Works. And she herself was just as happy to have the last few months in the big house with Mother.

My arrival was uneventful, as far as I know, except that Daddy was said to have observed at first sight of me,

"Oh, Girl"—"Girl" was his name for Mother—"she looks like Aunt Mary."

Aunt Mary was Grandfather Kimbrough's sister. She was a woman of sterling character and had the most generous heart in the world, but was so ill-favored in appearance as to be almost renowned for it.

That Winter Daddy had time to ride Lady a great deal, and he began to have coughing attacks again. Finally Mother made him go to see Dr. Kemper. When he came back he told her that Dr. Kemper said the cough came from riding, and that he had a kind of asthma, which people got sometimes from horses.

That was what he had had out in Colorado when he rode so much. He had never been threatened with consumption at all.

Mother was so relieved that the terrible threat of consumption was removed forever, that she dismissed the asthma and streaming eyes as uncomfortable but of no importance. She was, therefore, incredulous when Daddy told her a few months later that he had made up his mind to sell Lady because of it. She couldn't believe it was true, knowing how nearly she and Lady shared his heart. She told him that it was not in the least necessary for him to do it. She had never known him to be apprehensive about his health before, and besides it wasn't as if this could be anything really serious. It must be uncomfortable but the attacks didn't last very long. And perhaps he could wear something over his face to keep from breathing in whatever it was from the horse that brought it on. But Daddy was adamant, stern with her. He had never been that before, and asked her please not to speak of it again. His mind was made up. He was going to sell Lady.

He rode Lady every moment that he could, on Sundays, too, though Grandfather and Grandmother didn't approve of that. The curious thing to Mother was, that the asthma got no worse the more he rode. It was better, if anything. It had never occurred to her that he could be a physical coward and she tried not to believe it now. But she could find no other reason and was sick at heart over it. She wanted to reason it out with him but he would not allow the subject to be mentioned. She could see that he was wretched, too; ashamed, she thought. Sometimes she would see him walking home instead of riding, going past the house slowly with his arm up on Lady's neck and Lady nuzzling up and down the side of his coat.

He found a buyer, a man from Louisville, and he was glad, he said, that she was going back to the country she had come from. She was to be shipped on the first of June. The last month before she left, Daddy scarcely rode her at all. He would go out early every morning as if he were going to, saddle her, and then he would take the saddle off, put her in the barn again and come back to the house. Mother knew then that he was defeated by his fears.

Just about a week before Lady was to go, Mr. John Smith,

who was the head of the G.A.R. chapter in Muncie, telephoned the Bridge Works. General Andrews, from West
Point, he said, was coming to Muncie to make the Decoration
Day speech at the cemetery, and had sent word that if someone would provide him with a horse he would like to ride it
at the head of the procession. Everybody knew that Daddy's
was the handsomest horse in town. Would he lend her for
the occasion? Daddy said he would.

Decoration Day that year I was seven months old—was, I
suppose, much like all the Decoration Days I have known
since—sticky hot, with the smell of lilacs and peonies and
syringas heavy in the air. The streets were dusty and crowded
with people, the side streets blocked by the buggies of the
farmers who had come into town for the celebration; Main
Street was kept clear for the parade. Mother and Daddy
watched it from a balcony of the court house. I sat on Mother's
lap until I got restless and then Daddy took me over. Just as
he had settled me the parade came into view.

He leaned over to Mother.

"Look," he said, "here she comes."

Up the center of the street, ahead of all the rest by ten or
fifteen feet, Mother remembered always, came Lady with
the General from West Point riding her. Just as they got to
the corner where the court house stands, the city band struck
up the new march that was catching on all over the country
—*The Stars and Stripes Forever*.

"Da-da-*da*, da-da-*da*, da-da-*da*," the horns shouted into
the dusty heat, and Lady paused.

The General moved to touch her into place again, but she
was lifting her left front leg high. She stretched it forward
taut, and brought her foot down on the full beat of the
music. And then she lifted and stretched her right front leg,
placing her foot down just as Daddy had taught her, whistling for her in the back roads, her body swaying from side

to side in flawless rhythm, her lovely neck arched high, her head nodding to the beat.

And suddenly the crowd that lined the streets set up a yell such as, perhaps, had never been heard there before. But I, Mother said, startled by the noise, put my hand on Daddy's face. She saw then that his cheeks were wet with the tears which were spilling silently down them. He didn't speak, nor could she, and so there was no sound on the balcony, only the yelling below in the street, until Lady, high-stepping, sure and gay, had led the procession out of sight.

Daddy never owned another horse, and never rode again. I was nearly grown, too, before he told Mother that all the asthma in the world would not have made him let Lady go. But the cost of the baby was a debt he had not been able to pay, and the verdict of his father had been that selling Lady in order to pay it, was training for manhood.

Chapter Five

One of the incidental things which had contributed to Daddy's financial overload was the box of dirt from Grandmother Wiles, but Mother did not know about that for years.

Grandmother Wiles was an imperious and an impulsive woman, and she and my Grandfather lived in Indianapolis. *He* was the gentlest of men, Daniel Hough Wiles; handsome, too, with thick, startlingly white hair when I knew him, and deep-set blue eyes which humor almost always lighted. He suffered from asthma, and the only time I ever saw him show a sign of ill humor was when anyone asked him how he felt, and even then it was the expression which exasperated him.

"I *feel* with my fingers, of course," he would snap. "How else *would* I feel?"

Or if he were too spent with coughing to be able to speak, he would wriggle his fingers impatiently at the offender, his mild, deep eyes cold.

"I *am* better, or I *am* worse," he taught me very early, "but that is *not* how I *feel*."

Mildness in Grandmother Wiles, however, was as infrequent as was his departure from it. Not that she was disagreeable; she had a lusty and infectious enjoyment of nearly everything, but she was volatile and violent. Ideas came to her more quickly than to most people, and the period of time between receiving and acting upon them was almost imperceptible.

When Mother was growing up and attending the Girls'

Classical School, they lived on Delaware Street, and their neighbors were the Benjamin Harrisons. The gardens joined, I think, and one Christmas the two families made a little sentimental exchange of keys to the gate which separated them. Mother, even in reminiscence, always grew a little apprehensive over the telling of a meeting at this gate, so that I may easily be inaccurate about the details. However, Mr. and Mrs. Harrison moved to Washington to live in the White House, when he became President, and the house next door stood empty. One Summer evening, Grandmother, who was a passionate gardener—she could not conceivably have been an indifferent anything—was watering her flower beds after sundown. Suddenly a key turned in the lock of the garden gate, and when it opened, President Harrison stood on the threshold. Astounded, Grandmother cried out, "Why, Benjamin!" and turned the hose full force in his face.

He was astounded, too, and staggered from the impact into the shrubbery, revealing Mrs. Harrison just behind him.

"And *Mary*," Grandmother called, her voice high with pleasure at such a surprise—and diverted the nozzle with a jerk to Mrs. Harrison's countenance.

The little greeting evidently did not diminish for a moment the friendship between the two families, because it was in the Winter of that same year that the Daniel Wiles gave an "evening reception with dancing" for the Benjamin Harrisons, again home from the White House.

About an hour before the "evening" was scheduled to begin, Grandmother sat at her bureau under the ministrations of the French hairdresser—and how he had found his way out to Indianapolis I do not know. He went from house to house to "do" the ladies. Grandmother had on, over her corset cover and petticoats, a short, white dimity dressing sacque. Under the top petticoat she had on—I would have known, even if the hairdresser didn't—her bustle. She wore

Shook both hands above her head . . . and announced that the house was too hot.

one until she died in 1926; said it took away the sagged and swayback look women were apt to get and she liked the warmth of it, too.

But on the night of the reception she was too warm in it, and even in the sheer dimity dressing sacque. Not that she gradually became aware of this. She jumped to her feet as the Frenchman was twirling his iron preparatory to a dart on another curl, shook both hands above her head—her most characteristic gesture—until the heavy gold bracelet on each wrist was shaken down toward the elbow, and announced that the house was too hot. That was all she said, and that very minute she was gone from the room, the Frenchman left twirling his iron.

What she did was to go straight to the cellar and look at the furnace. Grandfather Wiles said later, benignly, that he didn't suppose she had ever looked at it before. Her answer was that you needed only one look to see that it was too hot. Even the door was yellow red, so she opened it with an iron bar standing near by, filled a pail of water from the spigot in the corner, and threw it in over the white-hot coals. The explosion must have knocked her ten feet or more, but when she sat up, she didn't seem to be hurt and the fire looked much lower, so she went back upstairs to finish dressing.

Her bureau was tall, walnut, with extended little round shelves and many little drawers, their handles made of glass drops. The mirror in the center was full length, and that was where she saw herself as she prepared to sit down again for the hairdresser to go on with his work. He was in no condition to go on with it—struck dumb and still waving his curling iron, but in a sort of warding off motion at her—and it was this curious gesture that made her lean toward the full-length mirror to see if her appearance was what ailed him. It was, indeed. From head to foot she was as black as the coal in the bin—all except the top of her head. That, well back to the crown, looked as bare and shiny as a darning egg.

When she had bathed—or rather, scrubbed—she found, too, that her eyebrows and eyelashes were gone. Nothing could be done about them, but she demanded impatiently that the hairdresser devise a "coiffure" which would cover the bald area, and be sharp about it. She and Mr. Wiles must receive their guests in half an hour.

They did, too, with President and Mrs. Harrison beside them, both somewhat dazed at her transformation. Grandmother was only exasperated at the Frenchman in spite of the superhuman work he had done. She had had to find her smelling-salts for him. He had said he felt faint.

She was impulsive, too, on the day when the Bishop came to call, and he must have been the one to tell it. Hurrying downstairs in a pleasantly nervous flurry when she was told that he was in the parlor, she tripped on the top step and fell the entire length of the stairway. She fell sitting, and struck the highly polished floor at the base with such force that she careened across it, together with a small prayer rug which she had encountered there. She only came to a stop well inside the parlor. The Bishop, after a momentary pause of surprise, hurried over to help her to her feet.

"I have never, Bishop Cunningham," she protested, as she took his hand and rose, "come downstairs that way before."

The box of dirt that nearly broke Daddy's back was only another impulse—a later one, because these things had happened before Mother was married. But working in her garden after Mother had moved to Muncie, Grandmother Wiles thought what a sweet thing it would be for Mother to start the garden of her own little house with soil from the garden of her childhood. To think of it was enough to put it into execution at once, of course, before she left the garden. She had a crate—the largest she could find—packed with the rich black loam. Then she sent it off immediately, express collect, to my father; but she didn't think of that—she was only pleased at having it as a surprise for Mother, by addressing it to Daddy.

It was a surprise for him, too; a surprise of fifty dollars, and he had to hire a dray besides, to bring it from the station; it was too heavy for the express wagon. He thought it must be something very important and did not question the payment, though he had to borrow the money from Grandfather, at interest. But when he and Mother opened the crate and found that the dirt on top wasn't used for protecting something, but was dirt all the way through—plain, black, garden dirt—he was very surprised again.

After the little house and the garden were finished, Grandmother Wiles used to come over from Indianapolis to visit. I was not very old when I began to sense that there was something momentous about these periods. They were *occasions,* attended with pleasure, tinged with awe, by the friendly neighbors. Perhaps it was her height which awed them. This was a little greater than average—Grandmother Kimbrough was only five-feet-two—or perhaps it seemed greater by reason of her grenadier's stance and carriage. It may have been her strong features, or the way she used them, compressing her generous mouth to a thin line and lowering her eyes to a slit when she was impatient or bored. She always dressed stylishly, wearing her hair—which, after the explosion, never grew long—in fine, short waves away from a center part, with a large figure eight, which was false, in the back. She wore, invariably, a pair of gold buckle bracelets which she would dislodge from her wrists half-way to her elbows, by shaking her hands abruptly above her head. I dare say *that* was to observers a somewhat disconcerting gesture. Her shoes were of as thin leather, it seemed to me, as her gloves, and fitted as smooth and tight. She wore her face veils pinned back very tight, too. She always put on her gloves by wetting the thumb and forefinger of one hand, and smoothing down between them each finger of the other. She said that she would as soon go out of the house with her corset strings hanging, as with her gloves unbuttoned. It was hard to fit the metal glove buttoner over the tiny buttons, and pull them into the buttonholes, but I learned to do it, even when she wouldn't stand still. Her Winter coat that I remember best was a short, sealskin jacket, tightly fitted at the waist, and edged with chinchilla around the collar and the big, wide revers that pointed above each shoulder. Her dresses were likely to be made with lace berthas; she loved lace and collected it. On the bertha almost always lay a heavy onyx necklace of pear-shaped stones joined with gold links, and supporting in the center a medallion edged with pearls, with a gold design in the center on one side. The back was hollowed out, covered with glass, and contained a picture of my grandfather. It was the only demonstration of sentiment toward him that I ever observed in her, although I did not think it as strange then as I did when I grew older, that although she bore him a child, she never spoke of, or to, him except as *Mr.* Wiles.

One Christmas she gave me a doll, and for a time after that I hated her with almost as deep concentration as I hated the doll. She had it dressed, from the skin out, by her own dressmaker in Indianapolis, and every article was sewn on tight, even the shoes. When callers came, during her Christmas visit, she would ask me to show them "Josephine," as I called the miserable wretch, and she would smile and bend her head in stately satisfaction as they twittered over the exquisite underclothes, "every stitch made by hand, and with *real* lace, and even black lace stockings." The dress was *black*, too—net over pink satin. I was, of course, forbidden to cut off the clothes, but after a while I think she sensed my venomous feeling toward it. I know that she remarked about my constant and devoted companionship with a doll Grandmother Kimbrough had brought me from St. Augustine. It was a baby at one end, but when you pulled the clothes over its head, you got, from the other end, a mammy nurse. Shortly after, she suggested putting Josephine away until I was older, when I would appreciate her more. I have never appreciated more that cold, white kid body stuck through with the stitches of her "hand-made" finery, nor the implacable, "hand-painted" French head.

I did, however, forgive her Josephine. I would have forgiven even greater indignities because of two superb gifts which she had, and which she gave generously—her gift with animals, and her gift for story-telling.

I had such a yearning for dogs that I hunted them more eagerly than any dog-catcher, up alleys, even into back yards, if Grandmother Wiles were visiting us. No matter how dirty or sinister each dog looked when, wheezing and panting, I carried him home from whatever remote spot I had found him, she would smuggle him and me into the cellar. There she would wash him, throwing her bracelets back on her arms, bending down to scrub, and to reassure the frightened animal with the gentlest words. Then we would present him clean and dry to Daddy—all three of us timorous—my heart knocking so that I could not speak; only hold the dog out toward him. Because Daddy, usually an understanding man, hated dogs with ferocity. Later I learned that it was because one had bitten him when he was a child, and he was really afraid of them. Those must have been the only times Grandmother even approached being timorous, certainly with her own son-in-law. And yet Daddy nearly always let me keep the animal.

Once he even bought me a dog from Mr. Meeks, our butter-and-egg man. A black, fluffy puppy with white paws. I

got his name out of a book, adding a last name, of course;
"Whitesocks Merrylegs Kimbrough," I called him, with no
abbreviation of so much as a syllable, even in the most anxious
moments when I summoned him back from a roam out of
our yard. The strays were extra, and generally very tempo-
rary. Usually they wandered off in spite of my surveillance,
ropes, and vehement pleas to keep the gate closed when I
was not there. Sometimes a distraught previous owner would
track down and claim my "find." I never made any effort to
keep it then, but after they had both gone, I would be possessed of violent grief.

It was in those first hours of loss that Grandmother Wiles
was my great solace, rocking forcefully in the big, tufted,
green velvet chair by the fireplace in our living room, and
telling stories, wedging me down beside her, my head knocking the back of the chair with the vigor of her propelling.

There was never anyone else in my life who could surpass
or even equal her at stories. About the Indians who would
come to the door, when her mother was young and alone
down in Brown County in Indiana, and demand to be fed;
and about the perilous trip her great-grandparents had made
in a covered wagon up from North Carolina, to settle in Indiana. The stories scared me, but they comforted me, too,
and salved my fierce anguish. At less critical times she would
tell, with a regal enjoyment, funny stories, escapades, absurdities, that had happened to her.

I could never be sure, however, just which incidents that
happened to her she would eventually enjoy. Once, at Easter
time, when we visited her in Indianapolis, she bought a white
rabbit for me, and hid it in the little conservatory off the stair
landing. On Easter morning, after I had found all the colored
eggs and fluffy yellow cotton chickens hidden in the rooms
downstairs, she opened the door of the conservatory and
called out to me,

"Why, here, I believe, is the Easter bunny himself. He's decided to stay with you."

Her voice rose to a shriek like the battle cry of the Walkyrie, and the Easter bunny rose on it and sailed through the door pell-mell down the stairs. I screamed with delight and set off to chase it round and round, through the parlor, library, dining room, den, over the glossed floor, leaving dunes of rugs in our noisy wake. Grandmother was just as active as we, investigating clamorously in the conservatory, the disaster there; for the Easter bunny, left overnight in that leafy home, had eaten almost every leaf, stems and blossoms too. What it had not eaten, the little pet had at least bitten and discarded on the ground. It made a very active Easter morning, and one to which Grandmother never cared to refer, though the original idea, and it was original, had been hers.

Another experience, however, to her discomfiture never ceased, in reminiscence, to give her pleasure. She had been paying us a short visit one June, and went on an evening to call on Grandmother and Grandfather Kimbrough. Uncle Lloyd had been in Indianapolis to have his tonsils out and was expected back with Aunt Huda, to convalesce for a few days at the big house. Grandmother sailed up Washington Street, her taffeta skirts crackling with the vigor and sweep of her passage, to inquire about Lloyd, and pass an hour or so with Mr. and Mrs. C. M. She thought, too, as she told it afterwards, that she and Mr. C. M. might even maneuver themselves into a good political discussion, for of the blood that flowed in the veins of both, three-quarters was fiery Republican.

But when she came up the walk she could make out, in the darkness, figures sitting on the porch. Grandfather came to the head of the steps to greet her.

"Good evening, good evening, Mrs. Wiles."

But Grandmother Kimbrough broke over his voice, calling from the swing at the end, where she was sitting, "Mrs. Wiles, this is Mr. Jones," and a figure rose up from a chair near by.

Why Grandmother Wiles thought that it was Uncle Lloyd, she could never explain, nor why she thought that Grandmother Kimbrough would call him Mr. Jones except, she said, that out of exuberance over his homecoming, and pride that he should have recovered so rapidly, a joke was being made. At any rate that is what she thought, and she entered into the spirit of play. Disengaging her hand from Grandfather's she swaggered over to the shadowy figure and slapped him on the back!

"Well, *Jonesey*," she said, "welcome."

There was an astonished silence, of which she was totally unaware. Grandmother Kimbrough came into it eventually; so did Mr. Jones.

"Thank you," he said faintly.

"And this is Mrs. Jones," Grandmother Kimbrough persevered.

Grandmother Wiles included her in her joviality. If they were going to call Aunt Huda "Mrs. Jones" she would respond in kind.

"Welcome to you, too," she said, and gave her cheek a hearty pinch.

Then she settled herself between the Joneses with a hand on Mr. Jones' knee, and launched into gay conversation.

Once Mr. Jones tried to speak, but she checked him.

"Don't talk," she advised. "Just rest," and she patted his cheek.

Grandmother Kimbrough succeeded in breaking in only once.

"I don't believe, Mrs. Wiles, that you have met Mr. and Mrs. Jones before, have you?"

"Oh, no, certainly not," she answered, and gave them each an affectionate slap.

No one tried to stem her after that, but some time later Mr. and Mrs. Jones murmured that they must go. She agreed with them heartily.

"Should have gone before, if you really mean to go home. It's much too late."

Grandmother Kimbrough tried, she said, to speak but could not seem to find any words. And at that moment Grandfather turned on the porch light to guide the Joneses down the steps.

Grandmother Wiles froze.

"Why," she said, in a little voice, "it isn't Lloyd and Huda at all."

Grandmother found her own voice.

"Lloyd and Huda?" she repeated. "Why, how could they be?" She went back to the beginning. "This is Mr. and Mrs. *Jones.*"

Sometimes I stayed alone with Grandmother and Grandfather Wiles, in Indianapolis. Mother and Daddy left me there when they went up to Chicago to hear some opera. Grandmother would let me go to sleep in her big walnut bed in the alcove of her bedroom. Some time later I would be moved into the room next door, but when I got into her bed, she would pull the cord on the light in the hall to the dimmer, and if it were Winter she would light the gas log that faced the alcove which the big bed nearly filled. She would sit beside me then, very straight, on a carved walnut chair, and tell me about when she was a little girl. The gas fire would flicker on the walnut dresser with the cut glass knobs, where she had first seen herself after the furnace explosion. That dresser had come in the covered wagon from North Carolina. If you pulled out the drawers you could see the diary of the trip written on the soft wood, because there was no paper. The bolster from the bed lay stiffly across a sofa under the windows—I would have been afraid of it if the dimmer in the hall had not been on—and I could see, from the dimmer and the firelight, the flash of the restless gold bracelets on her arms.

Grandmother could have told me, I know, a hundred stories or more, but I begged always for my favorites. There was so little time before I dropped off to sleep. It was too risky to try one that might not be quite so good, and so I heard the same ones over and over, loving them the more because I grew to know every word and every gesture the bracelets showed.

One Christmas time, when she and Grandfather were visiting us, they came to the Christmas party at my kindergarten. Miss Zenobia Stewart was our teacher, and the basement of the Universalist Church our schoolhouse. I loved everything about kindergarten, except cutting out and pasting paper rings into link chains. The marching and singing, especially when they were combined, was my idea of a rousing good kindergarten morning. But the paper business at long low tables, whose tops were marked off in little squares, for no particular reason, was dull business.

> "There's a wee little nest in the old oak tree
> Up so high, up so high.
> There are three little eggs blue as blue can be,
> Like the sky, like the sky,"

I liked to sing, at the top of my lungs, especially if I were leading the marching.

> "You dear little thumb, go to sleep, go to sleep
> And you, pointing finger, too."

This was not a marching song, but fairly entertaining in spite of that, because it had pantomime—thumb under, then first finger, and so on, until you had made a fist, which you swung around violently to the chorus of:

"So rock-a-bye, baby,
Upon the tree top."

We sang these for the Christmas entertainment, and Grandmother Wiles nodded at me as I marched by. The room was so crowded with parents and friends, there was barely room for our marching, but I shouted out the words happily as we skimmed the visitors' knees. After the march, we each took a little chair from our tables against the wall, and made a circle around the Christmas tree in the middle of the room. This was a complicated and deafening maneuver, and when it was accomplished, I could not see that very much had been gained. We were in a circle around the tree, but there was nothing much to look at there, trimmed with the colored paper chains and stars we had been cutting and pasting for weeks, though I had had enough of it the first morning. Underneath the tree was a mound of toys, but I had no desire to look at them. In the first place, they were for poor children and we had brought them—we were not to be given one of them. Furthermore, I had been over-susceptible to Miss Stewart's speech that if we picked out one of our toys which we loved especially, and brought *that very one* to give to a "poor" child, we would feel happier than we had ever felt before. My toy was there, under the tree, *that very one,* and I had seldom been less happy about anything. Sold down the river was my feeling about it, and I was about to say so when Miss Zenobia cut in.

"Emily," she said, "suppose you tell us the Christmas story."

I didn't know what she meant by *The Christmas Story*, and I was preoccupied, anyway. But a story was something I did like, either to hear, or to tell. If I were to be singled out on this especial occasion, with so many extra people there, I would give them one of my very best stories. I settled back in my chair, crossed one knee over the other, and began.

"Once upon a time, when my Grandmother Sarah Jane Wiles was a little girl, she went to visit her Uncle Amos."

A murmur broke out from the circle of grown-ups, and even then, as it has always been for me, an audience and a response made the headiest intoxicant. I launched more stalwartly into the narrative, over-riding without effort some murmur from Miss Zenobia about meaning the *Christmas* story, dear, that we had *all* learned—about Bethlehem; didn't I remember? I was away with Sarah Jane to Uncle Amos's, and I carried my audience with me.

Sarah Jane had not gone alone. She had been accompanied by her brothers and sisters, five of them, and all with sonorous names. I said them over as she herself had recited them beside the big walnut bed in the alcove, where the gas log flickered:

"Ezekiel Thomas, Jeremiah William, Zeno,"

The Muncie parents sat very still, their heads lowered in embarrassment for poor Mrs. Wiles, to be so humiliated in public.

"Amos and Phoebe."

Some of them, Mother always thought, were gratified inwardly by this disgrace. They were the ones who were self-conscious around Grandmother, but always oh-ed and ah-ed over everything she said.

Sarah Jane, I informed them all, was not a very good little girl. She got into mischief often, and she was not always truthful.

There was one in the eye for Mrs. Daniel Hough Wiles from Indianapolis, and her stuck-up city ways.

And, sure enough, at Uncle Amos's she got into trouble again. It was her idea to walk across a fallen log, over a churning stream, swollen beyond itself by the early Spring rains. The other children begged her not to do it. It was very cold, the log was narrow, the water would be icy; and, besides, if she fell in Uncle Amos would whip her. She was scornful, and she taunted them. They were all scared cats, she told them, and wouldn't dare to do it. But she dared them, she *double dared* them.

I stopped my narrative for a moment to allow the full impact of that to sink in on my audience, and there were clucking sounds in response. Everyone knew the significance of a double dare. You couldn't refuse it; that was against the law.

And so they had gone across, but not all together. I took them each, one at a time, over that perilous trip, just as Grandmother had taken them for me, while the gas log flickered in Indianapolis.

Certainly I was holding my audience. There was not a stir even from the children in the circle around the tree, and as I rose to my feet to demonstrate how the passage was made, every one of them looked up at me. Arms spread wide, I teetered to one side and then to the other, because the log was slippery, too, and not securely held. When Ezekiel lost his balance and fell headlong, there was a gasp from every member of the circle, and several sharp cries from the grownup audience.

One by one Sarah's family ventured out upon the log, and one by one they fell. Sometimes they almost reached the other side, sometimes their fate was swifter, but I was with them every step of the way.

Sarah Jane was the last to go. She had taunted the rest of them, yah-yahing them to their destruction until even gentle

Phoebe had been excoriated out and down. Only then did Sarah Jane herself set foot upon the bridge, and pausing a minute at the first step, run lightly and safely the rest of the way. She had learned from watching the others, that swiftness and not looking down were the only ways to accomplish the end.

Safe on the other side, she stood triumphant and opened her mouth for a yah-yah that would ring in the ears of the sissies floundering and shivering, out of the frigid water. There, on the shore she had just left, stood Uncle Amos, not saying anything, just standing and peeling a switch from a hazelnut tree.

Uncle Amos was a Quaker, I told my spellbound audience —so were all the children—and as each chattering wretch came up the bank he spoke,

"Ezekiel Thomas, did *thee* go in the water?"

If ever there was a rhetorical question! Nevertheless, that must have been what he said, for that is the way Grandmother told it to me. And the next observation, which followed close on was,

"Bend down."

A pause—"*Whack, whack, whack.*"

The audience gasped, and someone said, "Shame."

That was the way Grandmother had pictured it over and over again, when I lay shivering in the big walnut bed, and I followed her word and gesture.

"Jeremiah William, did *thee* go in the water?"

A pause—"*Whack, whack, whack.*"

But when it came to little Phoebe there was no whack, whack, whack.

"Run to thy Aunt Sarah," he told her, "and let her put dry things on thee."

Sarah Jane was the only one left, and she had had to watch

every whacking. But she *hadn't* fallen in, so it wouldn't happen to her. He changed the words.

"Sarah Jane," he boomed, "was it *thy* suggestion? Come here to me."

And Sarah Jane must go back across the dangerous log, over the icy roaring water, to a black-haired, angry man with a hazelnut switch in his hand, and four shivering, sobbing boys around him.

She did go back, and even then she didn't fall, but he gave her no credit for that.

"Bend over," he ordered, and Sarah Jane obeyed.

"*Whack, whack, whack.*"

But Mrs. Daniel Hough Wiles of Indianapolis was on her feet.

"He put me over his knee, Emily, and lifted my petticoats, one, two, three—the muslin with lace, the muslin with a ruffle, and the flannel—and then he——"

I remembered now.

"He took down your panties——"

"Pantalettes," she corrected.

"Pantalettes—and whacked your *bare skin.*"

Mrs. Wiles sat down again and adjusted her bracelets tranquilly.

"That is the way it happened," she said. "You must tell the story properly."

Chapter Six

Our neighborhood was full of interesting people. When we went down town, any member of the family and I, we would speak to most of the people we passed, but I didn't feel that I knew them as comfortably as I knew the people up and down the street. Some of the children I knew very well, even though, like Agnes Smith and Mildred Kitzelman, they lived clear at the other end of town. But we went to the same Sunday-school and always to the same birthday parties. Those two girls were cousins. Mildred was dark, with black eyes and very dark hair. Pretty as a picture, you always heard the grown-ups saying to each other when she was around. Agnes' coloring was fairer. "They make such an interesting contrast," the older people told each other. Agnes was quick and funny. I was always delighted to see both of them whenever we met, and always surprised, too, because I knew that they lived clear at the other end of town. I marveled whenever they arrived at the same places where I was, because it seemed to me they had come from such a distance, with surely many, many obstacles involved. Actually, they lived not a block farther from the center of town than I.

The territory which I personally covered almost daily was small; therefore I knew it well, and kept tabs on it. I knew the back door as well as the front of every house within a radius of two blocks. Furthermore, I knew on what day of the week every household did its baking. Naturally, I had my favorites. One establishment would, it seemed to me,

turn out better cakes; another excel in cookies. Mrs. Wildman's Emma made the best bread, crusty and with holes in
it like a mustard plaster's. I always paid a round of calls at
what I hoped were favorable times—favorable for food—
though I always carried home the loot because I was not allowed to eat between meals. There was nothing, however, to
prevent my snagging a little extra treat here and there to
brighten the dull fare at home. Other people's food always
seemed very much better than ours, so far as I could judge
from samples at the kitchen door.

I couldn't gauge it from birthday parties. Those were always alike in food wherever I went. Chicken patties, canned
peas—"French peas" we called them—tiny and very sweet, and
there wasn't a child among us who didn't beg for them rather
than the fresh ones. Birthday parties always included mashed
potatoes, too, with gravy, and ice cream and cake for dessert. Once in a very great while I did have dinner or supper
with a friend. I brought back the reports of those meals and
would repeat them over and over to the smallest detail,
savoring again in memory the wonder of such magic. One
time Mother, her patience spent, telephoned Mrs. Rich. I
had had dinner with Lydia Rich a week before.

"Will you," Mother begged her friend, "give me the recipe
for the cake Emily had at your house? And what on earth
did you have for meat? I couldn't even recognize the animal
from her description."

Mrs. Rich was mortified. She said it had been an economy
meal and she had never thought to have to reveal it. The
cake was only a "Two-egg" and the meat was calves' liver
with lemon juice and butter on it.

We ate calves' liver, too, once in a while but not very
often, not often enough for me to have been accustomed to
the taste of it. For the most part, Mr. Topps, the butcher,
gave some along with the regular meat order to his custom-

ers who had dogs. Everybody agreed it was the best kind of
dog meat. If you asked for enough for the family, Mr. Topps
charged ten cents a pound. Grandmother Kimbrough thought
that was very dear and didn't care much for eating that part
of an animal, anyway, except from a chicken or turkey where
it was small. Once, I told Grandmother, I had heard a lady
in our street say they were going to have kidneys for supper.
I asked what those were. Grandmother said not to say that
word again. Later I heard her say darkly to the daughters-
in-law that she didn't believe those people were very clean.

Once I asked another lady what was in a brown paper bag
on her kitchen table. Her back yard was across the alley
from ours. Playing in my swing, I had caught the smell of
baking and tracked it immediately to this source. I did not,
however, wish to seem greedy nor make the reason for my
morning call too obvious, so I was leading off with some
general social conversation. The contents of the paper bag
seemed a good opening. They were, the lady said, to*mah*toes.
At that my curiosity leaped to a fever point. Something of
which I had never heard was in that paper bag. I asked
breathlessly if I might be permitted to see. She tolerantly
lowered the bag, opened it under my nose. They were to*ma*-
toes. I backed away hurriedly and said I must be getting
home, I thought my mother wanted me. I did not even mention cookies because I felt suddenly as if I were talking to a
foreigner and that made me uneasy. I learned, as a matter
of fact, though I did not need corroboration, that she had
actually not been born in Muncie.

Mr. and Mrs. Hummel, who owned the bakery down on
Main Street, were German, but they gave me no uneasiness
because of that. I liked them both very much indeed. They
said they were German. They spoke German. They even
spoke English very differently from the way we spoke it in
Muncie. That was not what I understood by being "for-

eign." Foreign to me was something which you had every reason to expect to be familiar, turning out to be different and strange to you. That was a cause for uneasiness. Therefore, I mistrusted for a long time after that those people who said to*mah*toes.

There was nothing strange to me about anyone else in my neighborhood. Francis Gill Boyd lived as far down Washington Street, beyond me, as I was allowed to go by myself. He was deaf and dumb but I never thought there was anything remarkable in that. We simply talked on our fingers. He taught me how. We played together every day. "Such a handsome child," people said. I thought he was, too, slim and tall for his age, not chunky like me, with very large, blue eyes, but dark; bright pink cheeks and pale brown curly hair. He was fun to play with but serious, too, almost all the time. He always watched you anxiously. He never looked around and at other things the way the rest of us did when we were playing. He lived in a big red brick house with white columns across the front. Also, he lived with his grandmother and grandfather, not his own mother and father, and this, too, I thought was just as it should be. Only grandparents, I believed, lived in big houses. Parents with small children lived in small houses. Francis Gill moved to New York and the Elks bought the house for their Lodge. I visited the Elks a few times but found it dull.

Next to the Boyds' was the George Maring house. That was a big house, too, and also red brick. But the child Lavinia who lived there wasn't their own at all. She was a niece who lived with them. As I pointed out to Betty Ball to prove that she was adopted, *no* children who lived in big houses really belonged to the owners. Lavinia, who was my friend, always lived, from the time she was a very little girl, with Mr. and Mrs. Maring. Mrs. Maring was Grandmother Kimbrough's best friend. Lavinia was a quiet child who liked secrets. Mrs. Maring was even tinier than my grandmother, who weighed ninety-six pounds, and Mrs. Maring was not quiet at all. She was like a little bird, chirruping and twittering, holding her head a little on one side, looking at you out of very bright eyes, and bobbing her head up and down rapidly, as you talked, to show that she was listening. Her laugh was high, and quick to begin and to end. She was almost always surprised.

"Well, *mercy*," she would say, "is that *so?*" The Marings generally went away with Grandmother and Grandfather Kimbrough in the Winter. Usually they went to St. Augustine but sometimes they took longer trips together. Once, the Winter before I was born, they had gone to Mexico. They liked to travel, to bring home curios for their cabinets in the parlor, but they weren't comfortable while they were away. Mrs. Maring and Grandmother didn't mind being uncomfortable as much as Grandfather and Mr. Maring minded it. The two men were always homesick, Grandmother said, from the moment they got on the train, and only wanted to get home again as soon as they could. But Grandmother and Mrs. Maring loved to shop. They would spend their time looking through all the stores and buying things. Grandfather and Mr. Maring were very patient about it, Grandfather said. They just walked up and down outside and smoked their cigars and talked politics.

Sometimes, at home, I went shopping with Mrs. Maring and Grandmother and often to market. They nearly always marketed together, one stopping for the other with the horse and carriage. They showed me where to smell a muskmelon to see if it was ripe. I was suspicious, too, of the first person I heard call a "muskmelon" a "cantaloup." It sounded foreign again to me. They taught me, too, where and how to pinch the breast-bone of a chicken to make sure the meat was plentiful and tender. When they went to buy sheets or tablecloths, they always took off their gloves, wet their forefingers, and held them underneath. The way the moisture came through was proof of how good the linen was.

Once a man came from New York with fur coats. Grandmother was going to buy a new sealskin but Grandfather thought the price was too high. "A pirate," he called the man, and was very angry. You could hear his voice all over the big house. The man had the fur coats spread over the furniture in the hall. Grandmother had telephoned Mrs. Maring to come down to help her select one and had called Mother, too, so I was there. Grandmother and Mrs. Maring went from one coat to the other, blowing on them. They said that was the way to tell good sealskin. If the color were good and strong at the roots, then it was good skin. But Grandfather sent the man away without letting Grandmother buy one. Later, Mother persuaded him to read out of the Century Encyclopedia how sealskin coats were made and how the skins were gotten. Grandfather was impressed by that. He thought it was remarkable, he said, that they should be available at all and regretted having misjudged the man's pricing. He sent a letter of apology explaining that he had read about the industry in the Century Encyclopedia and found he had been ignorant. So the man came back again and sold Grandmother a coat—one she and Mrs. Maring liked best. They wanted it to look stylish, they both agreed, but most of all they insisted that it should be good quality.

Once a year a man came with Oriental rugs. Grandmother didn't always buy one though she said rugs, china, and good damask were the hardest things for her to pass by. Mrs. Maring, of course, always came to·the big house when the rugs were displayed. So did Mother, and sometimes the other daughters-in-law. The way Mrs. Maring and Grandmother judged the rugs was to walk from one end to the other watching the light change on the pattern. They said that was one way to tell a good Oriental. Even if they resisted a big rug, they usually bought one or two little ones. Scatter rugs, or prayer rugs, they called them. Grandfather abominated those. He said the day would come when he would break his neck on one. They gave you no purchase at all on the hardwood floor. Step on the edge of one of the pesky little things and you were worse off than on a banana peel. But Grandmother said they were so rich looking they colored the room. She even had them across the seats of two carved wooden armchairs in the hall.

Mrs. Maring's house was on the corner of Washington and Plum Streets. Mrs. Wildman was her neighbor on Washington but on the other side of Plum. Mrs. Wildman wasn't much interested in rugs or shopping. She was fat and jolly. She liked to sit comfortably on her front porch, watching people go by. Her hair was very white and her cheeks were bright. She wore round, gold-rimmed spectacles that fitted very close to her eyes so that it was a little like looking at goldfish through their bowl. Mostly she liked to talk about her husband who had been a Major in the Civil War. There was a big crayon picture of him in the hall. She always pointed to it when you came in, and she always dressed in mourning. Her son John lived with her. He seemed older than she, he was so quiet. He just went out in the morning and came home at night and scarcely spoke at all. Their hired girl, Emma, was very sociable. She was, everybody said, more of a companion to Mrs. Wildman than just a hired girl. She was a wonderful cook too. Ginger bread with powdered sugar on it was her specialty, as well as homemade bread. I always had some with each fresh baking, sitting on the front porch with Mrs. Wildman and holding the plate very carefully, not to get crumbs on the floor. Emma couldn't abide crumbs on the floor. But Emma was the one who always

telephoned to my house to ask if I might have a ginger
bread party there.

Emma was very brisk. She didn't like you to interfere
when she was working. Then her broad, open face would
grow tight with displeasure. I knew the signs and I obeyed
them. Sometimes she pinched off pieces of pie crust or bis-
cuit dough for me to work and put in a pan of my own. But
on the days when she was hurried and her face tightened
up, I thought of the James Whitcomb Riley poem:

> "Take yer dough, an' run, child, run,
> Er I cain't git no cookin' done."

And I did run.

Both Emma and Mrs. Wildman loved the evidences of
traveling. They never went away themselves (Mrs. Wildman
was much too comfortable on her front porch) but they
enjoyed few things more than the departures or home-
comings of friends along the street. The arrival of a visitor
from out of town brought an even brighter red-letter day.
Mrs. Wildman was always on sentry duty on the porch, until
the coldest weather drove her in to the big bay window in
her living room. That window was never obstructed with
boxes of ferns and rubber plants. The space was kept clear
for Mrs. Wildman and her rocking-chair. She and Grandmother Wiles were very great friends and spent much time
together when Grandmother was visiting us, but there was
never need for Grandmother to telephone that she had arrived. Nor could she step up to her friend's on a surprise
visit. Mrs. Wildman knew the moment the station hack
turned the corner of Vine Street.

The Woodburys, whose house was between Mrs. Wildman's and ours, traveled a good deal themselves. They had
an only child like me. His name was Mitchell and we were
companions all day long. Mr. and Mrs. Woodbury were

friends of Mother's and Daddy's. They all went out a great
deal to the same parties. Mrs. Wildman and Emma said
they liked to watch them coming out of the two houses, calling to each other and starting off together, laughing and
teasing. The Woodburys went away in the Summer even
earlier than we, and sometimes they took trips besides, to
New York or Chicago. When Daddy was out at the Bridge
Works, before he bought the Electric Light Plant, he used to
go away quite often, too, with bridge gangs on construction.
Mrs. Wildman said that all the comings and goings made it
one of the busiest neighborhoods she had ever seen.

The Rosses, who lived on the other side of us, had four
children . . . all of them grown up, two sons who had married
and gone to live in Indianapolis, and two daughters who
lived at home. The girls lived at home, we say in Indiana,
when we mean that they hadn't married. People said Mrs.
Ross worked herself to the bone for them. She made all their
clothes, even their underwear; washed and ironed for them,
too. The girls slept late in the mornings and then moved
out to the hammock in Summer. Mrs. Ross didn't like them
to lift a finger. She used to hold up her own red hand against
their long, white fingers. She would say proudly, "I don't in-
tend my girls ever to have hands like mine." The girls always
seemed to me to be drowsy, the way I was for just a few
minutes when I first got up from my nap.

There wasn't much for me to do when I went over to their
house, but there was always candy to take home. Young
men were always bringing them five-pound boxes of candy
—Lowney's, mostly—with pictures of a beautiful girl on the
cover, and the box tied with a wide pink ribbon. Sometimes
they gave me the ribbons, too, but mostly they kept them.
Mrs. Ross ran them through the bead-work on their petticoats or corset covers. The girls, people said, took after their
father. He was quiet and slow; he seemed to me older than

my grandfather but perhaps he wasn't. Perhaps he seemed older because Mrs. Ross was young in her activities and her yearnings; much younger than her girls. They seemed content to live the year round in the little house on Washington Street, getting up late, taking a long time to dress, sitting by the window buffing their nails, watching what went on in the street, and in the evening entertaining their beaux, on the porch in the Summer where the hammock was, or in the parlor in the Winter.

Mrs. Ross wanted to go away. She was always talking about the trip she would take. She wanted, too, to improve the house; make the property look pretty, she said. She was up, I heard Mother tell Daddy, before six o'clock every morning, turning out a full-sized washing before she got Mr. Ross's breakfast. Sometimes she would come over in the afternoon to sew for us, which was her way of resting. She taught Mother how to make clothes for me and to sew some things for herself, but Mother was too impatient, Mrs. Ross used to tell her, ever to be a really good seamstress. She would never even let Mother start a dress for herself, though Mother always had an impulse to try it every Spring. When they were sewing together, Mrs. Ross talked about the places she would like to visit or the things she would like to do for the house. She always sat in a rocking-chair, out on our porch in the Summer, or near the window in our dining room at other times of the year. She herself laughed at her fondness for a rocking-chair. She said she guessed it was because she liked to keep moving. She sewed very fast. Sometimes the material would catch on her rough fingers. She did hate, she would protest to Mother, to see threads roughed up on any goods. She would be very distressed about it as if she were to blame for what hard work had done to her hands. Mother would insist that the roughening of the material would never in the world show. She would smile and tell Mrs. Ross, "As my mother would say"—she meant Grandmother Wiles—"it will never be seen on a trotting horse."

Mrs. Ross would be somewhat appeased but would sew more slowly for some time. Often she would set up the folding work table when this had happened and sew on its smooth surface. Eventually she would take it back into her skilful hands again, rocking more violently after her brief inactivity. Her hair was dark but beginning to show gray. She wore it drawn severely back from her face; not severely enough for her liking, however, for her characteristic gesture was to push her palm flat and hard against either side of her hair. She was heavy when I first knew her, broad and quite tall; but as I grew bigger she grew thinner until she was lean and angular.

The place she most wanted to visit was Cincinnati. She had some cousins there whom she hadn't seen for thirty years. They were always begging her to come to visit them, but she had never been able to get away from Mr. Ross and the girls. She used, however, to tell Mother about Cincinnati as if she had been there over and over again. She had asked her cousins to describe it to her. In every letter over a period of thirty years they had sent some further detail until she could, she said, have walked out of the station and not have had to think twice to know just which way to go. It was a beautiful place, she told us. Some of the streets went up and down hill; it was not flat like Muncie. Wonderful big stores. She knew them all by name.

Grandmother Kimbrough, Mother told her, often went over to Cincinnati to do shopping. A great many people from Muncie preferred it to Indianapolis. Mrs. Ross agreed heartily with that preference, though she had never been to either city. Cincinnati things, she declared, had more style. She could even tell you how the windows of the best store had been decorated for the Spring and Fall showings and the Christmas displays, for, she would laugh and say, she didn't like to think how many years back. She knew about the theatre, too, in Cincinnati, and the plays that came there. She had some of the programs that her cousin had sent her. She had only once been to the Wysor Grand in Muncie. She declared scornfully that it was not really worth the bother, not when you considered what the theatre and the plays were like in Cincinnati.

Next to going herself, Mrs. Ross wanted her girls to see Cincinnati. She would have liked to go with them to show them the things. But Mr. Ross couldn't seem to get away from his business, she said, and she couldn't leave him to look after himself. The girls needed new, pretty clothes, too, if they were going to visit. It cost money for good materials. But one year she managed it. She sent them off by themselves to stay with the cousins.

The girls had had a good time, she guessed. She told Mother all about it, rocking back and forth in the bay window of our dining room. But the girls weren't the kind to talk much. They'd been to the theatre. They had seen two plays, but they hadn't even thought to bring the programs home. And they were both of them poor hands at remembering names, so Mrs. Ross couldn't figure out who the actors had been at all, though she would have known them if she could just have heard their names. The girls had said the town was pretty but an awful chore to walk up and down the hills to get anywhere. They didn't think the stores were so much better than Muncie's, but that the things in them were much more dear. And they didn't see much use in looking around at things if you weren't going to buy them. Mrs. Ross said that wouldn't have been like her at all. She would have looked and looked until her eyes would pretty nearly have spilled right out of her head. But then the girls took after their father. He never was one to make much of anything. She herself—and she would laugh and stop her sewing a minute to put her head against the back of the rocker—was just a natural born stewer, she guessed. And what was more, she would add, when she got over to Cincinnati she was going to let herself get into a fine big stew over everything she saw.

The only other thing in the world she really wanted, she would always say, was a cement walk around their house. Almost any time I went over to see them—when I would smell, from my back yard, chicken and dumplings cooking—she would tell me about the walk she was going to have. And she would caution me always about the one that was there. Rickety and dangerous she said it was and for me to watch where I was stepping. She could see me running across the yard between our house and hers, and she would tap on the window and point down to the wooden walk, shaking her head in warning at me. I would slow down and walk gingerly over it to the safety of the back steps. The reason it was dangerous, she said, was because it was full of knotholes and you could catch your toe in one of those and break your leg. There wasn't another house on Washington Street, she told Mother, that still had an old wooden sidewalk around it. She was so ashamed she didn't like people so much as to pass her house, let alone come up those rotten wooden steps. And she knew her girls in their high heels were going to have a bad fall, break their legs, most likely. It worried her at night sometimes so much that she couldn't sleep. A wooden walk was a dirty, messy thing, too, she said. You could never scrub it clean like you could cement. Look at the cement one we had. She would point out the window with pride, clucking and nodding her head in satisfaction as if it were a jewel of her own. That was something you could be proud of and could keep clean. Every Thursday she looked out her window and watched Chris, the man who came to us once a week to clean. She thought he must enjoy scrubbing it. Mother told her that she thought the wooden walk was prettier. She'd never really liked our cement one, it was so stiff and bare. Wood looked much softer. Mrs. Ross would snort at that. "Now, Mrs. Hal," she would say, "those are just some of your poetical ideas. You don't want a walk so soft that it will go through with you any minute. Always damp and soggy. Always full of rough splinters, and rotting away. You can't sit there and tell me that you don't enjoy looking down on that beautiful, clean cement of yours."

I told her about the one in front of my cousin Inez and Mac's house in Hartford City, and how much I liked it. But Mrs. Ross sniffed, and said she was sure there wasn't one in the length and breadth of Cincinnati.

Mother didn't try to argue any more after that. But she did ask, one time when I was there, if Mr. Ross preferred the wooden walk. Mrs. Ross said, oh, no, he didn't. He thought the cement one would be fine. But he was so busy he just couldn't seem to get around to it. But she was going to keep after him until he did.

One Summer when we went away in July, Mrs. Ross helped us get ready to leave. She did a lot of sewing and helped, too, with the packing. The day we got off she stood on her porch watching when Limpy came up with the station cab and got all our baggage. I rode by myself in it. Mother had said I could. Grandfather drove Mother and Daddy in the carriage. Mrs. Ross called to us as we drove off down the street to the Big Four depot, "Don't be surprised if you come back here and find something new around my house." Mother nodded and waved to her and kept saying, "Thank you so much for all you've done."

But Mrs. Ross cut over that again. "Don't be surprised, either, if I've been on a trip. You know where. I wouldn't ex-

change it for all your Atlantic Cities." (We were going to
Atlantic City.)

That night on the train I heard Mother talking about it to
Daddy. "Perhaps she'll really go this year," she told him; "it
almost looks as she might, Hal. She's been planning it for
thirty years."

I was sick on the train all the way. I was always sick on a
train from the moment it started until the moment I got off.
The smell from the locomotive started me as I climbed on
board. It always seemed to let out a puff of smoke just then,
and the stale coal and sulphur, or whatever it was, inevitably
caused Mother to go on a run for the porter to unlock the
ladies' room even before the train had left the station.

We stopped off in Philadelphia and were pretty bedrag-
gled when we got there, from all of my activities. We stayed
at the Bellevue Stratford Hotel. I had never seen such a
place in my life before, but I told Mother, going up in the
elevator, that I didn't suppose it could compare with Cincinnati. Grandfather had asked us particularly to walk past
the Union League Club. That was, he said, the very kernel
and core of the Republican Party, and he would like us to
pay our respects. We did walk by the red brick building. It
had some steps that went up on either side of a sort of entrance balcony. There were men in the windows, too. I told
Mother I supposed they were all Republicans and she said
they undoubtedly were. A large building a little farther on
had a figure which I recognized on its very top. I pointed it
out to Mother and told her that the building must be the
Quaker Oats factory. Mother said the figure was of William
Penn, whose picture is on the packages of Quaker Oats, but
that the building was the city hall of Philadelphia. In Muncie, we generally showed visitors our factories. I wasn't used
to public buildings such as that. The only public building I
knew at all was our court house, and that wasn't much. I felt

this place must certainly be far more like Cincinnati than like Muncie.

The next day we went on to Atlantic City. We drove in an open carriage from the train to the hotel. When we got off the train there were a great many carriages. The drivers were calling out the names of the hotels to which they belonged. The shouting was very loud and confusing, but we picked out a driver who seemed to be saying the name of the hotel where we were going. He took our satchels and valises and said he would take care of our trunks later. When we came to his vehicle we found it wasn't a regular carriage at all. It looked like pictures of old stage-coaches. Ten or twelve people could sit inside, facing each other, with a narrow aisle between. Two horses drew it. We clattered up the street with a great noise. The porters inside the hotel heard us coming and ran out to meet us. They took all the baggage down from the roof of the vehicle where the driver had put it. As soon as we were the least bit unpacked, which didn't take long, I persuaded Mother and Daddy to go out to see the ocean. I had heard so much about it, but I couldn't imagine how it would really be. They decided we might as well go for a little while because there was no use waiting for the trunks to come.

Everybody looked at us as we went through the lobby. They could tell we were newcomers from our traveling clothes and our color. They all looked brown and red. It made even Mother and Daddy feel a little bit shy, I think, to look so different and so new, so we hurried across the lobby and out the door.

Right in front of us, at the very door, was a wooden walk, like the one around Mrs. Ross's house. I could scarcely notice the Atlantic Ocean beyond it for my astonishment at this sight. The Atlantic City walk was much wider than Mrs. Ross's, and much higher off the ground, but it was, after all,

the same thing; not cement like ours. Just a wooden walk.
And everybody was walking up and down on it. Back and
forth, from one end to the other, although it was so long I
couldn't see either one end or the other. We walked along it,
too, and then I did notice the ocean. It was about the way I
thought it would be from the pictures I had seen, but I had
not expected a wooden walk. I whispered to Mother that
Mrs. Ross would be as surprised to see this one as we would
be when we got home and saw her cement one. And Mother
said yes, she would.

There were stores all along the walk. I couldn't tell whether
they were as good as the ones in Cincinnati because I had
never been to Cincinnati either, but they seemed full of
beautiful things. Very frequently there would be one with
no front to it. You could walk right in from the walk without
opening a door and sit down in one of the chairs that were
placed in rows. There was a man talking loud and very fast
at the far end, holding up in his hand or pointing to an
object of china or glass—all kinds of things. Daddy said that
was an auction, and that Atlantic City was famous for them.
There were places, too, called Japanese Alleys where you
could roll balls, and if they went into special holes you'd get
prizes. Daddy said I could do that some day but not this first
time when we were just taking a walk to see what it all
looked like. I couldn't take in everything at once so that it
was some little time before I was even aware of the chairs
on wheels which men were pushing and people riding in them.
I was distinctly uneasy about such traffic as that, remembering how Mrs. Ross had always warned me of the perils of a
wooden walk. It would, she said, rot away without anyone
knowing it until he crashed through and had his bones
broken for him. Daddy said we could take a ride some day
in one of the chairs but I looked at them then and throughout our stay with profound misgivings. Nor was I ever per-

suaded to ride in one. If the wooden walk were to rot, I felt
I wanted to be in a position to jump.

My delight was the beach. That, I felt, would not give way
under me. Nor could I ever have enough of the feel of the
sand through my fingers and between my toes—the hot burn
of the sun on my shoulder blades, and the constant cool
breeze that rustled my hair always from morning until night.
I knew so little about a breeze, living in Indiana. We had a
high wind sometimes, but if there were not wind the air was
still. This was such a lively air that I felt it and smelled it
with almost the same pleasure with which I had sniffed for
Mrs. Wildman's and Mrs. Ross's baking. I distrusted the
ocean, however, as much as I did the wooden walk and for
better reasons. The first day the ocean had turned me upside
down and rolled me high on the beach to my indignation.
When I righted myself, my mouth, nose and eyes were full of
wet sand. The inside of my bathing suit was clammy and
gritty with it, and I had lost my cap. I was from then on out of
humor with the Atlantic except for its fringes, where I could
dig for clams or make holes to fill with water.

We were the only ones in the hotel who had come from
so far away. All the others were what Daddy called east-
erners. There were a great many children. I made friends
with them. We played together on the beach, and I told
them about Muncie. I told them about Cincinnati, too, what
I had heard from Mrs. Ross. They all said they wished they
could go there some day. I warned them about the wooden
walk and they told their families. Their families said that was
foolish. The walk had been there for years and was perfectly
safe. I felt, however, that Mrs. Ross knew better than they.
She had one all the year round, so of course she would know
better what it was liable to do.

Daddy had to go home at the end of two weeks because
that was as much vacation as Grandfather thought it good

for him to take. But Mother and I stayed on all the rest of
the Summer. When we left the first of September we were
as brown as the people we had seen on our arrival. That was
one of the reasons I was reconciled to leaving. I wanted to
show everybody at home my new color. In Indiana, we never
got that way. Children weren't allowed to be in the sun as
I had been at the seaside. On the train, between dashes to
the ladies' room when a wave of nausea would turn me upside down, I counted off to Mother the things I was anxious
to do when I got home. I would show Grandmother Kimbrough my collection of shells. I would tell Grandfather
about the Union League Club and how we had passed it.
But best of all, I would tell Mrs. Ross about the wooden
walk they had at Atlantic City and I would see her brand
new cement one. She would tell me, too, about her trip to
Cincinnati and we would compare Atlantic City with it.

Daddy and Grandfather and Grandmother met us at the
station. They were surprised at our color; said we looked like
Indians. I told them I had brought them each a surprise
which was salt water taffy, but that I had had to go on a
wooden walk to get it. Going home, I asked if they had seen
Mrs. Ross's cement walk. But Grandmother and Grandfather
said they hadn't been down in our block since we had been
away. No one could tell me. I grew more and more impatient.

I was the first to see the Ross's house—with the wooden
walk around it, just the way it had been when we went away.
Mrs. Ross heard our clattering up the street and came running out on the porch. She was waving and waving. I jumped
out and started to run toward her. She shook her finger
quickly at me and called out, "Don't run on that wooden
walk, Emily The pesky thing might rot away from under
you at any minute." I tried to tell her about the one at Atlantic City and asked her where her cement one was, but just
then Mother got out and went up to speak to her. Mrs.
Ross said over my head to Mother that Mr. Ross had decided

that as long as it was so late in the year it would be better
to wait until next Spring for the cement walk. Winter would
be so hard on it. I broke in to ask how Cincinnati was and
she wrinkled up her eyes at Mother again over my head
while she said she had never got to go. There just didn't
seem to be the time. So we couldn't compare it with Atlantic
City.

We went on over to our house. The home-coming didn't
seem so exciting since the Ross's sidewalk was just the same.

All that Fall and Winter whenever Mrs. Ross came over to
sew, she would ask about Atlantic City and compare it with
Cincinnati. She could never get over the boardwalk. That
seemed to her a terrible thing for any place to have.

The next year we decided to go back to Walloon Lake,
where we had always gone before the trip to Atlantic City.
Mrs. Ross was working harder than ever all Spring, making
new outfits for her girls and insisting on coming over to us,
too. She was much thinner, and told Mother she guessed
it was from not sitting down long enough to let the fat
catch up with her. Then one day she told Mother that
one reason she was working so hard was that she was making clothes for herself, for a trip to Cincinnati. This time
she was really going and she was going to have clothes
to wear that her cousins wouldn't be ashamed to see her
in. She had the day all set on the calendar. She was going
to leave on the fifteenth of August and stay over Labor
Day. And while she was gone Mr. Ross was going to have
men up to rip out the wooden walk around her house
and put in a cement one. She used to stop talking about
it and lean her head against the back of the rocker.
She would rock, with her hands quiet in her lap, and her
eyes closed, just seeing how Cincinnati and the cement walk
would look. Mother helped her pick patterns and material
for her clothes and was as excited as she was about the trip,
she said. The girls didn't take very much interest. They said

if Mama wanted to go they guessed they could manage, but what she could see in Cincinnati they didn't understand. She told them she'd see everything she'd been dreaming about for thirty years, and then she could go on dreaming about them for the next thirty.

We left for Walloon Lake on the fifth of July, the day after we had the fireworks at the big house. Mrs. Ross waved us off, of course, and Mrs. Wildman from down the street. Mrs. Ross called out,

"I guess it won't be any surprise for you this year. You know all about what is going to happen to me while you're gone and what you'll see here when you get back."

Mother called back that she knew it would be beautiful just the way she had said the year before. When we turned the corner, the last thing I saw was Mrs. Ross waving with one hand and pointing to her wooden sidewalk with the other, nodding and grinning with pleasure over what was going to happen.

It was just two weeks later that she died. Urgent, the Muncie doctor had said, and he wanted her to see a specialist. He wouldn't operate himself. He recommended a man in Cincinnati. They had an ambulance waiting at the train there to drive her straight to the hospital. She didn't have to know for herself which way to go. She probably couldn't see much either, from the ambulance cot. The surgeon did operate, but it was too late. He couldn't do anything. She died in just a few days.

Mother got a letter from Daddy telling about it and the letter ended that Mr. Ross and the girls were staying on in Cincinnati for a visit with the cousins. Daddy wrote, "And as I look out of my window while writing this to you, the workmen are ripping up the old board sidewalk. They plan to lay down the cement tomorrow."

Chapter Seven

All Summer long, up at Walloon Lake, where we had a cottage, I heard about school.

"Don't worry about her, Lottie. School will make all the difference."

"Never mind, she'll be in school in the Fall, and you won't know her for the same child."

Things like that, until I thought I should pine away, the way people in stories did, with longing for that wonderful day. The day when I would be changed, everybody kept saying so, just like the six swans into brothers. A school teacher was a fairy godmother. She would change you—especially me—because I was already nearly seven years old. You would be able to notice the difference more. In an only child, they said, it was astonishing the difference it would make.

When Daddy came to join us for his vacation, I asked him at once if *he* thought I would be changed, and he said he did indeed. Also he had found out, he told me, that I was to go to the very same school in which *he* had started, and more than that, to the *very* same teacher. I wanted to know if she had changed him, and he assured me that she had, very much. People scarcely knew him for the same child. The same thing would happen to me. I made him promise that it would.

After that I could scarcely think of anything else. I put myself to sleep every night, imagining how I would be changed—tall and slender, with long, curling, yellow hair, and eyes like the sky. I was approximately square in build, with brown hair, uncompromisingly bobbed at the moment to make it come in thicker, and light brown eyes about the shade of golden oak furniture.

We didn't get home until the day before school started, and that passed fairly quickly, because there was so much to do. I had to have my hair washed, for one thing. Grandmother Kimbrough said, on the way from the station, that they had had a lot of rain the last two weeks, and she had had Father—she meant Grandfather—go to our house to make sure the cap was off the cistern. So there was plenty of soft water. That was why I had my hair washed, and Mother washed hers, too.

The rain water was pumped into a tank on the roof. The tank had charcoal in it to purify the water, and there was some kind of a filter. The spigot for it in the bathroom was in the center, between the regular hot and cold. It was higher, too, bent over in a hook. You had to be very careful not to get your head scraped by it, if you came up too straight from the basin. Zoe always gave me a dry wash rag to put over my eyes, to keep the soap out. It was Packer's Tar soap, with a stinging smell that I liked, and it made a yellow lather. Jap-Rose soap for regular washing was yellow and transparent, but its lather was white. If the cistern was dry, and we had to use hard water, we put Twenty-Mule-Team Borax into it as a softener for any lather at all. Sometimes, in spite of the wash rag, I got Packer's Tar in my eyes, which hurt like sixty. The wash rag itself always got soaked anyway, so I never could see anything, and nearly always I bumped my head when I raised it, and got scraped on the soft water spigot.

Mother and I sat out in the back yard in the sun and dried our hair, and talked about what dress I would wear to school. We decided on the yellow and black plaid gingham, which

I had known all along, because it was my favorite dress for special occasions. It had a square neck and short puffed sleeves. Grandmother Kimbrough had brought it to me from St. Augustine. I only hoped that it wouldn't change when I did, but I didn't mention that to Mother.

It was very hard to go to sleep that night. September is always hot in Indiana. Sounds carry farther in the still heavy air. And that night, wiggling about on my hot bed, I could hear Mother's and Daddy's voices from the front porch.

My room was on the first floor, at the back of the house. It was a new room, built on during the Summer while we were away. Daddy wasn't at the Bridge Works anymore, Mother said. He had bought the Electric Light Plant of Muncie. He would have to work until very late at night to make it go (when I was taken to see it I thought, therefore, that he wound up all the machines and kept them going), and so when he came home to sleep he must not be disturbed. That was why I had a brand new room of my own, downstairs. Zoe would be there, too, so that I wouldn't be scared, and they were moving the dimmer light down to the back hall, where I could see it. My new room was big, with a fireplace in the far corner, and windows on two sides.

All those open windows was what made me hear Mother's and Daddy's voices so clearly that hot September night. I couldn't make out what they were talking about, but I thought it must be about my going to school. So I got out of bed, and went to see them. I had to go through the bathroom and then the guest room, which had always been there on the first floor especially for Grandmother Wiles, and it had brass beds. That far it was dark, but when I turned the knob and opened the guest room door into the sitting room I was in the full light, because all four electric lights from the chandelier in the middle of the ceiling were turned on. They dazzled me for a minute, coming out of the dark, and I stood still to get used to them, and to get my bearings. Right beside me was the desk that closed up into the wall and always had a key dangling in the lock to pull it out by. There were books on shelves alongside.

How I loved some of these—not for what was in them, I never even asked about that; just the books. The set of Stoddard's *History of the World*, rich red with gold letters, and slippery smooth paper inside. Ruskin's *Principles of Art Criticism*, two volumes to that set. I loved to say the name over, not apropos of anything. Just talking to myself, or to anyone, I liked to say, "Ruskin's Principles of Art Criticism." But the best of all were on the bottom shelf. Three books in that set —*Abbeys, Castles and Ancient Halls of England, Scotland, and Wales*. The times I had put myself to sleep, pretending I was visiting Abbey in one after another of her Ancient Castles and Halls in England, Scotland, and Wales!

There were lots of other books on the shelves, of course, but those were the special ones for me. There were books on the reading table, too, in the bay window. To look out was almost impossible, because there were so many potted ferns on the floor in front of it. But the table was easy to reach, and had the *Muncie Morning Star* and the *Muncie Evening Press* on it every day—and books that Mother was reading. Lots of people had a copy of James Whitcomb Riley's *An Old Sweetheart of Mine* on their reading tables, with illustrations by Howard Chandler Christy and a cover of white leather. The book was always in a white cardboard box, though, to keep it from getting dirty. But we didn't have a copy on our table.

The lights were so bright that I could see across the living room into the dining room, and the parlor where the piano was, and the seat for two people where one faced one direction and the other the opposite way, like playing "Going to Jerusalem." I wasn't so confused by the glare now, and moved across the room, opposite from the bay window, so that I could cool my feet on the brown tile hearth of the fireplace. And then I edged past the green velvet rocker, where Grandmother and I rocked when I lost a dog. There was a tabouret beside it to be careful of. It was easy to knock over, it was so light, and it had curios on it, set around on its table scarf of embroidered black-eyed Susans. There wasn't a great deal of space from there to the green sofa that was along the fretwork partition from the vestibule. But the vestibule had quite a little space. The light wasn't on in there; we only turned it on when people were putting on their hats in front of the mirror in the hat-rack, where the seat lifted up to hold rubbers and junk. That was the same mirror between the pegs for hats, where one day I held up a page out of a magazine, the way it said to, and in the mirror the letters came right and spelled "Bon Ami" and underneath it "Hasn't scratched yet." I had never seen anything that astonished me more, and I always associated the vestibule with that day.

Through the window I could see the yellow arc lamp down at the corner; not very clearly because of the big trees all along the curb on either side of the street, but enough to know that that was what made some of the leaves stand out in shafts of moving, dusty, yellow beams while the rest were dark. Mother and Daddy were in the dark, too, at the far end of the porch, out of reach of the sitting room light. They were shut off from the street by thick morning-glory vines that climbed up the front railing and over wire netting to the ceiling. There were honeysuckle vines on either end of the porch so it was really closed in, except for the space where the front steps were. I stood a moment looking into the cool, sheltered darkness; I was just going to jump out to surprise them, when I heard Daddy say,

"We'll have to tell her soon, Girl. Her nose is going to be out of joint anyway."

While I was thinking about what a nose out of joint would be like, Mother told him,

"She'll be in Indianapolis until it's over, and then she'll just find a baby sharing her new room. I think she'll love it, like a live doll."

If this had anything to do with me, and they didn't want me to fuss, they couldn't have chosen a better time to acquaint me of it. No announcement would have distracted me. This was the night when the whole world was wide awake, only waiting for me to go to school in the morning to be changed. I jumped into the light; I heard them give a rustle of surprise in the darkness where they were. I said, "Did I scare you?" But I wasn't even really interested in that. How many hours, I wanted to know, until it was time to get up and put on my dress for school? I got sent back to bed pretty sharply, though Mother went with me through the light and dark rooms. And after she had smoothed the sheet out—where I had rumpled it, wiggling around—and folded the covers under so tight that I couldn't turn over very well, she sat for a little while beside the bed and patted me. Patting was tapping on my buttocks the beat of a song I knew, and I would guess what song it was. *Give, said the little brook,* or *Good morning, merry sunshine,* perhaps. But the beat itself, and the tapping, were so insistent that I always slipped away to sleep under them before I could guess more than a tune or two.

I did wear my black and yellow plaid dress the next morning, with the square neck and short puffed sleeves. It had eyelet embroidery, too, around the neck and waist and sleeves, with black velvet ribbon threaded through it.

I found it very difficult to eat breakfast. Daddy was evidently excited, too, because instead of peeling my orange for me, which he always did, he cut it across in half and I had to eat it with a spoon, which I detested. He kept opening his watch and snapping it shut again, and telling me one minute to hurry and the next to eat a good breakfast; that the engine wouldn't run well unless it was properly stoked with fuel. And he wanted it to run especially well for Miss Hutchins, who was the very same teacher who had taught him when he started school—as if I didn't know.

Mother seemed to be very quiet, and not at all excited. But she hugged me very hard when she put my hat on. And when she slipped the elastic under my chin she kept my face turned up in her hands, and looked and looked at me. It was a big moment, she said, I would never be really a little girl again. I was going out into the world, now. I felt as if I must burst with importance at that realization. I marched down the steps and up the street, stretched out into steps twice as long as I had ever attempted at kindergarten. At the corner I turned back to wave to Mother and suddenly I wanted to cry, because I might be so changed she wouldn't know me when I came back. Then Daddy and I rounded the corner, and we were really on our way to school.

The school building looked bigger that day than I remembered, though I had passed by countless times. All around it there were pleasant frame houses with yards. Big trees lined each side of the street. The building was set far back in its own yard, red brick with white steps. Very big, I thought, both the steps and the building.

We could hardly get up the steps for the jostling crowd of parents and children. I kept close to Daddy, held his hand tight and looked up at him. His cheeks were pink, his eyes were shiny and he was almost laughing. He looked excited. He spoke to other parents here and there, waved his free hand and called, "Takes you back, doesn't it? Makes you feel pretty old, I can tell you. Doesn't seem so long ago at that that we were coming up these steps."

I felt that for a father he did not look very old. His light brown hair was very curly. Even under the wide-brimmed straw hat he was wearing, I could see a little of the curls on either side of the middle part. He was wearing a very high collar because this was a special occasion. It pushed up his chin and made his face look chubby. He was wearing, too, in a pretty blue foulard tie, his best cameo stick pin.

We could hardly get up the steps of the building for the jostling crowd of parents and children. Daddy told me that these were the very steps he had climbed the first day he went to school. He pointed out, just inside the door, what he said was the principal's office. But I had no idea what the principal was, and all I could see was another crowd of grown-ups and children milling around a doorway. He didn't seem to remember the direction of the rooms where he had begun his education, and had to ask several people. But when he opened the door he said,

"This is it."

We stood on the threshold quite a little time, trying to adjust ourselves to the bedlam inside. There were about forty children, and at least one parent to each. A few of the children were sitting in their mothers' laps crying, because they wanted to go home. Some of the others were climbing over the tops of the desks, from one to another. We finally found where the teacher was, at the end of the room, but she didn't even see us until we had pushed our way down to her desk. Then Daddy said,

"Miss Hutchins, I am Hal Curry Kimbrough. I started school under you a long time ago, and now I have brought my little girl, Emily. It doesn't seem such a long time since I was here. But the years pass quickly, don't they?"

When he opened the door he said: "This is it."

Then the teacher looked up from the paper she was writing on.

"I am not Miss Hutchins," she said. "She is at the Jefferson School, if she hasn't retired by now. I have been teaching only ten years. Will you fill in this application blank, please?"

Daddy didn't answer a word but his face, starting just above the collar, turned very red. He stiffened his shoulders and stopped smiling. Suddenly he looked much older than when we had come up the steps—straight and dignified, but not so happy.

He pulled up a chair beside the desk, filled in the card, and gave it to her. She stopped her own writing again, and read it. I was at the wrong school, she said, according to our address. I should be at the McKinley School, and not here. Furthermore, if Daddy was Mr. C. M. Kimbrough's son who lived on East Washington Street then he must have started in at the Jefferson School; that was the way the districts were divided in those days. She didn't believe he could have possibly gone to this school. Daddy didn't say anything. She told him that if he would like to leave me there I could take part in the opening exercises, which they would get around to as soon as things settled down a little. And could I be called for in two hours? My father told her to telephone my mother, and gave her the number; he had no more time and must get down to the Plant immediately. He left me there without even saying goodbye, as if he never had had anything to do with my being there—because it hadn't turned out right, I expect.

Not a soul noticed my dress, no one even noticed me. I would have liked to sit at a desk with a lid and an inkwell, but they didn't assign me to one because I wasn't going to stay. So I sat on a chair against the blackboard. When the teacher finally got through writing she read off the names of the children, but she didn't read mine. So I spoke up and said my name was Emily Kimbrough, but it wasn't on the list. She said no, because I didn't belong there. That was the last mention, at any time, that there was of me. I suppose she must have telephoned Mother, who came to get me at eleven o'clock. I had been taken to the principal's office, which was empty now except for me in my best dress for special occasions. I didn't say anything. I just stalked out of the room, down the corridor, and out of the building ahead of her. Certainly I could not mention the real bitterness—the not changing. I ate some dinner and took a nap. Then I went out in the back yard and sat in the swing for a long time, convincing myself that this day could not really count about changing, because it had certainly not been going to school. Tomorrow at McKinley it would be all right. I told Daddy, when I said good night to him, that McKinley would be all right tomorrow. But he was very cross; just said he certainly hoped so.

I asked if he would take me again, and then he was really cross. He said no, certainly not, it was all nonsense. I was a big girl; it was time I learned to go by myself. That surprised me a good deal, but pleased me, too. It was the first indication that there was any difference between this and kindergarten with paper work and Miss Zenobia.

Mother actually did start me off the next day on my own to the McKinley School. I don't think it was as much because of Daddy wanting to forget that he had ever taken part in the ignominy of the day before, as it was the book she was reading. This, I think, was the one which said that children should not be hampered by over-solicitude. My manner of life changed so frequently and diametrically, according to the chapter and author of the moment, that it was sometimes difficult for me to remember just where she was in literature on a particular occasion. I had never before been farther from our house, by myself, than up the block to my grandparents'. But she told me, over and over, just how I was to go. I did go that way, too, I thought, counting on my hands the turns she said I was to take. It was very interesting and, of course, I had a great deal to think about, considering what was going to happen to me. So perhaps I didn't notice all the turns, and did walk farther than she had said I would. Because when I met up with Mr. Meeks, our butter and egg man, he asked me where I was going, and when I told him to school, he asked wouldn't I be tardy because it was after ten o'clock. He pulled his big silver watch out of his vest pocket and showed it to me. What school was I aiming for? I told him McKinley. And he said that perhaps he'd better help me get there, because I didn't seem to be going the right way for it.

He let me drive and we had one or two stops to make along the way, because it was right along his route and he didn't want to retrace his steps. So by the time we got to McKinley it was after eleven. Both my mother and father were there, and my grandparents, too. I recognized them at once, though there was quite a crowd on the front steps. This was the kind of reception I had expected the day before, so that it seemed to me only that this was a better school than the other. And the hub-bub over my arrival was exactly as I had pictured. It took me some little time to realize that the hub-bub was occasioned by my absence and not by my arrival. Mother had not been able to follow entirely literally the child authority who had recommended complete independence, so she had telephoned the school to make sure that I had reached there safely. It took quite a little while to prove that I was nowhere in the building, and that not a teacher had heard of me. But it took scarcely any time at all, after that, to summon my father from the Electric Light Plant, and Grandfather from the Bridge Works. He picked up Grandmother and Mother in the automobile and drove at a terrible speed, Grandmother said.

Daddy was on his bicycle and Mother was afraid that he might get sick, he had pedaled so fast in the sun. They all searched the building to see for themselves that I wasn't there. And then the principal suggested that they organize the older boys into a hunt of the neighborhood. When I pulled up behind Mr. Meeks' horse, they were just giving the boys the last directions for dividing into groups, each with a captain, and spreading out in different districts. The boys were so mad at me for coming at that moment and sending them back into the school again that they never were very nice to me. My family was nice to me, though, proud of me for finding Mr. Meeks and coming to the school. I thought it was silly to tell them that he had found *me* walking along, and that I was delighted to come anywhere he suggested, so long as I could drive the horse. I was contented, anyway. This was the way, I felt, to go to school, and McKinley was a place where I would enjoy this business of education.

I was wrong. I continued, throughout the day, to attract attention, but it was not favorable. My teacher had gray hair, a long nose, and a very large bust. Her hair was thin and she wore it in a tight knot on the top of her head; that is, some of it. Quite a good deal drifted away from the knot and trailed down the back of her neck. She wore eye-glasses pinched onto her nose. The glasses were attached by means of a gold chain to a button pinned on her bosom. When she wanted to say something, she took her glasses off. When she wanted to read she put them on, so that she was constantly moving them. The button had a spring in it. She held the glasses in the air, gave them a little jerk and then let go and they whirled up to the button. Then in a minute she would pull them out again with a sweeping gesture, as if she were going to lead a song, and fit them back precisely on the bridge of her nose.

Very close under her bust, crowding it up perceptibly, she wore, as anyone could have told at once, a long, tight corset. One of her most frequent gestures was to put her hand on either side of her waist and draw herself up, as if she were trying to pull out of the corset for a moment's release.

She wore a white, high-necked shirt waist that buttoned down the back, though there were gaps between the buttons and her bare skin showed through. Some of her hair would get caught frequently in one of the top buttons and she was constantly ducking her head down and trying to unwind it or break it, looking up again, very red in the face. She wore high laced shoes with very pointed toes. That first morning one of the laces got untied, but she couldn't stoop over to tie it again and asked one of the children to do it for her.

My teacher had convictions, and, I felt, little education. I had convictions, too. Also, I had a mother whose education had been admirable, and whose feeling about a discriminating use of language was almost fanatical. She had worked over my vocabulary almost from the time I began mouthing the first words. At least I cannot remember farther back than the time when she was saying,

"Choose a word that fits, Emily. How many other words like that one can you say?"

And so I had come to take considerable pleasure in polysyllables.

"Superfluous," I tossed at my teacher, within an hour of my arrival, apropos of two erasers she was urging me to buy. They turned out to be one for pencil and one for ink, but I termed them superfluous, and she stopped me.

"I don't like little girls to use words bigger than they are, especially if they cannot say them correctly. The word· is super-*flu*-ous."

"Superfluous," I repeated, in astonishment, and held to it.

That kept me for an hour after school, printing the word superfluous on the blackboard, with a line drawn under the syllable *flu*. I had enjoyed the beginning of the discussion, but it had led me beyond myself. Brief though it had been, I had managed to assert that I knew many long words, and could read and print, too. By the end of the hour, when I had covered the blackboard, I wished heartily not only that I had never mentioned writing, but had never learned it. This was like my metronome at home, which I always dreaded starting. Once you unhitched it, it went back and forth, back and forth, without ever changing. And once it started it was so hard to catch and hitch up again in its little notch.

Zoe came for me and waited until I had finished. And the teacher said it hadn't been a very happy beginning, had it? But she was sure we would never have to do this again, would we? Now we understood each other, didn't we?

I went home moodily with Zoe. And yet I had a certain feeling of pride, too. I had heard older children talk about being kept in at school, in a kind of boasting way, and it seemed pretty good that I should have achieved it the very first day. We were supposed to have only a half-day session the first week, but here I was coming home at half-past one, and without any dinner, either. I thought I would stop and tell my friend Lydia Rich about it. She was still going to Miss Zenobia's. But Zoe said she wouldn't mention it to anybody, not even to my mother. So Mother scolded me about coming home late, and said I must learn right away that I was not to dally but march straight home.

That night I cried in bed until I threw up. Mother washed my face and gave me a glass of cold water, while Zoe changed the sheets. Mother thought it was the excitement of the day, and getting lost in the morning. Zoe thought it was the shame of being kept in after school. But it wasn't either of those. It was knowing that I wasn't going to be changed—not into anything different, even at any school. I couldn't believe that people would fool you so, and I had retched into my bed.

Staying after school *was* like the metronome that I dreaded. It kept repeating itself over and over, just the same way, and I couldn't seem to catch it in time to stop it. Words generally started it, too. Once it was the bow of a boat, which I pronounced *bough.* And the teacher told me it was pro-nounced like the bow of a violin. I had not dreamed that a little word like that could bring me to the blackboard again, after hours. And I had been very careful not to use big ones. But at 3:15 I was standing at the blackboard writing "bo," with a long mark over the o, and "bow" underneath it. An-other time it was pho*tog*rapher versus photo-*graph*-er. When this challenge was thrown down between us I had just been, the preceding Saturday, to Mr. Neiswanger's to have my pic-ture taken for my baby book, to be pasted in on the page that said "First School Days," and I felt that I certainly knew where I had been. The struggle was brief, and I was up at the board again underlining *graf* and printing the word pho-tographer over and over again, the only distraction being the pleasure of slapping together two blackboard erasers at a time to clean them, and filling my eyes and nose with chalk dust. I enjoyed that. But I wasn't allowed to clean the boards. That was why the *good* children stayed after school, because they *asked* to clean them and help the teacher. I never told Mother any of these times, because Zoe didn't seem to want me to. I think she must have been so ashamed that I was kept in just like the bad boys. So on each of these battle days I was sent to bed half an hour earlier than my usual time for not coming home promptly.

I had trouble at home, too, something I was working on privately and secretly. Something I could only talk to God about, because it was so awful. The sole compensation for being sent to bed early was that it gave me an extra half hour for this. I would climb into the dirty clothes basket in the closet off the bathroom, which was my praying place, and try to get God to help me out of the other secret trouble. I thought *it* could at least be kept secret, but it was my teacher who brought that out in the open too.

She was telling us about what she called the government.

There was a president, she said, and she told us his name.
I knew that name—Theodore Roosevelt. He had come once
to the big house. But no one had called him a president.
Grandfather had said he was campaigning. He had stood on
the porch railing and made a speech, hugging the pillar beside him to keep his balance, and laughing because it was
such a funny position. The street had been full of people.
They had even crowded up on the lawn. The family had
stayed inside and listened to Mr. Roosevelt from the library.
I had listened for a little while, and then just watched the
people. I had known that speeches were something I could
not understand. I had listened to Grandfather make a great
many of them, down town, or out at the cemetery, though
never from the front porch. I had never understood any of
them.

She named the vice-president. We repeated the name of
the man who went from Indiana to Washington, to be what
the teacher called a senator—Senator Beveridge. I knew him.
He came to the big house sometimes. He was a friend of
Grandfather Kimbrough, and Grandmother and Grandfather
Wiles. People called Grandfather Kimbrough "Senator," too,
but Grandmother didn't like to hear it.

"What in the world your father had to get himself into
that for," I heard her say to the boys, whenever there was
something said about a senator. "As if there weren't *enough*
ructions at the Bridge Works. He'll wear himself out. I've no
patience with politics!"

"By the way, Emily," the teacher said suddenly, turning
with a sort of sneer to me, "what is the name of our state
senator from here?"

I didn't know, I told her. She pushed out her lip, which
I knew was the sign of trouble for me—I had learned that on
the first day. Don't act naughty, she told me, adding that we

didn't want any trouble, did we? My private opinion was that we were out to get it, whether we wanted it or not, but I said nothing. She shouted at me and banged her ruler on the desk, which made me jump.

"I don't like little girls who won't speak up, and want to be coaxed. That's not a pretty way to act."

Acting pretty did not appeal to me particularly. But I would have been willing to oblige if I had known how, because I had been interested in what she had been saying about a president and vice-president. I liked the sound of the words, and I wanted her to get on with more of them. I didn't know how to act pretty. So I just sat there at my desk, in the front row, looking up at her behind her desk on her platform in front of me. She waited a minute, and then she jumped up from her chair, leaned across her desk down toward me, and her face got very red.

"It's your grandfather"—her voice was shrill and loud—"and you know it. Trying to act stuck-up with me, are you?"

It had never occurred to me that she could be talking about my grandfather. I didn't know that "senator" was anything but part of a name, like Senator Beveridge, or Senator Kimbrough. I didn't know either that it had anything to do with the word "state." I wasn't sure even now that it had, or that she was right. She had never convinced me about super-*fluo*us or bōw of the boat. She was not going to convince me of this. If a state senator were not something terrible *she* would certainly not have mentioned it, because everything she said about me was always bad. A state senator, therefore, must be something awful to be, like being crazy. I spoke suddenly back at her. I yelled,

"He is *not* a state senator! He *never* is!"

She came down from behind her desk on the platform and walked to mine. I watched every step getting nearer. Not a soul in the room so much as moved. She came all the way to my desk, reached out her hands suddenly, and shook me up and down in my seat. She gave me a last thump, and stood back with her arms folded. She was very red in the face, and breathing hard.

"Don't you talk back to me."

I couldn't have talked back if I had wanted to, and I was doing the best I could to keep from crying. It hurt me where she had jounced me on the wooden seat.

"Your grandfather is in the state senate, because he wants to reform the State prison laws, and you know it. Trying to show off. Look at your shoes. They're made by the *prisoners*."

And there it was, my secret trouble yelled right out in the air, before I could stop it, and all over something to do with a state senator. This was what I had prayed about, all those hours, crouched down in the dirty clothes basket, begging God to help me about Grandfather and prison.

The first time I had heard about it I couldn't even pray. Grandmother Kimbrough had said to Daddy, right in front of me, one afternoon up at the big house, before I even started school,

"Your father is away, Hal," she had said. "He's up at the prison, and I don't know what time he'll be back."

That time, the first, all I could do was to bury myself as far down as I could in the dirty clothes basket, with my teeth chattering and my stomach going up and down.

A day or two after that he was home again. I was so glad that he had gotten out that I went right back to the dirty clothes basket and thanked God. But not long after that I heard Grandmother say that he was at the prison again. And that was when I began praying. I had to sneak to get in there because when I was discovered I was always jerked out by Mother or Zoe, and looked at very crossly and searchingly, and asked if I had been doing anything naughty. They never explained what it was. And I wasn't sure whether praying, the way I did, was disrespectful or not, so I didn't know if I wasn't being naughty. Anyway, it got Grandfather out.

The time, however, that he came back with the ideas about the shoes I felt that we hadn't gotten him out quickly enough. I had heard that he was back, and rushed up to the big house to see him and make sure it was true. When Mother and Daddy came to get me he told them about the shoes. The prisoners could make them, he said; they knew how long he had been working to start some industry there. At last he had the equipment and permission to start. And it was at that moment he had the idea they would start with shoes for me. They could be tried out on me. It wouldn't be wasting so much leather if they made mistakes on small shoes, and also the shape would be easier.

We were in the den. He swung around in his revolving chair—the one I liked to whirl myself around in until I had to hang on to the high sides to keep from falling out—and unlocked the desk that let down from the wall. He took out a big sheet of paper and a pencil. I stood on it on the hearth, which was cold but smooth, while he drew a line around from my heel, up around my toes, and back again, which tickled. Sometime later, when God and I got Grandfather out of prison again, he brought the shoes back with him. They looked exactly like the line on the paper, including the place where I had wiggled because the pencil was tickling me. One pair was black and the other was brown but they were both stitched in red. Perhaps that was the only thread they had. The soles extended almost half an inch all the way around. I thought it was just part of the design but perhaps those artisans were not entrusted, at that early stage, with knives for cutting them down. When I first wore them I fell down almost constantly, because I kept stepping with one shoe on the extended sole of the other. But I learned to walk wider apart, and farther ahead on each step. Then Grandfather told Mother he would like me to wear them to school and tell about them. There was no getting out of wearing them, but certainly I had not opened my mouth about telling where they had come from. That came too close to the terrible secret about my grandfather going to prison all the time.

I would just stand in the yard at recess time and let the children jeer and yah-yah at me, and call "Clod-hopper, clod-hopper!" Nothing would have made me tell about Grandfather. And now the teacher was saying it out loud in front of everybody. I scrambled out of my seat, on the side away from her, and made for the cloakroom. She whisked past me, and got to the door first. She stood with her back against it, and her hand on the knob, and sneered at me.

"Just where do you think you are going?"

Somehow I think I knew that here was my moment. It wouldn't help Grandfather. I would have to tend to that later. But perhaps it would help a great many other things, and make me feel better than I had felt for a long time. My chin was just about on a level with the doorknob. So I stood on tip-toe, opened my mouth, and bit. I don't know how close my teeth came to meeting through her thumb. I tried to bring them together. And I didn't let go for quite a while, in spite of the commotion.

The principal telephoned for Mother, and she came and got me. But she didn't spank me, even though I didn't explain anything. I think when she saw the way my teacher was carrying on, she guessed a little what she was like. But she didn't ask me anything about her, nor about what had happened. We didn't, as a matter of fact, talk at all on the way home. She sent me out in the yard to play. And she came out and sat on the swing for a while with her sewing, and talked to me about Grandmother Kimbrough making grape jelly the next day, and that I could help her strain it with a cheese-cloth if I wanted to.

I didn't get a chance to go to the clothes basket until I was supposed to be in bed that night. But I had a long session in there then. I told God that being at school so much of the day, and being kept in so much of the time besides, didn't give me enough hours to work with Him about keeping Grandfather out of prison. And now it had all come out, because of this school business. But I wouldn't stop trying. And if He would watch over Grandfather harder than ever, then between us surely we could keep him from going to prison again, or from being a state senator.

Chapter Eight

Betty Ball came to school about ten days after I had started. She was my oldest and best friend, and her mother was my mother's. She had hay-fever, too, like me, only worse. That was why she was late starting school. They stayed up in Northern Michigan until the ragweed was over. We always did everything together, although Betty believed more deeply in fairies than I did. I hoped for them with all my heart, but I doubted a little. Betty had not the slightest doubt.

In the Spring, when I sometimes went out to spend the day with her, we would mix up magic concoctions from leaves and grass and acorns, and one or two secret ingredients. Then we would fill little candy boxes, which we had collected and saved all Winter, and tie them to the trees all over Betty's place. This was to attract the fairies. Betty went out early every morning before breakfast to look for them. She told her mother one morning that she almost thought she really had seen one, and it made a very exciting day. She got her mother to bring her in to town to tell me about it. They lived about three miles from me, out beyond the town itself, on Minnetrista Boulevard along White River. Whenever she came in to spend the day she nearly always thought she saw fairies, but it wasn't the same and she told me privately she knew it wasn't. When we were eating our dinner, at noon, she would say to my mother,

"I cannot eat any more spinach, because there is a fairy sitting on it."

Mother would ask if she couldn't suggest to the fairy that

it sit somewhere else, but Betty said the fairy wouldn't understand her. And if Mother said to try taking bites around it, Betty said that would frighten the fairy. But if I said, "I see a fairy, too, on mine," Mother always answered to me, "Eat your spinach, Emily."

Betty was little with blue eyes that were nearly always solemn and usually anxious. Her hair was yellow and it was bobbed, with a bang across the front. The cut of her hair closed in her face, making it more tiny.

Her mother brought Betty to the schoolroom the first day, and said that we were best friends, so that it would be nice if we could sit near each other, because Betty was a little shy. The teacher said yes, indeed, and called me up to her desk. She put her arm around my shoulders while she talked to them, and said I would tell Betty what a jolly time we were all of us having together. But as soon as Mrs. Ball had gone, she put Betty across the room from me, where I couldn't tell her anything, and she said that all the seats had been assigned; she was sure Betty would be just as happy in that lovely desk by the window, and that there was nothing for her to be shy about in this happy, friendly room. But she *was* shy that first day, and scared, and she never got over it.

I was scared when I got into one of the moments that led to the blackboard, but Betty was scared all the time. We always stood together at recess, out in the yard, and she was brave about staying with me when the boys jumped around and yelled about my prison shoes. Sometimes, at recess, we walked to the little school supply store at the corner, and bought a writing pad or a pencil, because we got two long sticks of licorice with either of those. It never occurred to us to buy just the licorice. We accumulated as much of a collection of writing tablets and pencils as our finances would allow, in order to taste the bliss of those twelve- or fourteen-inch-long pieces of candy. They were in ridges, like our

ribbed stockings, but they were so soft that you could tie
them into knots or shapes and untie them again, without
breaking them. We were neither of us really supposed to eat
between meals so we never bought any jaw-breakers or hoarhound—which we really liked very much, too—or candy-fried
eggs in a tin skillet with a little tin spoon to scoop them out
with. The licorice wasn't really buying candy, because you
had to get a tablet or pencil first.

On the way back to school there were generally some boys
watching for us who would jump out and try to grab the
licorice. The biggest bully of all was a boy named Ralph,
who was in our class. He had a very white face and tiny blue
eyes. I wondered that he could see out of them at all, they
were so little. His hair always looked sticky, and it wasn't
very much of a color; blond, perhaps, that wasn't very clean.
He was a favorite of the teacher, and she almost always let
him go up and down the aisles to collect the papers. All the
time, while he was walking past our desks, he sucked in his
lower lip with his big upper front teeth way down over it,
as if we had all done something awful that he knew about.
Sometimes he would wrinkle up his forehead, too, as if he
had found something especially bad and ought to tell. I
hated him for that. He knew, too, how easy it was to get me
into trouble. Sometimes he would stand longer at my desk
than anywhere else and look down on the top of it as if he
saw something there. Then besides pulling in his lower lip
with his teeth, he would whistle by drawing in his breath,
and shake his head. He would do this until the teacher would
notice him, and she would always say, in a very sweet voice,
"Is there anything the matter, Ralph?"

He would jump quickly, as if he were surprised, let go of
his lower lip, and say that oh, no, there was nothing the matter, and then smile at me as if he and I knew what it was but
that he wouldn't give me away to the teacher. I would squirm

in my seat, not daring to say anything to justify myself nor do anything to him. *How* I hated him. Betty took me way into the back corner of the cloakroom one day at recess, when it was raining so hard we couldn't go out, and whispered that she thought that he changed the things, too, on the papers of the people he didn't like. And she had seen him dip the end of Helen Jackson's braid in his inkwell—Helen sat in front of him—and then smear it over her paper when he took it up to the teacher. Helen had to stay and do it all over again for being untidy.

He tried at the same time to get in well with all of us children. When the teacher wasn't there he did things we wouldn't have dreamed of doing, right up to the minute when she came back and opened the door. We were all, in spite of hating him, fascinated by his daring. He could draw better than anyone there, better even than the teacher. He used to draw things on the blackboard for us, when she was out of the room, and just get them erased when she came back. We would pretend at first not to look at them, so as not to give him that much satisfaction, but eventually we always did. The pictures would make us laugh and get obstreperous and then, just as she came in, he would erase the pictures quickly and say, "Shhh!" to us, standing up in front of the room where he had been drawing on the blackboard, but looking as if he had gotten up and gone there to try and quiet us down. Lots of times, after something like that, he would be the only one who got out of school on time, and the whole rest of us would be kept in.

One day, when the teacher stepped out, as soon as the door shut behind her, he ran up to the front of the room and drew a picture of her and the principal kissing each other, with sparks coming out of their mouths. Just as he had finished it and stepped off to one side so we could see it, the teacher herself came hurrying in for something she had forgotten. She saw him up there at the blackboard, and before he could get in front of the picture, or smear it, she saw what he had drawn. She just looked at it for one minute and then she began to breathe hard, which was a signal I knew well. She started toward him, and then I guess she thought he was too big for her, for she said, in a voice that sounded as if she were strangling,

"Go to the principal's office—get out of here."

He went, too, past her and out the door. His little pig-eyes were open as wide as they could go, from fright. Just then the twelve-o'clock bell rang for noon recess, and everybody rushed into the cloakroom for their wraps. We only had an hour in which to go home for dinner and come back again. Everybody ran and pushed. Betty was so little that sometimes she had been knocked down, until we got to waiting until the rest had gone. So we were the last to leave, coming down the stairs by ourselves and talking about what Ralph had done. We had reached the bottom of the stairs before we heard the terrible sound, and then we didn't know where it was coming from. It seemed to be coming from all over, a high screaming, and someone saying,

"Oh, please, oh, please, *please* stop!"

We kept on moving; we didn't know what else to do. Suddenly we were in front of the principal's office. The door was open and just inside was Ralph, bent over a chair. The principal was beating him with a big, thick, wooden paddle, and it was Ralph who was screaming. He was facing us, too. He looked right into our eyes, as we stood there, and he didn't care. He just screamed and screamed.

I think if we had only *heard* that he had been paddled, we wouldn't have minded so much; maybe we would even have been glad. But to see it happen, with Ralph, the big bully, staring right at us and not even caring that we saw him like that! He didn't *care* that we heard him screaming. He wanted *us* to help him, anybody, to stop his being hurt. And the principal wouldn't stop. He was liking it, sweating and grinning over him, and saying—twice we heard him over the screaming——

"*Draw pictures,* will you?"

I don't know how we got out of the building. I remember Betty fell down, somewhere, and I jerked her up again, without even stopping. We both just ran and ran and ran. Finally we came to my house; I don't know how we ever found it, but we came lurching up the front steps and got the front door open, somehow. Mother met us at the door. She called Zoe, I suppose, because Zoe came running. Then they both took us up and carried us to the bathroom. Zoe sat on the toilet seat, with one of us on her lap, and Mother sat on the rim of the tub with the other. They washed our faces and just kept saying,

"There, there," until we got quiet.

I suppose we must have looked like crazy children, trying to talk and not being able to get our breath from the running we had done, shaking and hiccoughing, and trying to breathe, and trying to tell Mother to go and get Ralph, until finally she did go to find out for herself what had happened.

We never went back to the school again, either of us, not even to get our books, pencils, or erasers, and all the tablets we had collected, buying licorice. Our mothers got them for us, and said a few things to the principal about what we had seen. But Daddy and Mr. Ball said that it was useless to try to do anything about it. The law said that a principal could punish, with corporal punishment, a misbehaving boy. Our mothers and some others set to work about it, however, and after a long while the law was changed. Meantime, we went to school at the Frank Balls', and Miss Reba Richey taught us.

There were five Ball families who lived in a row on Minnetrista Boulevard, along the river. All the children were cousins, because their fathers were brothers. At the far end was the Frank Balls' house. The Frank Balls had five children —Arthur, Lucy, Frank E. (who was called Frankie), Margaret, and Rosemary. They had a playhouse, too, which was big enough for a schoolhouse. The Ball mothers, and some others, including mine, decided to have a teacher for all of us in the playhouse. All the fathers were holding out for a regular public school education. But the mothers said they had tried that, and now they thought they would just try *education*. Miss Richey was a friend of all of theirs, and had studied to be a teacher, so they persuaded her to take us, though we children were of different ages. She was young, gay, imaginative, tender, and an inspired teacher.

Every morning she collected the town pupils, took us out on the trolley and home again in the afternoon. The trolley ran along the length of the Ball houses in the back, dividing them from the Fair Grounds across the road. In the afternoon, when we would wait at the back gate for the trolley to come, we found that if we pressed our ears hard against a telegraph pole we could hear when it was coming, long before it was in sight. The humming that was always there inside the pole, far off and lazy, grew deeper and stronger. We all got so that we could shut our eyes and say when the trolley was coming around the corner into sight, and sure enough it always was.

The Fair Grounds were used only once a year for the County Fair, when people showed their horses, cattle, sheep, hogs, poultry, pies, cakes, quilts—the things that were their specialties. People came from all over the County; the Fair lasted three days, and there were big prizes. There was also a merry-go-round, and there were side-shows. You could buy balloons, too. It was hot always, because the Fair was in early September, and dusty, with the crowds shuffling slowly round and round past the booths, looking at everything.

The rest of the year the grounds were deserted. The frame buildings which held the exhibits were empty, and the track where the animals were shown was overgrown with tall grass and weeds. In the Spring there was nowhere around so good for wild flowers. They grew like a thick, tufted bedspread —the kind some women showed at the Fair—all over the grounds. Violets—purple, yellow, white—Spring Beauties, Trillium, Bloodroot, Wild Hyacinth.

Miss Richey said we could take plants from there for our own gardens. We were each to have a wild flower garden and take care of it. And on almost the first day of school, we went over to the Fair Grounds to gather nuts. The Grounds really were in a grove of trees, walnut and hickory mostly. We stamped on the hickory nuts when we got back to the playhouse, and smashed them in, because the shells were so thin. It was hard to separate the meat, but we pried it out with pins, and ate a good deal of shell, too, sitting on the steps in the sun. When we opened the walnuts with the green outside shells, we got our hands stained dark brown, and had to put the nutmeats to dry before we could eat them. It was fun, having our hands so brown.

While we were waiting to recite, if we had finished studying our lessons, we could go out and work in our gardens, or just play around—never off the place, of course—and certainly never alone as far as the Fair Grounds; but we didn't have to sit still in the house if we weren't studying; I loved that part especially. I loved every part of it, for that matter. Perhaps I wouldn't have enjoyed it so much if it hadn't been for the McKinley School days. I was so happy here that I wanted to shout all the time, or rush up and hug Miss Richey. That exuberance was probably why I was sent out to my wild flower garden a good deal.

The first thing we did in the morning was to assemble on the stair landing in the main house. A piano was there; not one that pushed against the wall like ours, but one that stretched out like Grandfather's, and had room underneath. We crouched there every time we sang a song about butterflies. We were cocoons under the piano, and when we crawled out and skipped around the landing, flopping our arms, we were butterflies. The boys never played that song; they just sat on the lower step and waited until it was over. Mrs. Ball always came into the upstairs hall and leaned over the railing while we sang the morning prayer.

"Lord, we thank Thee for the night, and for the pleasant
    morning light.
For rest and food, and tender care, and all that makes
    the day so fair."

Then she would say good morning to each of us, and go away, and that was all we ever saw of her, unless we had a special new song. We would practice it for days. Then one day Miss Richey would ask Mrs. Ball, after the prayer and the good mornings, if she would like to hear a new song. I used nearly to burst with excitement and pleasure over these occasions—acting out the part of a tulip, or a rooster (in the song *Mr. Rooster Wakes Up Early in the Morning*). That was one of my most stirring performances. Or I *would* be, if forced, though restlessly and impatiently, one of the baby chicks that just slept. But it was all friendly and gay, with lots of music—learning to read music, too, and singing, divided into parts—and nothing to be afraid of.

After the exercises we went to the playhouse and had our real lessons. There was nothing to be afraid of, even then. We did some things together, and we also did things by ourselves. One day Miss Richey asked Arthur to gather up all of the inkwells on the desks, to be filled. And somehow, when he came along where we were sitting, it made me think of Ralph, although Arthur was the nicest boy and always very polite to us younger ones, and didn't tease. But just seeing him walking along, collecting things that way, made me think of Ralph. I looked over at Betty, she was looking at me, and we both felt sick. But that was the only time I ever thought about the old school.

Every morning I was out at the curb half an hour before Miss Richey came, I was so impatient to get into the day at this place I loved so. And yet this was the school I ran away from. It never occurred to me to run away from Mc-Kinley, even hating it as I did. After all, when we ran from seeing Ralph, we were supposed to be going home for dinner, anyway. But I ran off from the place I treasured.

It was all on account of my temper, which I was always being told at home to keep down by counting ten. I got mad one day. We had, all of us, been out on a walk, saying the names of trees, and telling what their leaves looked like. We had gone along the river bank—the river was just on the other side of the Boulevard. Though it was called a boulevard, it was really only a dirt road. The river bank was muddy; there had been lots of rain that week. I got my rubbers thoroughly covered. We picked some bitter-sweet to bring back and hang in the playhouse, until it would burst open into orange-colored berries. We found two big gray cocoons of the Cecropia moths—one for Betty's collection and one for mine. Miss Richey told us about rivers and we learned the names of some of the big ones, and where they were. I saw a big brown flicker hammering on a tree. The day was sunny, with just a little chill in the air—not close to you but as if it were waiting around on the horizon until the sun fell. The horizon was smoky with the haze of late Indian Summer, and in it was the smell of leaves burning. It was a golden day. And I walked through it, smelling the haze and the smoke of leaves, hearing the flickers drumming on the tree trunks, watching the sunlight on the leaves just turning, feeling the sun between my shoulders, and the little faint chill waiting for the dusk. All my senses were spilling over, like Daddy one day saying, "Hold out your hands," and then pouring popcorn down into them, until it spilled out over the sides, hot and buttery, more than your hands could hold. That was the way I felt. There were more nice things that day than I could hold, even if I had both hands out.

Then Miss Richey said I had to clean my rubbers. They were muddier than anyone else's. Where *could* I have walked? She wasn't cross about it, and she brought me a stick for scraping, telling me to sit on the steps in the sun. But then they all went in, and she shut the door. I could hear their voices, but they had already forgotten about me. They might never remember about me, alone in the cold. No one would do that to me at home. Very well then—I would go home where I could be sure of being taken in.

I slid off the steps, stood up in the golden sunlight, looked around to see in what general direction my house might lie, and set off down the driveway to find it, clumping along in my muddy rubbers. I did find it, too, though it was four miles away by a very circuitous route which I had never before covered on foot.

I was not in the least surprised to find my house. After all, it was what I had set out for. But I was tired. Mother and Zoe were surprised to see me, and asked what in the world was the matter. I had a leg ache, I told them. I saw no point in going into the business of the rubbers. And after the four-mile trudge, I did have a leg ache. Growing pains, Zoe said, and Mother told her to put me down for a nap, and rub my legs a little. She was going out. It never remotely crossed her mind that I had come in alone. Someone, of course, had brought me and so, obviously, it would not have occurred to her to telephone the Balls to say that I was home.

Miss Richey always declared that she allowed only a few

minutes to elapse before opening the door to see how I was getting on with my rubbers. And when she opened it I was nowhere to be seen. For the first few minutes she was not even vaguely alarmed. She thought that I had gone off to find something that would clean the rubbers more efficiently, and that I was going to appear with them, showing off with pride how well I had done the job. Then she thought perhaps I had been a little put out by the arrangement and was hiding in the shrubbery to scare her or surprise her. She was not quite ready to be surprised, so she went back into the playhouse and closed the door. A few minutes later she came out again and called out that the game was over, and for me to come from my hiding place and let her see how nicely I had cleaned my rubbers. There was, of course, no answer to this suggestion. It was then, she said, when the story was told later, over and over, that she began to have a first, faint stirring of uneasiness. She set the children some tasks to do, and came out into the shrubbery, still calling as one does a recalcitrant puppy. She got down on her hands and knees and investigated clumps under which I might have wedged. There were considerable lawns, gardens, and clumps, and she investigated every one of them. Only then did it really penetrate that I was *not there*. In all her search she had never stopped calling my name. And as she came back toward the playhouse again, completing the circuit, Mrs. Ball from the main house heard her and came to the window upstairs. She smiled benignly down at Miss Richey and asked in her gentle voice if I were hiding. She had heard Miss Richey calling me. Miss Richey looked up. She was hot, dirty from crawling in and around the shrubbery, out of breath, and frightened. The best she could muster was a reedy croak, and she sent it up to the second floor.

"Emily is lost. She's gone!"

Mrs. Ball's reply was a wail of anguish reminiscent of

Ball Brothers' whistle on a Saturday noon. Mrs. Ball had never before been known to raise her voice above a murmur. It was small wonder then that this strident departure brought the entire household on the run. Mrs. Ball had only one real fear, she managed to tell the group around her. Anything else she was prepared to face. But haunting her waking and sleeping hours was the terror that a child would be kidnaped. And now a child entrusted to her, the child of one of her best friends, had made this fear a reality. And with this pronouncement she fainted.

Such a dramatic contradiction to her usual serene behavior destroyed the last vestige of restraint in the rest of them. Daddy always maintained that, from this moment on, the entire affair became about as rational as an opera bouffe, and with much the same quality. Miss Richey's retort was that the men behaved no more sensibly than she, and furthermore, that no one had ever before seen Bessie Ball faint. The men's sheepish justification was that the household had certainly sounded excited when the call came through. Besides, at the Bridge Works, and Ball Brothers, at all the factories, they were jumpy. Daddy knew that, they protested. In the last year the town had nearly doubled in size, with the factories growing so fast. It had gotten so you could walk down town and see people up and down the street, that you didn't know at all. Foreigners, too, every one of them, not even speaking English. On top of that, this business about unions, with threats, and ugly talk. Time had been when you'd known every man in your plant by his first *and* last name. Now you didn't know half of them by name, and you scarcely knew how any of them felt about you any more. It would make anybody fearful about what might happen to his family.

That, they tried to explain, was why Mr. Frank Ball and two of his brothers came from their factory when Miss

Richey telephoned, and Grandfather joined them from the Bridge Works, with Uncle Frank and Uncle Lloyd. She had called the Electric Light Plant first of all, but Daddy was out of town. To Daddy's later and bewildered query of why they hadn't telephoned the house at once, to see if I were there, they answered clamorously that the last thing in the world they wanted, was to let Mother know that I was gone, or what they feared.

But, Daddy explained, my routine method of expressing displeasure was to make for home. That was when, in the re-telling, they all grew somewhat ill-tempered. Not having the dubious pleasure of knowing me so well, they retorted, they were not acquainted with my habit of going home. They had only resorted to their own devices for finding a child who was reported kidnaped.

They searched the grounds again to satisfy themselves that I was not hiding.

By this time, of course, the other children were highly interested in what was going on. And so Miss Richey told them that Mrs. Ball had lost something, and that the men had happened to be out there to talk business, so they were just helping her to look. The phrase "to talk business" was as familiar to any Muncie child as "it looks like rain." From the time we first heard the word "Union," our fathers were always gathering at someone's house at odd hours, after supper, or Sundays. We were always hustled out of the way, because they had come to "talk business."

The Ball and the Kimbrough men came back into town in the middle of the afternoon. They asked the police to help comb the town, and each of the men set off with a small posse, to an area assigned.

Uncle Frank and his group came out of the police station and started for the district they were to cover. Not fifty feet away from them, coming along the sidewalk toward the police station, was my mother. She came on inexorably. Uncle Frank would, he said, have given anything to have turned and run as far and as fast as possible; she was the last person he wanted to meet. He was afraid he might betray some of his awful terror, and he must hold it all inside himself. He couldn't turn away, nor could he push her back. He could only watch her come, with every smallest detail about her, he said, standing out with extra sharpness, the way trees, just before a storm, stand out from the landscape. She walked quickly, as she always did, with short, brisk steps, tall enough, holding herself so straight that there was no effort in her walk, almost as if she were blown toward him by the light Fall breeze. She had on a new suit—dark brown. The coat fitted into her waist, and was long enough to reach her knees. The front was filled with frothy white; it was the jabot of her high-neck shirtwaist. Her brown hair was in a pompadour, and her brown broadcloth hat had two gold hatpins stuck through the knot of her hair on top. She came up to Uncle Frank and the three policemen. And to his thankful disbelief her gray eyes were shining with amusement, her head a little to one side. She spoke as she passed, low and demurely, glancing around at the three uniformed companions.

"I *am* sorry to see you in this difficulty, Frank dear, but I'll say nothing to Father Kimbrough about it, I promise you."

Uncle Frank managed a wan smile in return. And she was gone, swiftly and lightly, though her coming toward them had seemed interminable.

"That," said Uncle Frank wryly, "is the mother of the child we are trying to find."

Two hours later they all returned to the police station to report that the child had not been found, and that they could no longer postpone breaking the news to Mother. It

"I am sorry to see you in this difficulty, Frank dear."

was the time when the children were brought home from our school and she would, of course, demand to know why I had not returned. Uncle Frank was the one delegated to tell her, and Mr. Frank Ball went with him. They neither of them spoke all the way up Washington Street. They were both so tired Uncle Frank always said, when he told this part of the story, that it took considerable concentration to put one foot in front of the other.

So they came up the steps of our house without a word, and rang the bell. Mother came to the door, still wearing the brown suit. She must just have come in. She had her hat in her hand and was sticking the hatpins back into it. She was very surprised to see them, but pleased, welcoming them. And how was Bessie, she asked Mr. Frank. Mr. Frank, remembering that Bessie, when he had last seen her, was just coming out of a faint, said nothing at all, but managed a weak smile. Uncle Frank thought it was better to waste no time.

"Lottie," he said, "we've got a little bad news for you I'm afraid. But you mustn't be too alarmed; everything is being done. We have the situation in hand, and I'm sure we'll have her back to you in no time. But right now we don't know where Emily is."

Mother looked from one to the other of them in astonishment.

"*You* don't know," she repeated. "But *I* know. She's *here*. She came home early today, about two o'clock. She said she had a leg ache."

Uncle Frank's mouth was dry; it was not easy for him to speak.

"Was she here," he asked, "when you passed me this afternoon with the policemen?"

"Certainly," Mother told him, "she was here taking a nap. She's in the dining room now, eating her supper. Would you like to see her?"

There was a long pause, and then Uncle Frank moistened his lips, and spoke again.

"No, Lottie," he said, "I wouldn't. Not, I think, for a *long* time."

Chapter Nine

All through the month of October we practiced a lovely song about the goldenrod.

"The Autumn is the evening clear that comes before the Winter's night," it ran ... "Along the roadside, up and down, I see the golden torches flare like lighted street lamps in the town."

We had an elaborate pantomime to the song which began: "The leaves had a party one Autumn day, and invited the north wind bold."

We were the leaves preparing for the party and enjoying ourselves until we were set upon by the obstreperous guest, the north wind bold, who blew us round and round until we lay upon the ground, though *we* never lay down until we had been sharply enjoined several times by Miss Richey.

Autumn leaves were burning and Hallowe'en was coming. All up and down the streets, piles of leaves smoldered in the gutters, never flaring up into a bonfire; more leaves with each fresh raking were stamped down so there would be no sharp blaze. The smoke drifted up day and night, and the smell hung over everything, until the air was heavy with it. Sometimes my eyes smarted a little, but my nose quivered always with the delight of that sometimes sharp, sometimes sleepy, sunny smell. Nothing in the world was more fun than scuffling up the block along the gutter, dragging my feet through the leaves, dust coming up and making me sneeze, and sometimes a little flame licking out and scaring me into a jump over the next pile. Walking home from the big house at anytime was a more involved process than anyone gave credit for, but this time of year made it more ceremonious. Ordinarily there was the necessity of stepping in the center of each cement square because, of course,

"Step on a crack and you break your mother's back."

Then along the grass between the sidewalk and the curb were, occasionally, round caps. Some of them said "Water," others said "Gas." If you could jump from the middle of a cement sidewalk right square onto the top of the cap reading "Water," you would have good luck. If you missed it, it was not good, and if you had misjudged which one it was, and landed on a "Gas" by mistake, that was terrible luck, so that you had to go all the way back and start again to counteract it. It was also bad luck to shuffle through the leaves in the gutter, and not take care of any of the caps or cracks. So the best thing to do was to go back from the corner, if you had gone through the leaves, and start again on the pavement. It made the trip home much longer, but if I ever omitted any part of the ceremony a disaster was sure to follow.

I was always aware of impending disaster—not with a sense of apprehension, simply a recognition of its recurrent visits. I was, however, not caught by them unaware.

Across the street from us was an iron fence which surrounded the house and orchard of Mr. Cassidy. Mr. Cassidy was a mysterious little man, who lived by himself and played the flute. At least Mother made him mysterious, because she used to call to me to come with her to listen to him whistling as he went down the street. It was a strange, uncharted music, she said, sad and wild. He must have been in far-off places and learned native chants. It was very unusual, she told me, and we tried to recapture it. She tried, too, to win

his confidence in order to find out what far-off lands he had
visited. But he was so shy that at sight of her he would bolt
into his house, and she could never cajole Daddy into pur-
suing him there to make a formal call. When Daddy discovered and brought home the news to her that the strange,
sweet music that he whistled was the second alto part for
the flute in the selections for concerts by the city band, of
which he was a member, she lost interest. He was still a
source of interest to me, however, because I used his fence
as a graph of current events, and of my expectations.

In my philosophy, "It must follow as the night the day,"
that when something nice happened to me there would follow something unfortunate. And the bigger the pleasure the
harsher the subsequent misfortune. Mr. Cassidy's fence was
my chart.

I had a cache of yellow and white chalk, and I took these
over to mark off the good and the gloomy events. Sometimes
it was hard to decide whether the misfortune was of a pro-
portion sizable enough to count, so that I could justifiably
look forward to a good event as the next in line on the
calendar. If I marked with a yellow piece of chalk a line
that did not come to the edge of the iron paling it meant
that it was anybody's guess as to what the next event would
be—good or bad. On the other hand, if it were a double line
of yellow, from one edge of a paling to the other, then that
had been a genuinely bad time, and I could look forward to
a rip snorting good one ahead.

That October went along fairly evenly, more indifferent
than good or bad, and I was apprehensive. Almost inevitably
a spell of temperate weather would, for me, be followed by
a bad storm. And I wanted the bad part to be over with in
plenty of time to assure a good Hallowe'en, because this was
to be such a one as I had dreamed of. I had been told that
for the first time in my life I could dress up and go *down*

town after dark, to the Hallowe'en parade. The whole town turned out for this occasion—nearly everybody in costume—a few just to see the sights. It was a carnival. Not that I had ever seen it, but Zoe and other people had described it over and over. I had thought I would be old before I could see it, when, out of a talk about our new songs at school, Mother suddenly said that she would take me. I could not believe it. The only way for me that it could become credible was for something so bad to happen before the date, that a tremendous good thing must be the inevitable sequel. *That* would be the parade.

I *had* had one yellow mark from edge to edge, but I wasn't sure whether I could call it justifiably a double one or not. Certainly it was a misfortune, but I had known worse.

It was just that I had asked Roberta Franklin to come over one evening and have supper with me. The only detail that marked this invitation as a little different from average was that Mother had told me I could *not* have her for supper. She and Daddy were going out. I would have accepted her veto, if it had not been for the kind of party Mother and Daddy were going to, and the shock it was to me. They called me into their room and asked if I would like to see how they looked before they left.

I knew it was a party that Betty's mother and father were giving, and I had heard them talking about its being a children's party. But I certainly had no idea that I would walk into their bedroom and find my mother in a white eyelet embroidered dress, just below her knees, with a Dresden sash and a hair-ribbon to match—they were mine. Her hair was in curls down her back. She wore long pink stockings and patent leather slippers like mine, with one strap that buttoned.

My father had on short, black velvet, tight pants, above his knees, a white blouse with a great big sailor collar edged with embroidery, and a pale, flowing blue tie in a bow in front. He wore black ribbed stockings and dancing pumps. And he had his hair all ruffled up in curls, parted on one side curling all over his head. On the back of his head he wore a straw hat with the brim turned up all around, streamers hanging down the back, and an elastic under his chin. I stood in the doorway staring at them, and Mother said,

"Would you let me take your baby doll, Emily? I'll be very careful of it. Run and get it for me."

I was so humiliated and disgusted at the sight of them that I had nothing to say. Of all the shameful things for my own mother and father to go out to a party looking silly like that! To take my doll besides was sickening.

"Hurry, dear," Mother said, and there was nothing for me to do but to go and get it. My favorite one, too, she had chosen. I held it out to her with loathing. But she just said, "Thank you," without even meaning it.

And she told me that Uncle Lloyd was going to be dressed like Buster Brown. He had sent to Schwarz's in New York for a stuffed dog like Tige, the dog Buster always had with him in the funny papers. Two other men—she told me their names—were going to be dressed like the Katzenjammer kids, and another one like Little Nemo. They were *all* going to be dressed like children—not just she and Daddy.

She took out of a box—while I watched, dumb—a little two-wheeled cart with a long handle, the kind of toy I hadn't played with since I was three or four years old, and handed it over to Daddy. He said it was *wonderful*, and ran it up and down a few times in front of him. Then he held Mother's evening cape for her, which I had loved to see her wear. It was black velvet, except for a wide band of black moire, and it came down to the ground. It was lined with a strawberry-pink moire, so heavy and stiff that the cape could stand by itself, and it had black frogs across the front all the way down. It was terrible to see her put it on over that silly, short white dress with my sash, and see her pulling out her curls over the collar, and standing up the bow in her hair. I didn't even say good night to them. Zoe was laughing and slapping her apron, and telling them they looked as pretty as pictures and no older than their own child. The most shameful sight I had ever seen.

The moment they had gone I decided that I would have Roberta Franklin for supper. I went across the street and got her. She lived down at the corner on the other side. But I did not stop to check up on Mr. Cassidy's fence to see what I was due for. If I had, I might have been a little more cautious, because the mark there was white—meaning, of course, that something nice had happened and I was due for a balancing bump. Roberta came back with me, and I didn't mention what had happened to my mother and father. We just talked in a very grown-up way, because she was about three years older than I. I was impressed at having her, and I didn't want her to be bored by eating with someone so much younger. But right in the middle of my conversation I had a feeling of uneasiness. It was a very positive feeling, enough to make me stop talking and look over my shoulder, and there in the doorway stood Mother. She and Daddy had got half way out to the Balls' before they realized that they had forgotten the anniversary present for them, which was the reason for the party. So they had driven all the way in again. As if Mother hadn't done enough to shame me that night, she said to Roberta that she was extremely sorry but there had been a misunderstanding. I had been told I could *not* have her for supper; therefore, she would have to ask Roberta to run along home.

"Run along home."

As if she were exactly my age, instead of three years older. And Roberta went without saying anything.

Mother, in the silly white dress, took me into my room, took down my panties, and spanked me with Daddy's bedroom slipper, her cape thrown back over her shoulders. Then they went out to the Balls' again.

Of course the whole thing ought to have warranted a double yellow bar across the iron paling, *but* the spanking hadn't been very hard—Mother was in a hurry. And also Roberta had telephoned me later to say that she thought it was the meanest thing she had ever heard of, and that she was saving two pieces of divinity fudge for me. *That* from someone three years older would certainly counteract a double yellow bar. So I felt that something else bad ought to happen, if I were to be guaranteed a good Hallowe'en celebration.

I was to go with Mitchell Woodbury. He was an only child, like me, just six months older and lived next door. We played together all the time. Daddy had had Mr. Hammond, the carpenter, come and make me a tree house up in the apple tree over my sand pile in the back yard. Mitchell and I played there. It wasn't really a house, of course, just a platform with sides and a roof. But it had a regular door, and a window too. And there were boards nailed up along the tree trunk to make it easier to reach. We had two chairs and a table, and dishes. Sometimes we were allowed to take blankets up and have our naps there. Mitchell was very good at inventing games, but one time I scared him so that he pretty much did what I wanted to after that.

We were not in the tree house. We were playing over our outside cellarway—that was his idea too. He said it would be "Knight rescuing princess from the castle." He would be the knight, and I would be the princess. The outside entrance to our cellar was down a flight of stone steps to a small cement areaway and a door about eight feet below. Around the rim, at the head of the steps, was a wide cement band. Mitchell had me walk this until I was against the house with the steps and the areaway below me, and the distance across to the other side, about five feet. He left me there and went way off. Then I heard him pretend to be galloping up on a horse. When he came, he had a board that wasn't very wide, but was long enough to reach across from where I was standing to his side. We made up some acting then, about how I was being held prisoner by a cruel giant and I could hear him coming up the stairs after me. The knight was going to save me if he could, but we must get the drawbridge down. So he pretended to wind it, and did put the plank down, little by little, across to me. I stepped out upon the drawbridge looking over my shoulder fearfully, lest the ogre catch me. I did not give a thought to the drawbridge under my feet until it gave an ominous crack and split in the middle, piece of kindling that it was, dropping me the eight or nine feet down to the cement floor below. Mitchell gave one fearful look over the edge, and then lit out for home. Zoe, sitting sewing under the apple tree, saw him go, and came strolling over to tell me it was time to come in and get washed for supper And there I lay, stretched out flat, at the foot of the steps. Zoe wasted no time over me either. She turned and made for the house and Mother as fast as she could move, calling out hoarsely ahead of her,

"Mrs. Kimbrough, Emily's dead at the bottom of the cellarway."

Mother's chief complaint, later, was at the total lack of substance in her knees. But somehow she managed to get out and to the top of the cellar steps. I sat up then, opened my mouth, and let forth an elephantine roar that shook me— and Mother, too. I wasn't a bit hurt, but I was jarred. The reason it was made indelible in my mind was that I may have been knocked silly for a minute, but I had my first crystal clear realization that it was no use my beginning to cry until there was someone around to hear it. It also marked the beginning of a period when Mitchell played whatever I said, because he stayed scared for a long time. So when I told him about going to the Hallowe'en parade, he said he would, though *he* didn't like to dress up much.

Grandmother Wiles came over to visit us about a week before Hallowe'en, and was very surprised and pleased to learn that Mitchell and I were to go downtown after dark with costumes on. We discussed the costumes every evening as I prepared for bed, though the discussion was somewhat limited in scope owing to the fact that Mitchell had only one costume. But it was a wonderful one, and I described it over and over to Grandmother. A real Chinese costume for a little boy. His father had brought it to him from San Francisco. And there was a wig that went with it with a long pigtail. All that he had to get was a Chinese false face. Every evening we went over that Chinese costume, thread by thread. Mine, however, presented a wider field for discussion. The only actual costume I owned was that of a fairy, made for me for a fairy party at the Frank Balls'. And that, Mother said, was too chilly to wear at this time of year —unless I wore my long-sleeved underwear underneath it, or my blue serge reefer on top. Either of these, I felt, marred the spirit of the occasion. Grandmother flung herself into the problem, and was instantly on my side.

"Preposterous," she declared, "for a fairy to have long-sleeved underwear sticking out."

She knew, too, how I abominated that underwear, how I suffered physically under the scratchiness of it from early Fall until late Spring, when a violent attack of prickly heat would finally induce Mother to let me take it off. And how I anguished spiritually over it every Friday afternoon at dancing class. The galling garment was a one-piece union suit with a round neck. It buttoned down the front, and had, in the rear, what was humiliatingly known as a drop seat that buttoned across the back. Under ordinary clothes the garment didn't show so much because I wore, for the most part, a Peter Thompson sailor suit with a dickey which came tight around my neck just under my chin. I wore, too, long, ribbed cotton stockings and high buttoned shoes. But for dancing class my thin party dress—usually white with a little Irish lace somewhere and always a Dresden sash—was slightly lower in the neck, coming probably to the lower rather than the upper rim of my collar bone. (I wonder why the sashes inevitably worn with party dresses were called Dresden. They were wide, of stiff taffeta with a flowered pattern, and there was always a hair-ribbon to match. Perhaps the pattern was a copy of Dresden china; I can think of no other reason. I only know that all little girls either wore plain colors, pink or blue perhaps, or, if it were patterned, it was always a *Dresden* sash.) At any rate with this party attire I wore white ribbed stockings, but instead of high buttoned shoes, I had patent leather slippers, with a single strap across the instep. I did not wear these to the class; I carried them in a slipper bag, brown linen on the outside and lined with pink taffeta. When I changed from my buttoned shoes, in the cloak room at the Commercial Club, where our dancing class was held—over the Sterling Cash grocery—out sprang the bulge of underwear around my ankles. I was, as a matter of fact, lucky if it had stayed around my ankles. Putting on stockings over long underwear was always a hazardous business. You folded the surplus around your ankle, holding it with your thumb, and then pulled the stocking on. But obviously, at some point, the thumb had to be released. Occasionally the fold stayed where you had started it, at the ankle. More frequently, however, it slipped as the thumb let go, and traveled up the calf until it came to rest at some careless point between ankle and knee, where it presented an unsightly and somewhat sinister looking bulge. This sometimes happened on both legs. The sleeves of the union suit were rolled up to accommodate the short sleeves of the dancing school dress. By the time the folding reached that height it was thick enough to give a very unnatural appearance to my upper arm, more in the nature of a malformation than a muscle. The two top buttons of the union suit were opened, as a further concession, and each side turned under and pinned with a small safety pin. These always felt icy cold. The general appearance of abnormality was, I felt sure, accentuated, furthermore, by the fixed elevation of my eyebrows. This was due to the fact that my hair was pulled so tightly back off my forehead, and attached so firmly with the hair ribbon on top that they rose to an expression of constant surprise, in order to ease the strain a little.

Grandmother's contempt for this ensemble was ill-concealed; in fact, it was not concealed at all. On the occasions when, during her visits, she walked into the dancing class, she would observe audibly and indignantly,

"That underwear, that underwear, Lottie! What if she did catch a little cold? A sniffle wouldn't make her look as unsightly as she does now, bulging out like that. Above her elbows she's got the arms of a blacksmith. As for those legs, do you think any boy is going to dance with a child with lumps?"

Small wonder then, feeling as she did, that she should throw out at once the idea of the fairy costume. And yet we came back to the fact that it was the only costume I had. Back and forth we discussed it. As I undressed in my bedroom, she sat, on a stiff, straight chair, which she took with her all over the house. She disliked, probably because she laced herself so rigorously, any seat that was either cushioned

or low. Sitting there one evening, just as I was getting into
my sleeping suit, she hit upon an idea. How would it be,
she demanded, if I were to wear a costume of hers—not a
costume exactly, but one of her dresses, or a skirt and blouse,
her hat with a veil, and my hair would be done on top of
my head? I could wear her black feather boa, too. If Mother
insisted on that outrageous union suit, it would not be discernible.

The suggestion met with my instant approval. Several
children who were to be allowed downtown on Hallowe'en
were going to wear their fairy costumes, because they had
been to the Frank Balls' party, but I would look quite different. I would be completely disguised; best of all I would
look old. And, I confided to Grandmother, stylish, too. Yes,
she said, confirming it with a judicial nod of the head, I
would.

From then on the time until Hallowe'en itself seemed interminable. I was, furthermore, tortured by the agreement
which Grandmother and I had made that I was not to tell
a single living soul what I was going to wear, not even
Mitchell Woodbury. He was not to know until the moment
when I stepped out from my front door to join him. The
strain of this was almost unbearable. We started off with
Miss Richey every morning, my lips clamped tight together
in a muscular effort to keep from revealing the magnificent
surprise in store for everybody. And though I did relax mus-
cularly as the day wore on, I kept mentally on the alert not
to betray myself. And every night I repeated to Grandmother my success of the day. Together, smacking our lips in
mutual enjoyment, we visualized the furore, the stupefying
surprise I was going to give everyone. Not a man, woman,
nor child would recognize me until the dramatic moment
when I would remove my false face. Just where and when

that dramatic moment would be, took up another twenty minutes, before I could detach myself from savoring it, and be reconciled to going to sleep.

Hallowe'en Day—it did come at last—was sunny and clear, except for the Indian Summer haze that is always on the horizon—at least on the Indiana horizon. The playhouse was gay with paper pumpkins on the wall and a real pumpkin hollowed out into a jack-o'-lantern on the window sill. A few paper witches on broomsticks hung from the ceiling on strings. And in one corner there was a sheaf of corn, not husked, the ears full and tawny. There was no surprise in any of this decoration; we had been making it for weeks. And we had brought the corn ourselves from a field near the Fair Grounds. But it all did, somehow, spring into a gala atmosphere when we opened the door on it on the very day itself. We had a special ceremony, too, on the landing, singing the song about the goldenrod which we had practiced all month. And singing and acting, too, the one about the Autumn leaves. We acted with vigor, and shouted lustily another one,

"Swing the shining sickle."

Mrs. Ball said they were all splendid and she thought we sang them with fine spirit.

At noon Miss Richey told us that we were to go home; she was giving us a half holiday for Hallowe'en. No one had expected that that might happen, and we were beside ourselves with excitement—screaming and jumping all the way down the back path to the trolley, pushing our ears impatiently against the telegraph pole to hear it coming, and then rushing off to play tag, only to return anxiously to listen, as if it would not come unless we anticipated it.

I suggested, as soon as I came into the house, that I start getting into my costume. But I was persuaded to wait for a little while, on the grounds that if I were dressed too early,

while it was still bright daylight, there was a possibility that
I might be recognized. So I went out into the yard to play.
I started to call Mitchell, who had come back from school
with me, but I was afraid that my self-control might not
last, owing to the excitement of the day, and that perhaps I
would blurt out the momentous secret. So I climbed up into
the tree house, and stayed all alone the rest of the afternoon,
just thinking about how it was going to be with everybody
wondering who that mysterious "woman" was. At supper
time Zoe went up and down the street calling for me. She
went all the way up the next block to the big house, so she
was a little cross when she found me in our own back yard,
but I hadn't heard her from the tree house, because I had
had so much to think about.

The minute supper was over—and I was not able to eat
very much—Grandmother, Mother, and Zoe came with me
back to my room and they all, at last, started to dress me.
Underneath I wore my regular underwear, and not the
Winter kind because I wasn't really into that yet. Over my
panty waist and panties Grandmother laced a *corset*. It belonged to her. She was slender. I was *not*. And then she put
on one of her bustles, tying the strings in front. Higher on
my front, Mother pinned on one of her ruffles that she always
wore because she wasn't very big there and wanted to be.
Then they put on a shirt-waist that was high-necked and
buttoned all the way down the back, and then a gray broadcloth skirt that was quite full around the bottom, too. Zoe
had made some tucks down near the edge where they wouldn't
show, she said, because of the fullness, so that it was just
right for me, barely touching the ground. It had a train out
behind, which was the best part of all, and Grandmother
hooked around my waist a black, taffeta belt with shirring
and whalebone stitched in at the back and sides. Higher in
the back was a little fan-shaped fluting of the taffeta across

the top. Mother fixed my hair in a big pompadour on top of my head with rats underneath to keep it puffed out. They set on top of it a gray hat almost covered with black feathers. I put on the black kid gloves myself, but Mother buttoned them with the glove buttoner. I didn't wear the suit coat that went with the skirt, because it couldn't be made to fit me very well. Mother said that I didn't need to—she thought I would be warm enough. But I did put on the black feather boa, which I loved. Zoe tied the false face on. It had bright pink puffed-out cheeks and a dimple in the chin. Grandmother said, in a whisper, but I heard her,

"Why, Lottie, that looks like a baby's mask."

But Mother said, "Hush, Mama."

I didn't pay much attention to them. I hurried into the parlor; I couldn't walk very fast because I wasn't used to the long skirts. I tapped on the window, which was my signal for Mitchell. He was waiting at his parlor window, too, and tapped back. And then we came out of our front doors at exactly the same minute. He looked across at me coming down the steps, and said,

"I've been ready for twenty-five minutes."

His voice was as if he had his head in a bucket, because of the mask. But it made me angry just the same. How did he, I demanded in fury, know it was me? Did someone tell him what I was going to wear? Nobody would recognize me. He said nobody had told him, but since I had knocked on the window pane that was our signal, and had come right out the front door, he didn't know that it could be anybody else. But, he added, and crossed his heart, that if he had seen me downtown, he honestly wouldn't have known me. I was mollified, and told him that I wouldn't have known him either, even if I had remembered the least little bit that he had a Chinese costume. His false face was Chinese, too. It was a little better with his costume than my combination, but I didn't mention it because I preferred not to acknowledge it even to myself. Mother and Grandmother came out after us, and Mrs. Woodbury called good-bye from the front porch. Then she said quickly,

"Who is that with you, Mitchell? I thought you were going with Emily." My heart leaped with pleasure, like turning a somersault, and I could hardly find breath to call,

"It is Emily, Mrs. Woodbury. I guess you didn't know me in my costume." She said, no, that she never in the wide world would have guessed who it was. I went off up the street in a shining dream of success. It had all been planned that Mother and Grandmother were to stay behind us, far behind us, and pretend not to know us at all. And that is the way we went up the street.

When we got to the big house we rang the front doorbell, just as if we were strangers. Grandfather opened the door, looked down at us for a long minute, and then said,

"I am sorry, I think you've come to the wrong house. This is Mr. C. M. Kimbrough's, and I'm afraid we don't know any Chinese people nor elderly ladies." Once more I nearly suffocated with delight. And then I called out,

"It's me, Grandfather. It's Emily Kimbrough."

He took two or three steps back, in astonishment, and called Grandmother, who came hurrying out of the library, and said,

"Why, Father, I thought I heard Emily's voice. Where is she?" Grandfather told her—he was such a wonderful man—that Emily had gone off; she was in a hurry. But this was somebody that he would like Grandmother to meet. And he introduced me as Mrs. Robinson, with my friend Mr. Hop A. Long. Grandmother shook hands with both of us, and invited us into the library. I walked all the way into the room before I told her who I was. And she had to sit down in a chair and fan herself, she was so astonished. Great-grandmother Curry was there, too, Grandmother Kimbrough's mother. She was just going upstairs to bed, because she was quite old, but she came back all the way down the hall from the stairs to the library, leaning on her cane and looking at us very sharply. She said to Grandfather,

"C. M., I don't believe I know these people."

He introduced us again, just the same way. She said she never would have guessed. And then she offered us each a little piece of peppermint candy which she took out of her apron pocket. She always wore either a gray or lavender dress with a very thin, white apron tied over it. It was a small apron with little pockets that had ribbon run through them, pink or blue, or lavender. And she wore a lace cap on her hair with little bows the same color as the ribbon on her pockets. She always carried tiny pieces of peppermint candy there. She would break one piece into four or five, and she sucked one of these always just between her front teeth. It was good for them, she said, and for the digestion. We couldn't get the candy into our false face mouths, however, so we gave it back to her. Grandfather walked the length of the hall with her, to the foot of the stairs, and saw her start up them. She always turned at the landing, and called down to him,

"Good night, C. M."

When she was gone this time, Grandfather told us that he had a surprise for us too, not as big as ours had been, but maybe we would like to see it. Mitchell and I said we would, and sat down in the hall. Mitchell sat on the couch across from the fireplace, but I had to hump myself up on a carved, hard, ebony armchair, because Grandmother had laced the corset on me too tight. Grandfather called up the stairs,

"Are you ready?"

Somebody's voice that sounded like Uncle Frank's called down the steps that they were coming right away. We heard a bedroom door open, and footsteps. I heard someone say, "Good night, Grandmother."

I thought it must be Uncle Frank speaking to Grandmother Curry, but when they rounded the corner past the landing it was the Gold Dust twins, both of them, all black from head to foot, faces and hands and everything, with black wigs, and around their middles stiff tarlatan skirts which stuck straight out. They capered up and down in front of Mitchell and me, rolling their eyes. And then they put their arms around each other's waists, and did a Buck and Wing dance. I was rather scared, and I think Mitchell was a little, too. But when they stopped one of them said,

"My name is Frank Kimbrough. I don't know who you are."

It really was Uncle Frank, though I never would have believed it. When I told him who I was he said he couldn't believe it either. The other twin was his best friend, Phil McAbee, and they were going to a Hallowe'en dance at the Commercial Club where they were going to do a stunt. Then Mother and Grandmother Wiles came in; they had waited out on the porch, as they had promised, until all of the surprise about us was over. When they saw Uncle Frank and his friend they began to laugh right away. They laughed and laughed but didn't seem really surprised, and knew who they were. It made me uneasy, and I asked anxiously how they had known. Would people guess about me like that? Everybody said quickly, not at all. It was only because Uncle Frank and Mr. McAbee hadn't been able to keep the secret, the way I had. They had told. I was completely reassured by this, of course, and Mitchell and I swept out the front door, and down the steps in triumph.

We went next to call on Mrs. Little, and then on down the opposite side of the street to see Mr. and Mrs. Hageman, where the sky-rocket had gone in on the Fourth of July. Nobody knew us at all. Mother and Grandmother Wiles waited each time by the gate at the sidewalk. At Mrs. Bowman's gate we were almost betrayed, because Mitchell started sneezing, either from a cold coming on, or something from the false face. It ·got worse and worse until his nose began to run. That made the face all around it get soggy and cave in. He couldn't get underneath it to use his handkerchief. I told him, over and over, to sniff, and he said he was sniffing. But the false face got soggier and soggier, and sucked in and out when he breathed. It didn't look as Chinese as it had in the beginning. Mother thought she had better untie his mask and have him blow, but we persuaded her not to. We were so afraid somebody would come by. We went on, right into the very downtown itself.

Neither of us had ever been there before, after dark. It looked quite different. There were not only the corner lamps over the street, the way they were up on Washington Street, but the store windows were lighted, too, and there were lamps on posts on the sidewalk down the block. The saloons had music going on inside, and people going in and out through the swinging doors. That was what brought on the awful trouble.

Ever since we had come to the very edge of downtown we had been in a crowd, everyone in costume with masks on, all shoving, jostling, and laughing. It was very confusing at first, with the lights and the noise and the costumes. But Mitchell grabbed my arm and said,

"That's Bennet Heath."

We both called his name out at him and sure enough, although he was in a clown's costume, it was Bennet. He turned around and said hello, but he didn't know who we were. We saw several people after that whom we recognized, and we told them their names, but they didn't guess ours.

They tried several names, but we only shook our heads—they never said the right ones. If they had we would have said yes, we were those people—we had agreed to do that—but they didn't say it. We were still safe when we came to the part of Main Street where the saloons were. Mother and Grandmother had kept far behind us, just as they had promised, but they said, when it was all over, that it was the crowd of people and the saloons there in that block—not a nice section of town—that made them anxious. So they moved up closer, but we didn't know that. We were looking ahead at the children coming our way. They were all together in one group. Suddenly I saw that several of them had on the green fairy costumes from the Frank Ball's party. Almost in a minute I began to recognize them, and Mitchell recognized them too. We called out, in deep changed voices,

"I see you, Lydia Rich. I see you, Ruth Stone. I see you, Eleanor Spencer. I see you, Abbott Johnson."

They came up close to us saying, "Who are you, who are you?"

We just shook our heads. The whole crowd came up and circled round and round us.

"Who could they be, who are they? Go on, we'll tickle you until you tell us."

But Mitchell and I just stood and shook our heads. I had never felt such exultation as rolled up inside of me.

"Is this your mother?" they asked Mitchell about *me*.

I thought I would burst with pride. He shook his head, and they went on,

"Who is it, who is it, and who are you?"

But we didn't say; nobody could guess, not one single person knew who that Chinaman and the older woman were. I had been so afraid that something would give us away. I had guarded the secret so anxiously, for so long. All of those people were bewildered and curious, and circling round and round about us. "We are, I guess, the best disguise in the town." I said that to myself under my breath.

At that very instant Grandmother Wiles pushed her way through the crowd and came straight over to me. I couldn't believe my eyes. She kept on walking toward me, and when she reached me, she was hurrying. She stooped down and lifted my skirt, shaking out some leaves that had caught underneath. She straightened up and called back,

"It's all right, Lottie; she only picked up dry ones. They're not smoldering."

Everybody in that crowd—everybody in the town for that matter—knew my Grandmother Wiles and my mother. They laughed and jeered and said,

"Good evening, Mrs. Wiles; good evening, Mrs. Kimbrough. Hello, Emily, hello, Emily Kimbrough. I knew it was you all the time; hello, Emily." And then to Mitchell Woodbury:

"Hello, Mitchell Woodbury and Emily Kimbrough."

Over and over they taunted until at last the tears came boiling out, and I couldn't hold them back any longer. I ran stumbling through the crowd, past Mother and Grandmother, and up Main Street toward home as fast as I could run, not seeing very well, with the mask dissolving on my face, and not running very well, with the full skirt tripping me, but crying with all my heart and strength.

Grandmother and Mother came, after Mitchell caught up to me. They explained, over and over, that I had walked over a pile of burning leaves, because I hadn't seen well enough to avoid them, and that I had caught some under my skirt. Mother and Grandmother had seen them, because they *had* to come up closer in the crowded part where the saloons were, and they were afraid I would catch fire. That was why Grandmother had hurried into the crowd, and had forgotten her promise. They were sorry, very sorry, but I had fooled everybody until just that minute.

What difference did that make? I hadn't fooled everybody, and I might have. What was the use of all those weeks of keeping a secret? What was the use of all that planning of costumes to fool people? What was the use of a corset that wouldn't let you breathe, and a bustle, and a ruffle? It was not, any of it, any use at all. I should have known being spanked for having Roberta come to supper hadn't been a big enough bad thing. I should have marked it better on Mr. Cassidy's fence. I had *had* to have a bigger bad one. Hallowe'en had brought it.

Chapter Ten

Two weeks after Hallowe'en we were making paper pumpkins again, this time for Thanksgiving. Turkeys, instead of
witches, and stories about the Pilgrims. Margaret Ball was
chosen to recite by herself, on the stair landing where we had
morning exercises,

"The breaking waves dashed high on a stern and rock-
bound coast."

So I never cared much for that poem.

The bittersweet we had gathered and hung in the playhouse burst into flames. In the Fair Grounds, we gathered
nuts now that were ripe enough to eat. Along the river bank,
across the road, the ground was soft underfoot as if it were
let down for a Winter rest, before the Spring activity started
up again. We wore our arctics when we walked there, high
overshoes with metal frogs to fasten them. Winter was coming, the trees were bare overhead, the leaves soggy underfoot.

Soon it would be time to put on our leggings—abominable
things—cloth for every day, leather for Sunday, both button-
ing all the way up each side from the ankle to the hip. The
leather ones were the worst; if you got them wet by lying
down in the snow to make an angel they stiffened, and made
you walk as if you had been cut out of cardboard. They were
cold and clammy, too, and they stayed that way. Beaver hats
were for every day in Winter, too, and silk beavers for Sunday, both made exactly the same, with drooping brims, a

ribbon around the crown, and always elastic under the chin. You always worked the elastic up over the chin, however, so that you could suck it until some grown-up, passing by, jerked it out to fly back to its allotted place with a cold snap. It made the area under the chin almost always wet and cold, therefore, and chronically chapped.

There was usually another sore place just below the chapped area. This came from being pinched by a too vigorous fastening of the hook and eye which closed the velvet collar of all Winter coats. The long underwear, of course, was on inexorably until Spring. The flannel petticoat was postponed, like the leggings, until the first heavy snow. But the low shoes had gone into a box in the attic, or, if outgrown, to a box for the missionaries. The high buttoned ones, cloth tops for Sunday, would be the only choice for some months.

These, however, were only external irritations. For the most part it was a good time of year, especially because there was Thanksgiving at the end of it to mark going through the gate to Winter. But also because there were other things along the way, popcorn on Sunday afternoons that Daddy made over the fire in the sitting room, with a bowl of butter melting and sizzling on the hearth, the salt put in first. People came in to call; they had cider, and popcorn from the big bowl with the butter and salt mixed in. I only had the popcorn, but handfuls of it sometimes, running over and dripping between my fingers.

Once, when Daddy was out of town on Electric Light Plant business, Mother popped the corn. She couldn't find where he had put the popper, so she did it in a big skillet on the stove in the kitchen. Zoe told her it was better that way, anyway. But Zoe didn't think she needed to tell Mother to put a lid on. She should have though, because Mother didn't think of it. Some people came to call and heard Mother, just as I opened the door, calling Zoe and me, and saying,

"Quick, help!"

Everybody rushed to the kitchen, and there was Mother in a shower of popcorn which was coming up from the skillet like a Roman candle peppering all over, and she hopping around a little bit like the corn. It was hard to get through to her with the skillet lid, and by the time we did it was almost all over, that is, the Roman candle display. Underfoot, it was like walking on fragile marbles. It tasted just as good as Daddy's, however, when I had scooped it up after the grown-ups had left the kitchen, and put butter on it with salt mixed in first.

We toasted marshmallows in front of the fire, too, when Mitchell Woodbury came over, and Lydia Rich, and the other children from up and down the street. Our faces got burned, and so did the marshmallows. We liked the marsh- mallows better that way, both the taste, and the excitement of blowing out the flame, and seeing how fast we could pop the charred, black remnants into our mouths without burning our tongues.

There were children at our house every day. The side yard was a good place for games. It was the neighborhood meet- ing place, not on the side between us and the Woodburys, but the other side, where the Rosses lived. We played,

> "How many miles to Banbary Cross?
>   Three score and ten.
>   Can I get there by candlelight?
>   Yes, and back again—
>   Look out! The witches don't catch you."

Ten and fifteen of us on a side, screaming our way to safety out of the clutches of the witches between.

For Hide-and-Seek we used the whole block, clear up to Mrs. Wildman's on the corner beyond the Woodburys, but never across the street. That wasn't allowed. Late afternoon, just as it was getting dusk, was the time when playing was best, the shadows stretching out toward us across the grass, and the sharpened air carrying sounds more vividly. When the "It" called out,

"Olly, olly out's in free,"

the words would reach the uncaught stragglers all the way to the corner.

Then, just as all the shadows met, and it was really dark, the very best time for playing, other calls would come from the porches up and down the street—

"Ly*dia*—*su*pper time!"

"Hus*ton*—Huston *Frank*lin!"

"Evelyn *Hag*eman—Eve*lyn!*"

Immediately all my friends would scatter, hurrying to their mothers, while I stood at my side door, calling after them urgently, in a momentary desolation, that I would see them to*morrow.*

They always came tomorrow, even Sundays. All our families were Presbyterians, so we weren't allowed to play games that day, not things like Hide-and-Seek, or Hop-Scotch, Still Pond, or Statuary. We could play School, because it was a quiet game. All of us sat on the front steps, except the teacher. That one stood in front of us with a pebble in one tight fist. He held out both fists to each of us in turn, and we tapped the one we thought held the stone. Everyone who guessed right was promoted and moved up a step, the one who got there first became the teacher.

If we came into the house, we could sing and Mother would play the piano for us. At our house, we could sing any songs, but at lots of the children's houses only hymns were allowed. The toasted marshmallows and the popcorn took the place of games, too.

After my birthday party we played indoors, even on week days, because of the wonderful present I got.

The party was a week before the Hallowe'en disgrace. I should have counted it on Mr. Cassidy's fence, as a great big good thing; then I would have been prepared for the disgrace. But I was misled and put it down wrong, because Leo Ganter promised me and crossed both arms over his chest, which was a swearing promise, that he would give me a pony. Of course, I believed him. I could not, however, make my family take steps toward making ready a barn. We didn't have a barn, because we didn't have any horses. We never had a horse after Daddy sold Lady. We used Grandfather's. But I wanted my own pony, at my own house. I suggested that I would even sacrifice my tree house. It could be taken down and put out in the back for the pony, a Shetland pony, Leo had said, so it wouldn't take much room. Neither Mother nor Daddy did anything about it. And sure enough Leo Ganter came walking up Washington Street to my birthday party with a present in his *hand,* which turned out to be a copy of the *Sunbonnet Babies.* So I chalked up the whole party as a bad thing, but that was inaccurate. The rest of the party was good.

Mother said I could invite all the children I wanted. She told Daddy, and I heard her, that it would be the last time for me before my nose was out of joint. I had heard before that prophecy of a nose out of joint, and mine was still all right. Certainly nothing to bother about when I was saying aloud to Mother for her to write down, the names of all the children to be invited. The list, completed, numbered forty-five. Mother said she wouldn't have thought there *were* that many children my age, but when I had finished the names of everybody I wanted, which was almost everybody I knew, forty-five was the total. Then she discovered that they weren't all my age. There were some much older—I liked them best —and a few were younger. I was inflexible. She had *said* I could have all I wanted (that blood-chilling battle cry in the war between parents and children), and she had to keep her word. She kept it, and except for the pony it was a wonderful day. Lots of mothers helped her, and they got the kindergarten tables from the Universalist Church to put our supper on. Our dining room wasn't nearly big enough for all the tables, so they had to be put in the parlor and the sitting room and the guest room that was Grandmother Wiles's, behind the sitting room.

We had chicken patties and mashed potatoes, canned peas and ice cream in bricks with tutti frutti down the middle. There was a birthday cake for each table, too, because everybody had to have a chance at the thimble, the ring, the dime, and the button inside. I went from one table to the other, making a wish, blowing out the candles, and cutting the first slice, giddy with such importance. Of course, I should have gone right over to mark it down on the fence, as the biggest possible good thing. It was just that I was preoccupied with Leo Ganter and his perfidy.

Every child had brought a present; I asked each one at the door, and they all said yes, and gave it to me—but there was no pony. After supper we had toasted marshmallows. We weren't allowed to do them ourselves, because there were too many of us. So they were pale brown and insipid compared to the crisp, charred ones we could make. While we waited for them we played games, different groups of us, some in the parlor, some in the sitting room, and some in the dining room with the tables all moved away, and mothers to take charge of them. In the parlor, because that was where the piano was, we played "Going to Jerusalem," with chairs set up the length of the room, and my mother playing the piano. In the sitting room they played "In and out the window, In and out the window, In and out the window, as we have done before." And then "Stand before your Lover, Stand before your Lover." Only they could scarcely hear themselves above the "Going to Jerusalem" shrieking. The dining room ones played "The farmer's in the dell, the farmer takes a wife, the wife takes a child, the child takes a cat." They had trouble hearing, too.

That was the end of the party. The mothers who hadn't been there before, began to arrive to take their children home, and the mothers who had been helping said,

"Lottie, go to bed. You can tackle this in the morning. We'll help clean up now. You have no business to be on your feet like this with your time so near."

That was the kind of thing they said. The time was half-past six—the party had been from three to six—and the day was the 23rd of October. Furthermore, the time was not near, it was gone. The birthday was over. I did not, however, stop to point this out to Mother and her friends. I was anxious to get across the street to mark it down on Mr. Cassidy's fence and I did not want to be caught, because it was almost dark. Going out of the house near dark was forbidden, and I knew it.

When I got back Mother had gone to bed. Grandmother Kimbrough, Aunt Helen, and Aunt Huda were straightening up the house; everybody else was gone. They told me Zoe was looking for me. I was to go to bed right away; it had been such a long, exciting day. Where had I been? I didn't answer this, but I asked to wait up until Daddy came home from the Electric Light Plant to show him my presents. Of course I wasn't allowed to. And by the time he did get home (they said he was working late that night) I was asleep. Zoe had hustled me, too, so that I had had no time to go over the presents. I put them all in a pile by the window near the fireplace where I could see them the first thing in the morning. I wanted to count them, but counting took me quite a long time, and Zoe wouldn't even let me start. She said I had to say it over too many times; she hadn't time to wait. She wouldn't even count them with me. The best I could do was to lie in bed and see them outlined by the dimmer light in the hall.

That was the night the burglar came. The very night when my birthday presents were heaped up by the window, and that was the very window he entered, because we found his footprints. I don't know what time he came; none of us heard him. Mother was so tired from the party, and Daddy from working late at the Electric Light Plant. Zoe and Ruby, the girl, were tired, too, from the party. And Daddy said I wouldn't have wakened up if the house had been on fire. Whatever time he got in, he went upstairs and took the money out of Daddy's trouser pockets.

That was the first thing Daddy discovered in the morning when he started to dress. But the next minute he found that his watch was gone. The money was important, but Daddy said the watch mattered even more. So I knew it must be about the most important thing in the world. He told me it was the watch his father, my grandfather, had given him on his twenty-first birthday, a gold watch. But Zoe told me later that even *that* wasn't the most important thing. It was a picture of Mother cut out and pasted inside the lid of the watch that counted for him the most of all. There was something special about it, she didn't know what, but she said he set more store by it than anything he owned.

Two policemen came to the house while we were having breakfast; Daddy must have telephoned them. And he told them about the watch. He said it could be identified by his initials on the outside, and also by a picture pasted on the inside of the lid. He said it was a picture of Mrs. Kimbrough taken several years before. And if they did recover the watch he would like them to be particularly careful of that picture. He would appreciate very much having that back again. One of the policemen said he guessed Daddy would like to have the watch back again, too. But Daddy didn't answer him.

When the policemen had gone Mother patted him, and told him it was foolish to care so much about it. He said it was the only sentimental treasure he had, and he did care about it. They were both very quiet through breakfast, though I kept begging them to tell me every detail about what had happened.

I was the one who found the footprints, myself, inside the window when I went to go over my birthday presents. I set up a yell that brought them running. My temper was up, way up, and I had no time nor inclination for counting ten to push it down again. There was my pile of presents; and there was a footprint right beside it. He had probably taken one of my presents, or a lot of them, and I would never know, because Zoe wouldn't allow me to count them the night before. They had come so fast at the party that I had had no time to look at them enough to remember them. I would never know whether they were all there or not. I provided, I daresay, a little distraction for Mother and Daddy, but they provided no comfort for me, saying they were sure he hadn't taken any of my presents. Why were they sure? Had *they* counted how many presents there were? No, nobody had counted, and wouldn't let me count. Of course he must have taken some—lots of them.

Mother said we would count them now, and if there were as many as there were children at the party yesterday we would know they were all safe. Besides, burglars really didn't care for birthday presents; this last I brushed aside as sheer nonsense. The other suggestion I had little use for either. More people had given me presents than had come to the party; some mothers had brought some, and there had been some in the mail.

It was then, poking dismally through the pile, that I found the one that had come from Aunt Lulie in New York. I hadn't, in the excitement of the day before, even opened it.

So I untied it, half heartedly, now. Out came a cash carrier and basket for packages, exactly like the ones at Mr. Vatet's or Mr. McNaughton's store, with lines by which to string them up overhead. You could play store, put the pretend money in the little, round carrier, pull it up by a rope until it joined the crossway pulley with a little tinkle of a bell, exactly like the ones at the store, the basket with the packed parcels swinging underneath. At the other end, wherever you put the cashier, it would stop, and she would take out the packages, wrap them up, take out the pretend money, put back pretend change, and push it on its return trip. I was allowed to set it up immediately, overhead in my own room, with Zoe helping me. It did distract me from the ill-gotten gains I felt sure the burglar had had from me.

The cash and package carrier was, immediately, the neighborhood's favorite toy. That was what brought us indoors to play, even on week days. In my experience there had never been anything more exhilarating than to conduct a transaction over the ironing board placed between my doll's carriage and doll's bureau for a counter, put the cardboard money, which had come with the game, into the carrier, the parcel into the basket, pull the rope until they clicked with the ring of a bell, and then send them off all the way across the room, where Mitchell sat up on a chest of drawers and was the cashier.

On Sunday, of course, we were not allowed to play with it. But on the first Sunday after my party and the burglar, I went in and looked at it for a little while, after I came home from Sunday-school with Zoe. Mother and Daddy had stayed for Church. Then I went out to the back yard and to my sand pile, where I was allowed to be on Sundays. The sun was so bright that it made a warm day, even on the last of October. I couldn't really play in my sand box, because I still had on my Sunday clothes, my rose challis dress, and my button shoes. I had on my gray cloth Sunday coat, too, with the velvet collar, though I had taken off the gray beaver hat that went with it and left it on the bed in the guest room.

I just wandered around the yard looking at things, when I saw a strange, flickering shadow on the back of the house. I thought it must be a butterfly, a Monarch perhaps as late in the year as that, and I wanted it for my collection. So I ran inside and got my butterfly net out of the hat-rack seat in the vestibule. When I came back the shadow was still there, and I crept up on it very slowly and quietly on tip-toe. But on the wall where I had thought the butterfly was fluttering, was the picture of my mother out of the back of Daddy's watch. I began jumping up and down, screaming for Zoe, and she came rushing out of the house in a panic. She thought I had fallen out of the tree house, or something; she always thought something terrible had happened to me. And she was cross when she saw that I was all right. When I pointed to the picture, and she leaned close enough to see what it was, she got nearly as excited as I was.

We both hurried off up the street, and walked all the way to where we met Mother and Daddy coming home from Church. They were in their best clothes, too, but we made them hurry just the same. We didn't tell them what we had found; we just said it was very important. So they did hurry with us all the way back to the house, up the steps, and around to where, on the shingle, Mother's picture was pasted, so tight that the wood underneath had to be cut out before the picture could be taken away. Mother and Daddy were so happy about it, hugging each other right in front of Zoe and me, that they didn't even begin talking about how it got there until at dinner. Dinner was at the big house, of course, on Sunday. And it was after Grandfather had said grace, and begun to carve the roast, that Daddy told what I had found. Then he said, for the first time, "How did it get there?"

We never knew. We talked about it all through dinner at the big house, and many, many times after. But we never could find out how it happened. Did the burglar see the picture when he was leaving, and pull it out of the watch in order not to be identified? But why didn't he tear it up then? Why did he stop to paste it on the back of the house? Did he find out, someway, how Daddy felt about the picture? Mother said she liked to think that he did, and that he had enough sentiment himself, to come back and risk being caught. And that some night that week, he had tip-toed into our back yard to paste the picture there, firm and tight so that it would be safe when it was found. She said it couldn't be that tight in the wood, if it had been put there immediately after coming out of the watch, because the glue on the back was old and hard and wouldn't have held it. She said he was a nice burglar, a Robin Hood kind of burglar. Not to me he wasn't. He never marked up on the back of the house, nor anywhere else, how many birthday presents there were by the window when he came in.

All November the store game never flagged. The store supplies crowded my room. So did the children every afternoon, except for one week when I lost my taste for it. This was because I got spanked in Mr. McNaughton's store, and it left, temporarily, a disagreeable association with all store matters.

Mother had taken me there for a pair of kid gloves for Sunday. I sat at the counter with my elbow pushing down on the glass case, so that Miss Wood could try them on. She said she remembered the first gloves I had ever had, and how Mother had held out my hands while she tried to put them on. She couldn't believe that now I was big enough to sit up at the counter, keeping my hand steady myself by pressing my elbow down, and holding my fingers stiff and wide apart. She wet her thumb and first finger and pushed down each finger of the glove over my hand, and buttoned it around my wrist. That pinched a little, but she bent my hand to move the fat part away from the buttons, and got it secure. Mother said they were fine, and that she would like a pair, too.

I got down from my stool, and wandered along the aisle. When I got to the end it occurred to me that a pleasant diversion would be to turn all the stools until they were as high as the one had been made for me to sit on. I twirled the first one, and Mother looked up. She was holding her arm on the counter as I had held mine, with the elbow pushed down to keep it steady. She looked across it to me and called in a very low voice,

"Don't do that, Emily. The stool squeaks."

I didn't do that one again, but I went on to the next. I thought it wouldn't squeak, but it did. Mother looked up again, and so did Miss Wood. Mother said, a little bit more strongly,

"Emily, I said not to do that. It disturbs people."

I was very disappointed in that stool for squeaking, but I did wonder if all of them did. Furthermore, it occurred to me that suppose I were to go ahead and twirl all of them, which was what I was longing to do, what could possibly happen to me there in a big store? It wasn't like doing something at home that I was told not to, because there I was on the spot for punishment. Here was a big, safe, public place. I broke into a run, and twirled three stools, one after the other. They all squeaked rackingly, like chalk on a blackboard, or pulling a nail out of a board. Mother pulled off the glove she was trying. She did it very slowly, and looked at me. I turned my back on her, and went down to the end of the row to start again. I think I must have been intoxicated by my own idea of daring and safety. The next thing I knew she was beside me, taking me quietly by the hand. And the next thing after that we were back at the glove counter, and she was saying to Miss Wood,

"Would you mind letting me come back there a moment?"

Miss Wood looked dazed and frightened, too. Mother pulled down the little folding seat, that the clerks could sit on when they were tired. She sat on it herself, put me across her knee, pulled up my clothes, and spanked me, just exactly as if we had been at home, except that it was her hand, not Daddy's bedroom slipper. I yelled, of course, but I was more astonished than pained, and indignant that my idea of safety should turn out so false. Mother put me down, and got up herself. She apologized to Miss Wood. She had wondered what to do, she said, but had decided that she had to take steps to disabuse my mind of the feeling that there were places where disobedience was safe. And she would never inflict delayed punishment, threatening what would happen when we got home; she believed in it at the moment and on the spot. Miss Wood only nodded; she was still shaken. So was I, though I had stopped yelling. I couldn't get over the surprise of my miscalculation.

Two days later Betty's mother brought me home after I had spent the day at her house. She told Mother that she had taken us into McNaughton's on the way to do an errand, and that I had gone straight up to the glove counter, and pointed out the stools to Betty. If she twirled them, I had told her, they would squeak and Betty would be taken right back to that seat, which I pointed out, and spanked. This was the first Mrs. Ball had heard of the incident. But she said that everyone else in the store who had not previously known of it learned its entire proceedings from my recapitulation. Mother admitted it, and said that she had not known what else to do at the time, and still thought it was the only procedure. They both suddenly *laughed*.

I retired immediately to my own room, and sat on my low

chair before the fireplace. But I could see the whole cash and package carrier over my head. They were too strong reminders of the episode, so I did not look up at them for a week, nor did I let the neighborhood children come in to play.

We were back at it again, however, the following week, and from then on we marketed in my room for Thanksgiving. From every visit to the big house I brought back new items for us to purchase; cranberries, of course, for cranberry sauce, sage for the turkey stuffing, and extra bread to be kept until it was stale, for the stuffing, too. Sweet potatoes, and marshmallows to go on top, nuts, especially almonds, some of them in the shell, some to be blanched and roasted. Erna, at the big house, was making fruit cake, and I tried to remember all the things that went into it. We sent back and forth across the room pretend ingredients for mince meat, and pumpkin pie filling, too. The real ones were being assembled in the big house.

Every few days I sneaked off there, to smell and hear about what was cooking. As the days grew crisper outside, the smells, it seemed to me, became more acute. They seeped out through the kitchen, and could be savored the minute I opened the front door, although I had to go through the wide front hall and the den and the back hall, before I could come into the room where they really lived. One day Mother sent me down with three jars of mustard pickle which she had made herself and wanted Grandmother to have for the Thanksgiving dinner. Grandmother said it was very good, and for Mother not to mind that she couldn't make many things. The ones that she did, like Thousand Island dressing and mustard pickle, were just fine.

The day before Thanksgiving, Erna set the dough for fresh bread and rolls. I watched every manipulation, and licked what was left in the bowl from my fingers, just as I had sampled the mince meat and the pumpkin filling. Erna was a tease. I knew that, but when she told me Grandfather had said not to get a turkey this year, we didn't really need one, I couldn't make up my mind whether she meant it or not. I said to myself, going home that afternoon in the dusk, that it was just another teasing, but I couldn't be sure. I asked Zoe when I went to bed, and she said how did she know, but she expected my Grandfather would have a turkey all right. I felt she really didn't know, and I went to sleep with a deep uneasiness, worrying too because I had not gotten away from Zoe on the way home, to check on Mr. Cassidy's fence what I was due for.

I was up early, but I wasn't allowed to go to the big house until we were all ready. The first snow came while I was waiting, and I watched it from the parlor window. It was not very sure of itself, coming in thin little spurts like the rain water out of the spigot when the cistern was low. I saw Mitchell across in his parlor window, watching it, too. I pushed my mouth against the pane, and made him understand me asking if they were going to have a turkey. I understood him, too, when he nodded and also when he asked if we were. I couldn't tell him positively, so I pretended not to understand him. I felt more and more uneasy. I didn't see how I could explain to him and Lydia Rich that we hadn't a turkey, and I didn't see how I could swallow all the good things I did know about, if they weren't around a turkey. Everything would be spoiled.

I was very subdued when Mother and Daddy and I finally started off up the street, although I was in my best clothes, and Mother did say wasn't it fun to be starting off up the street for the big house, and a wonderful turkey dinner? Daddy said he was certainly ready for it, and she said she was too. I hadn't the heart to tell them that Erna had said that maybe there wouldn't be any turkey. And my heart sank lower and lower.

We were the first to arrive, and had to wait for Aunt Helen and Uncle Frank and Uncle Lloyd and Aunt Huda. I wanted to go to the kitchen at once, to end the awful suspense, but Grandmother said I couldn't. Erna didn't want anybody underfoot. And Harris, who was the hired man, was cross that day.

"He always is," Grandmother said to Mother, "when he's not sure that everything will go all right."

I knew what that meant. It meant that he knew there wasn't to be a turkey. I went into the library and pulled out one or two of my favorite books that I wasn't allowed to take home but could only read there. They had belonged to the boys, and were part of a series—*Frank on a Gunboat*, that was one of my favorites, and the other was *Frank Before Vicksburg*. But they had no flavor for me today. The flavor of turkey was what I wanted, and was so anxious about. I went over to the folding doors that were closed between the library and the dining room; I put my face to the crack and sniffed and sniffed, but I couldn't make out any turkey particularly. I could smell hot bread and mince pie, but I knew about those. There seemed to be no turkey rising above them.

The door bell rang, and I went back into the hall where Grandmother and Grandfather were letting in the boys and the daughters-in-law. They were all laughing and talking, the daughters-in-law knocking the snowflakes off their muffs, and shaking their hats, after they had pulled out the hat pins and taken them off. We went into the library, but we didn't stay very long. The folding doors opened, and Harris said dinner was ready. Everybody was laughing and saying not a moment too soon, they were hungry enough to eat a house.

I couldn't tell them then that they probably weren't going to eat turkey; Erna had said Grandfather thought it wasn't necessary. I hung back and Grandfather said impatiently for me to come along, come along. What was I waiting for, didn't I want any turkey? I wanted to tell him that I couldn't remember ever having yearned for anything so much, but I kept still. Everybody kept chattering about how pretty the table looked.

It did, too, with Grandmother's best lace centerpiece over the table cloth, the plain linen part covered by a cut glass bowl with asters and ferns in it. The silver candelabra were at either side of the bowl with pink candles in them, not lighted of course, and pink silk shades dotted with pearls.

We had the cut glass water tumblers, too, and the nut dish with the blanched almonds I had seen roasted—a flat dish, but cut glass, with peppermints in it from Craig's in Indianapolis. I looked up toward Grandfather, and there was even the cut glass roller beside him, that little piece shaped like the second joint of a turkey, and made to hold the carving knife and fork propped on it, after they were used. A carving knife and fork for a turkey we probably wouldn't have. For a chicken, maybe.

Then there was silence, because Grandfather was going to say grace. We all bowed our heads, and closed our eyes, and he said the grace. It was never the same; it was always made of the words that he felt at the time, except for the ending. That never varied. He came to it today, paused a moment, and then gave it in his deep, grave voice:

"Bless this food to our needs for Thy Son's sake. Amen." And in the next breath he added, "Mother, would you like a little turkey—a little white meat, a touch of dark?"

I looked up, and there stood Harris in the swinging door from the pantry, smiling at all of us. He was holding high in the air the great big silver platter, and on it the biggest turkey I had ever seen.

Thank you, God, I said to myself. It was like the Pilgrims getting the fruits after the long year of anxiety. It *was* Thanksgiving Day, and I held out my plate to my Grandfather.

Chapter Eleven

One morning after the others had gone to the playhouse, Lucy Ball held me back on the stair landing in her house, where we always had morning exercises. Lucy's hair was red-gold, not so harsh as a marigold but a little that color. Added to that advantage, she was a little older than I. Singling me out made it an event for me. Her mother had said, she told me, that she could ask me to go the next Saturday to the Wysor Grand Opera House to see a play. It was called *Babes in Toyland.* Her mother couldn't go because the Conversation Club was meeting at her house, but Miss Richey would take us. My sense of pleasure ebbed rapidly.

I tried to thank her politely, and said I would ask my mother. It was not a prospect that pleased. My experiences with public entertainment had been anything but fortuitous, and I was more than willing to forego that kind of pleasure. My presentiment was not lightened when Margaret, Lucy's younger sister, came out to her garden later in the morning, when I was working in mine. Margaret was a grave child, but usually optimistic; tall for her age. She asked if Lucy had spoken to me about going to the Wysor Grand on Saturday. I told her she had, and I was going to ask my mother. Margaret's forehead wrinkled anxiously. Well, she said, she hoped it would be nice. Her mother had said we would sit in a box. I knew then and there that my foreboding had been well justified. I could not think of a more doleful way to spend an afternoon than by sitting in a box.

"Are there holes in it?" I asked Margaret.

She said she didn't know. And when I asked how we would see out of it, she said she didn't know, and that was troubling her. I ventured the hope that we might stand up in it.

At this point Miss Richey came out on the playhouse steps. Margaret asked her if it would be possible for us to stand up in the box at the Wysor Grand on Saturday. Miss Richey said decisively, certainly not. We were to sit very still. I said quickly that I didn't think my mother would let me go. Miss Richey said nonsense, of course she would; she wouldn't want me to miss it—and she went back into the playhouse. I continued my digging in a moody silence, remembering the other time.

The other time had been when I went to the Wysor Grand with Zoe. I had not known that we were going; neither, I think, had she. But one Saturday morning, walking down town together on an errand for Mother, we heard music coming along Walnut Street toward Main. Zoe began to hurry.

"It's the *Uncle Tom's Cabin* parade," she said.

I knew about parades, circus and political, but I had never heard of an Uncle Tom's Cabin. Circus parades had a band and animals. Political parades had a band, too, but no animals—just carriages and flags, and torches if the parade were at night. They were pretty. Daddy said you had to make sure that it was a parade before you cheered it. Once when they were little he and Uncle Lloyd and Uncle Frank had cheered and cheered a parade, shouting, "Hurrah for Garfield!" until it was out of sight. Then Grandmother had hurried out of the house and dragged them off the fence. It was a funeral, she said, and she was mortified.

Zoe promised me that this was a real parade. We ran the rest of the way to the corner. There it was, coming head on toward us—not as big as the circus parade, but dazzling. Remembering every detail, I stopped digging and included

Margaret. I would like to tell her about it. She said she had seen it, so I went on remembering it by myself.

First there were men playing the music. They were dressed in black trousers and red coats, with red caps on their heads. Behind them walked a big man by himself. He had on a red coat, too, but it had long tails in the back. He had on a white shirt and a white tie, and a big broad-brimmed hat. His hair underneath was black, flowing to his shoulders. He had a black mustache, too, and in his hand he carried, curled up, a long black *whip*. He scowled toward one side of the street and then the other. Twice he unfurled his whip and cracked it with a noise louder than a Happy Hooligan fire cracker. Behind him, straining at heavy chains fastened to their collars, were four big dogs, yapping and slobbering. A man dressed like the band players was holding them. Zoe held my hand harder.

"Simon Legree," she said, "and the bloodhounds."

Then came the really dazzling part. It was a white cart, drawn by a white pony. Standing up in it was a little girl in a dress of blue silk covered with net, and with rosebuds around the neck. Her hair was bright, bright gold, hanging in curls below her waist. Her cheeks were the brightest pink I had ever seen, and her lips the brightest red. She was blowing kisses to everybody as she went by, and even sent one straight to me. I couldn't speak to ask Zoe who it was. I was cold with awe over her beauty. Zoe told me it was Little Eva. I emerged from my reverie for a moment, and asked Margaret if Little Eva had blown her a kiss. Margaret said yes, she had. I hurried back to remembering by myself.

Behind Eva a dark brown child was skipping along. She had pigtails all over her head, each one tied with a different colored little rag. Sometimes she would stop and turn a cartwheel, then run ahead and jump onto the back of Little Eva's carriage. There she would sit swinging her feet down into the dust. Eva would stop blowing kisses, and reach down and pat her on the head. Everything Eva did was beautiful. The little brown girl rolled her eyes and waved at people. Zoe waved back at her and laughed. She called out, "Hello, Topsy!"

Some more people walked back of Topsy in a group, all of them grown-up, and in old-fashioned costumes. Zoe said they were people in the play, and the play would be that afternoon at the Wysor Grand. I knew what a play was—all of us children made them up all the time. I thought if I could see this one, it would be the most wonderful thing in the world. I could scarcely get the words out; I just managed a whisper to Zoe. Did she think we could come to see it? She didn't know, but she would try.

We walked on to do the errands, not talking any more. I was still thinking about Little Eva with the long curls almost to the bottom of her blue silk dress. Zoe stopped and showed me a picture on a wooden stand. It was a picture of the same people from the parade, and the sign told about the play. I could read the big printing at the top—*Uncle Tom's Cabin.* I remembered something my father had said sometimes, when he had been working hard at the Electric Light Plant:

"I'm so busy, I'm doubling in brass and leading the blood-hounds for an *Uncle Tom's Cabin* parade," he would say.

That was where I had heard the words before.

We went home to dinner, and Mother and Daddy weren't there. Ruby, the hired girl, said Daddy had telephoned Mother that he could get off from the Plant and would take her over to Indianapolis to a matinee. She had flurried around, Ruby said, and they'd gotten off just a little while ago, on the Interurban. I asked what a matinee was, and Zoe said it was a play like *Uncle Tom's Cabin.* I said I would like to go to a matinee, too. Zoe told me to hush, and get into bed for my nap.

All of a sudden she came into my room, pulled me out of bed, and put clean clothes out for me as fast as anything. I couldn't make out what she intended doing, or what was going on. And she didn't say until we got all dressed and my hat on, and she was hustling me out of the house.

"We're going to the Wysor Grand to see *Uncle Tom's Cabin*."

She must have made up her mind with a rush.

We ran nearly all the way, but when we got there the man was closing the ticket window. He said we were just in the nick of time.

Inside it was pitch dark except for way ahead of us, where there were people moving around up on a lighted platform. I told Zoe I couldn't see, and out of the darkness I heard, "Hush! Hush! Hush!" at me from all sides. I kept still after that, and held on to Zoe. She followed somebody else, who took us down to two seats. We felt our way in and sat down. Zoe pointed to the lighted platform, and said,

"The play is started. Watch up there."

I couldn't make out anything that was going on, except people going back and forth and talking. I could understand the words, but I didn't know what it was about. Someone ran on to the stage, and I stood up. Zoe pulled me quickly down into my seat again. It was the little girl from the ponycart—the beautiful, golden-curled princess who had blown kisses that morning. I said to Zoe, but I was careful to whisper,

"That's the princess."

She whispered back to me,

"It's Little Eva."

For me it was the princess from Never-never-land. And I watched with a catch in my throat so troublesome that I could scarcely swallow. The platform went dark, something came down in front of it. Lights went on all around us. It was the end of an act, Zoe said. I blinked in the sudden light, and sat back in my chair, not wanting to talk. Zoe nudged me, and pointed into the aisle.

"Look who's coming."

I looked out perfunctorily. I didn't care about seeing anybody; but it was she, Little Eva, coming toward me up the aisle. She was dressed in white this time, but her curls were just as long. She held a basket on her arm, filled with pictures. As she came nearer, I saw that they were pictures of herself. She came closer and closer, and then she was beside me. She stopped, I looked up at her dumbly. She put a picture into my hand.

"Want one?" she asked.

I was barely able to nod. I didn't look at the picture. I never took my eyes off her face.

"Ten cents, please."

She spoke beyond me, to Zoe.

"It's a cabinet photograph."

I said aloud, "I have a cabinet photograph of Little Eva." Margaret said she did, too. I retreated again.

Zoe pulled her purse out of her pocket, and gave Little Eva the money. I sat holding the picture in both hands, and turned my head around to watch her pass. Somebody behind me said,

"Forty-five if she's a day."

I didn't know how they could be talking about anything else, when someone so lovely as that princess was passing us. She went all the way up to the end, and then I couldn't see her any more. But a minute or two later the lights went on, the covering was raised from in front of the platform, and the people were there again. My princess was there in a big bed. Grown people were standing around it—all of them crying. Topsy was there, too, from the parade—only not rolling her eyes now, but crying, too. Zoe leaned over to me.

"She's dying," she said. "Little Eva's dying."

I thought my breath would stop. Eva smiled at all of her loved ones; then she closed her eyes and was still, the way a dog of mine was when it died. But just as I thought I must scream with horror, she moved again. She rose right out of the bed, and the back of her nightgown turned into wings. She floated in the air. She flew higher and higher, and went right on up into Heaven where she lived, I knew. So she was all right, and I was reconciled. Not long after that, terrible things began to happen.

There was a man called Uncle Tom. He was black. He had loved Little Eva and she had loved him. After she died I could tell that he was unhappy. The man with the long hair and the black mustache came in—the one I had seen in the parade carrying the whip. He had it now, and the first thing I knew he cracked it across Uncle Tom's head. Uncle Tom fell on his knees, and the man whipped him over and over. The *next* thing I knew, except that it happened at exactly the same moment, Zoe was giving a piercing yell that rose up over all the talk on the platform.

"That's the way it was," she said. "That's how it was."

Then she clapped her hand over her mouth and drew herself in, ashamed I suppose of having made a commotion. But this was Zoe, my fortress and my strength, my solace and my protection. A brief second I looked at her, stupefied. And then I followed her voice with a roar of dismay and incredulity that put to shame and rout the pipings on the platform.

Our joint demonstration did not last very long inside the theater. We were almost immediately requested by the man who had taken us to our seats to follow him outside. We did stumble out, I still wailing, Zoe quiet except for trying to pacify me. She kept saying to the man who had taken us out, and several others who had gathered around outside, that she didn't know how she ever came to do such a thing. She

was just taken all over, because it was so real. It took me all
over, too, for some time. And though I treasured the cabinet
photograph as something that had come straight out of
Heaven, delivered by a princess angel, I had no desire to go
back into that place again.

A good part of the town had been there that afternoon,
too. I didn't see any of the people, because it was so dark,
but they all heard Zoe and me and saw us taken out.
They told Mother about it, too. She wasn't cross about our
going and she loved the photograph. But people were always
stopping us on the street to ask if we had seen Uncle Tom
or Mr. Legree lately.

I started to tell Margaret a little about it, but she said she'd
been there, and had seen us taken out. She'd wished she
could go, too. It got worse after we left. The only consola-
tion, we agreed, was that if this *Babes in Toyland* were as
bad as that we might not mind it so much, because if we
were sitting in a box we would be able to see very little of it.

A circus, I maintained, was different and better. We
stopped raking our gardens, and went over to sit on the playhouse steps to discuss a circus, pushing our rakes absently
ahead of us in the gravel path. Circuses, in the first place,
were light all the time—you didn't stumble around in the
dark. And, certainly, I had never seen any boxes there with
children in them. Margaret said even circuses scared *her*, on
account of the elephants' trunks. Her family, she said, always
sat way down in the front, so that the children could see
better. When the elephants came along they swung their
trunks right at her. She had heard, for a fact, that if they
sucked in when their trunk was pointed at anything, they
could attach it, just like a magnet. It could never be de-
tached. So she said she always wiggled around in her seat,
in order not to let the elephant get a direct aim at her and
attach her. But she knew some day it would happen. She said

you died from the suction, and you could never be pried off. We contemplated that grisly prospect for a moment, savoring it with awful relish.

Dog and pony shows, I put out tentatively, were nice. And to my relief she agreed. She had never, she declared, found anything to worry about at a dog and pony show. We reviewed them happily.

Sometimes they came alone, but other times they were part of a regular circus—the best part. They had only dogs—mostly fox terriers, white poodles, or something about that size which you couldn't identify—ponies and monkeys, all very small. All the equipment was small, too, the ladders they climbed, the chairs they sat on. The ponies, of course, and the monkeys, did tricks, too. There wasn't an animal you wouldn't have liked to take home. They had a parade in the town in the morning, just like the regular circus, only with no big cages holding roaring, snarling animals, or sealed up so that you could only guess what awful thing was inside. These parades were opened with a monkey driving six and eight ponies at a time, and a man sitting beside him to see that everything was all right. And dogs riding in a cart, leaping in the air and turning somersaults as the procession passed. Clown dogs following on foot, plodding along with dunce caps on their heads, and ruffles around their necks. Monkeys riding bicycles, the dogs standing on the bar behind with their front paws on the monkeys' shoulders. It was the best thing in the world to see, every part of a dog and pony show. The finest of all was at the very end; it was always the finale, and it never varied from year to year.

A little house was set up at one end of the tent, all rings were cleared. The little dogs lived in the house, and you could see them going in and out on their hind legs, sitting down on chairs at the table. Then suddenly the house caught on fire. Flames leaped out of the roof. Little dogs leaned out

of the windows, and yapped for help, but just as it seemed
inevitable that they would all be burned up, in through the
opening at the other end of the tent, with a great clanging
of bells, swept the hook and ladder wagon. It was drawn by
ponies, and driven by monkeys who were the firemen. They
rushed down the ring and drew up in front of the house.
The monkeys jumped down, set up the ladders, scampered
up them, helped some little dogs who climbed, actually
climbed, down the ladders from the upstairs windows. Other
members of the dog family ran out of the burning house.
The monkeys turned the hose on, real water came out, and
the fire was extinguished. Those were moments to remember,
and we sighed happily over them.

We returned morbidly to the topic of circuses. There were
other things, I said darkly, that could happen, besides getting attached to an elephant's trunk. Margaret said she supposed there were, but she had never heard of them. Well, I
said, with certain pride, I had had one happen to me. It
had happened only that very Summer.

I had had a searing experience at the circus, though God
had been the instrument more than the circus itself. Certainly it had made a lasting impression, and I told Margaret
about it.

Mrs. Woodbury had asked Mother if she could take me
with Mitchell. The circus was coming, and she thought it
would be exciting if we were taken to see it unload in the
morning. Then we were to come home, later go to the
parade, and then see the performance in the afternoon.
Mother was very dubious about so much for one day. But,
in the end, I persuaded her; Zoe helped me. Mother agreed
on one condition—that I would promise not to eat a single,
solitary thing at the circus. She said to Mrs. Woodbury that
excitement always went directly to my stomach, anyway, so
that the less I had there the better it would be for everybody.

Furthermore, she didn't want me to eat any of the dreadful stuff sold there. I promised, my left hand above my head, my right hand on my heart, which Mother said was unnecessary, but which all of us children knew meant sealing it. Then, to my incredulous delight, she said that I could spend the night before at Mitchell's house, so that I could be waked up very early there when it was time to start for the circus unloading.

I had my supper at my own house, and then I went next door with my sleeping suit, toothbrush, brush and comb, and a dress to wear in the morning. I persuaded Zoe to put them in a valise. It was really like going on a long trip to walk down my steps and up the sidewalk to his, instead of across the yard, and carrying a valise, too. We were put right to bed, but we didn't sleep much. Mitchell kept running into my room to ask if I thought it was time to get up, and I kept running into his—we were next door to each other. And his mother and father kept hushing us, from across the hall, so perhaps they didn't get very much sleep either.

We did drop off, though, because at five o'clock Mr. Woodbury had to wake us both. It was just beginning to be light. I had never seen that time of day before. The willow tree in our side yard was shaking itself in the dawn breeze, drying from the dew. The birds were talking now and then, to their families, like Daddy calling out things from the bathroom while he was shaving. Far off a rooster was crowing. A wagon went by, clattering as loud, out of the silence, as a bag of marbles which had spilled one day unexpectedly on our parlor hardwood floor. The sun was coming up, but the heat of the day had not yet come with it. We went outdoors into a pale light, and an air that was just wakened and stirring a little.

The circus always came to the big lot down by the C. & O. depot, at the foot of Vine and Plum Streets. It was only about three blocks away, straight ahead of us. We walked there very quickly. Mr. Woodbury went along with us; he held on to Mitchell, and Mrs. Woodbury held me. We both promised not to squirm or wiggle.

The circus train was lined up along the C. & O. track. The sides of the cars were let down. All over the lot a great, big canvas lay flat; it was going to be the tent when it was lifted. We saw elephants pushing wagons with their heads. We saw other animals rolled across from the tracks in their cages. The horses were led out. Lots of little boys were there, running back and forth with buckets of water for the animals; they would get in free that afternoon, Mr. Woodbury said, for doing that. Mitchell and I wanted to join them right away, but we weren't allowed. There were such clouds of dust raised up by the wagons and animals that we couldn't see very clearly, but enough to be too excited to eat breakfast when we came back home. I packed up my valise, and went down the steps and home. But not long after that, Mitchell and Mrs. Woodbury called to me to come out again and start for the parade, so that we could have good seats.

We sat up in one of the windows of the Commercial Club, and had a wonderful view. Beautiful ladies rode by on horses. Some of the ladies had long skirts, and hats with plumes. Some of them had very short skirts that stuck out all around, and they wore pink dancing slippers. Mostly these rode on white horses without any saddles on—just a big broad band around the horse that they held on to. I myself was wearing a white pique dress that was scalloped around the neck and the edge of the short sleeves. It had pleats, too, all the way down from the shoulder to the hem, and a wide, red leather belt that went in and out under the pleats. I had white socks on, and high brown shoes. Mother thought that with all the walking I was going to do it was better to have my ankles supported.

The animals went by in their cages, most of them asleep. The clowns were very funny, tumbling in the street. The band played every now and then. But the best music of all was at the very end when the calliope, steaming and tooting, wound up the whole procession. I told Mitchell that was my favorite kind of music, and he said it was his, too. We came home, and had a little dinner, and both of us had to lie down for a while, because we had already had such a day of it, our mothers said. Then we started out again to go to the circus. Just as we left, Mother reminded me again of my promise not to eat anything, and I told her of course I wouldn't.

We sat quite far down in front, but I didn't know then about the elephants' trunks. So I enjoyed it, until I began to feel a little bit tired and sleepy, and my head hurt from all the band playing. The tent seemed especially hot. A man came by selling lemonade that was pink. Mr. Woodbury asked me if I wanted some; he didn't know about my promise to Mother. I said quickly that I did. And I said to myself that this wasn't eating something, it was drinking.

Telling this to Margaret, I stopped and asked her if she didn't think that was right. I had promised Mother that I wouldn't eat anything, but nobody could say that you ate a glass of lemonade. Margaret said, well, she didn't suppose you could, but at the same time she wasn't sure that your mother wouldn't count it. Well, I said, it wasn't Mother, but God.

The circus ended; we didn't stay for the Wild West Show. It had so much shooting, and cost ten cents more. We did go into the other tent and look at the animals. But Mr. and Mrs. Woodbury didn't want us to see the side-shows; said they weren't good for children. I was ready to go home, anyway, by this time. I had sort of a leg ache from the long day, and I felt hotter and hotter. The heat had come up quite soon after the sun, and had stayed all day, and the air had gone back to sleep again—it wasn't moving anything at all, not so much as a leaf. The dust was so thick that my legs were dirty way up above the tops of my socks. When I got home, Mother asked how would I like to get into a nice, cool bath and bed, and have my supper there. I said that would be all right. And she looked very surprised. So did Zoe. But I had never kept up with as much of a day before, I told them. I didn't tell them that my head hurt, and that I felt very tired. I was afraid they might think I needed a dose of Syrup of Figs, or even the terrible business of calomel.

I ate some supper, and then I started to go to sleep. But all of a sudden there came back to my mind—it had never really left it, I had just pushed it into a corner—my broken promise. I began to feel very miserable. I thought perhaps I would tell Mother, but then I didn't want to. I got up, and went into the bathroom, and climbed into the dirty clothes basket, where I always prayed, and asked God to forgive me. And I asked Him if He thought it really was breaking a promise, since it wasn't eating, but drinking.

I started to go through into the front of the house and tell Mother and Daddy, who were sitting out on the porch. I could hear their voices in the hot, still night. But at the door into the guest room, I turned back. I didn't feel like going any farther. In bed again, I decided I would never tell. I would count it not breaking a promise, and nobody could say that drinking pink lemonade was eating something.

Margaret interrupted me to ask if I *ever* told anybody, before her. That, I said was what *God* did.

The next morning I woke up; I felt a little bit queer. Zoe came in my room. She looked at me, then she came closer, pushed up the shades all the way, and looked at me again. And what do you suppose she said? Margaret didn't know. She said—I paused, shaken again by the memory—she said,

"What you got in you, honey? You're all pink."

I couldn't *believe* such a thing could happen, but it had happened. Zoe got Mother, and Mother got the doctor, though I told her there was nothing the doctor could do about it. I told her everything then, about breaking my promise, because I didn't think drinking was eating. I explained that God had brought the pink lemonade to the outside, and that I would never break a promise again. She said she didn't believe I ever would. But she thought we would just have the doctor, anyway. I asked her if she would have to tell him about the promise, and she said no. So what do you suppose he said it was? Margaret didn't know. He said it was measles—German measles. I just looked at Mother, and she looked at me. I whispered,

"Promise you won't tell?"

And she whispered back,

"I promise."

Of course, I knew *she* wouldn't break hers, and I knew I would never break one again either. So Dr. Cowing still thinks, I said to Margaret, that I had the German measles. Of course, I repeated, I wouldn't have broken a promise in the first place, if it hadn't been for going to the circus.

We both realized what I meant. Going to the Wysor Grand on Saturday was not very different from going to the circus. We put our rakes up against the playhouse, and started back inside, because Miss Richey was calling us. Margaret turned back and whispered to me,

"At least let's not promise anything."

I nodded my head. I had no intention, anyway, of committing myself to a promise not to stand up in a box.

When I got home I found out that Mrs. Ball had already telephoned Mother, and Mother had said she would be delighted. She told me that she had a wonderful surprise for me. When I found out it was the Wysor Grand, I was disgusted. Margaret and I didn't talk about it much the rest of the week; there wasn't anything more to say. Friday, when I went home from school, Margaret said, "I'll see you tomorrow," and I nodded gloomily.

Zoe took me down to the Wysor Grand. Miss Richey was waiting there with all the children; there were eight of us. We said hello to each other, and then stood around glumly. Somebody in the crowd coming into the theater spoke to Miss Richey, and said weren't we all excited? Miss Richey said we were too excited even to talk. She had never seen us all so quiet. She had our tickets in the suède bag with the fringe and the drawstring, which she always carried. She marched us in ahead of her, counting us all to make sure nobody was left behind.

The inside of the theater was light, not dark, as it had been when Zoe and I came in late for *Uncle Tom's Cabin*. There was a man to show us the way. He took us over to the side, and down a little path. Then around behind a pillar, he pulled a red velvet curtain, and stood to one side, saying, "Here you are." We walked on ahead of him. And there was a big round space with a railing in front, and chairs on it, hanging out a little above the rest of the seats in the theater.

"Here we are," Miss Richey said. "This is your box."

I was so astonished that I stood stock still, looking over this sumptuous balcony out of a palace. People calling it a box. *Why* would they do that?

Miss Richey poked me between my shoulder blades.

"Sit down, dear. You're blocking the way."

I sat down on one of the chairs. It had a gold back. But Uncle Frank, I thought, wouldn't have liked the velvet seat. He couldn't bear the touch of velvet, nor anything like it. Even the sight of me licking the fuzz off a peach disturbed him. He always turned a piano stool from underneath, so he wouldn't have to touch the plush seat.

I settled back happily, and looked across at Margaret. She was grinning at me from ear to ear. Miss Richey said to take off our coats. We spread them over the backs of our chairs, but I was sorry to cover up the gold so that the rest of the people in the Wysor Grand couldn't see it. Margaret looked all around her, then leaned across Willie Ball and Ruth Stone, and whispered,

"Why do they *call* it a box?"

I shook my head. I was watching the people down below coming in. I knew most of them. And I could hardly wait for them to get through taking off their wraps, so they would look up and see me sitting there in a box, leaning against a gold-backed chair. It was a very funny thing about words, I thought, sitting there waiting to be seen. You could never tell how they might come out, like the time in Sunday-school when we sang the marching song, holding the left arm crooked and pretending to gather something from it with our right hand, and scatter it about. Mrs. Ball had stopped Betty and me, and said we weren't singing the right words. That they weren't "This is the way to spread disease," but "Thus the farmer sows the seeds."

Cousin Susie Marsh took off her coat down in one of the seats below, and folded it over the back of her seat. Then she sat down and began to take off her gloves, pulling the tip of each finger between the edges of her teeth, so as not to wet the kid.

She was an artist, and had very black hair, black eyes and long white fingers. I watched her wiggle her fingers after the stiff gloves were off. She had five children who were my cousins, and Cousin Susie was teaching them the Bible by having them all paint the walls of the parlor with a Biblical

scene. Even the youngest was doing it, and I had been allowed to help on a corner of sky.

I leaned over the rail, and waved and waved to her. But
she didn't see me until she had gotten the gloves off, and was
blowing into them to keep their shape. She was so surprised
to see me sitting up there in the box that she waved both
her gloves, and smiled and nodded her head. Then she had
to blow into them again, to put the shape back.

Miss Richey leaned forward—she was in the back row—
and whispered not to be conspicuous. That was a word I
knew; I heard it a good deal. It was a troublesome word to
me, but there was no mistaking what it meant. I sat still
again.

Lots of people were seeing us from down below, waving
and smiling. Miss Richey told us to wave across to the lady
in the box like ours on the other side. That was Mrs. Wysor,
she said. Her family owned the theater, so she always sat
there at every play.

That was the moment when I saw the big picture between
us and Mrs. Wysor, a picture of Walnut Street, with printed
signs on it. The Owl Drug Store. The Sterling Cash Grocery.
Star Vaudeville, Two Shows Daily. The Braun House. Roller's
Candy Store, Try Our Dark Secrets. As I spelled out the
signs, the whole picture rolled up out of sight, disclosing
another one more beautiful than I had ever seen. A lady
wearing a white wig, and a gorgeous pink ball gown sat in
a swing made of ropes of roses. Two beautiful gentlemen
were swinging her. They wore wigs, too, and satin coats and
knee breeches. There were other people sitting around in
what seemed to be a garden, but I barely noticed them. I
was being that lady, dressed like her and being swung in
my backyard by the two beautiful gentlemen. There was
music playing, which had distracted me only enough to have

Miss Richey leaned forward . . . and whispered **not to be**
conspicuous.

me place it also in my backyard as an accompaniment to my
swinging.

In the midst of my pre-occupation, this picture too began
to rise in the air. At its lifting, my throat tightened to a knot,
my breath caught in it. I clenched my hands, and the palms
were cold. It was to be like this for me all the rest of my life,
whenever the curtain in a theater was lifted.

When the picture disappeared out of sight, there were
real people on the stage—little girls—and they began to sing
to the music. There was a toy shop, and the toys came to
life. They had a parade. A little girl sang a song about having
a hard time at school. With an uneasy sense of disloyalty, I
whispered to myself that she was as beautiful as Little Eva.

"Put down six, and carry two." She hummed in anxiety.
"Gee, but this is hard to do." Again she hummed. "You can
think, and think, and think till your brain is numb. But I
don't care what the teacher says, I can't do this sum."

Behind her a whole line of little girls, almost as pretty as
she, sang it, too, the next time, and then they danced. They
were beautiful. The music was more wonderful than anything on Grandmother's pianola. The dancing was like the
fairies that Betty and I tried so hard, with our boxes of
magic, to catch. This was *all* magic, real magic, not pretending.

It must be God who made this magic. It must be God
showing me that when you didn't go without telling your
mother, like *Uncle Tom's Cabin*, and when you didn't break
a promise, like the circus, there weren't bad things at a play
at all. There were beautiful things, beyond any pictures in
any book. I knew, and I whispered to Him, that never, never,
until perhaps the day I came to Heaven, would there be, for
me, an experience so wonderful as sitting in a box at the
Wysor Grand.

Chapter Twelve

To go to the big house was always a treat, whether it was Thanksgiving, Christmas, or just Sundays. Thursday was the only other day when I went regularly, because Great-grandmother Curry's *Christian Advocate* came in the mail, and she read me the jokes on the back page. Mother said I would be a nuisance if I went too often. Perhaps that was one reason why the visits remained occasions.

I liked every aspect of the house itself. I thought its construction of brown brick, with a red tile roof, a fine combination. The heavy cement blocks, which ran parallel with the front steps, were, I thought, a sound piece of architecture, too. To jump off one of them onto the grass, or, more daring still, onto the front walk below, elevated one to a position of real prestige in the neighborhood. The front porch was bigger than ours and, therefore, better. The swing was better than ours, as well.

Immediately inside the front door was the vestibule, cut off from the main hall by an elaborate fretwork. Not only did the vestibule have a mirror and a hat-rack, like ours, but a bench running along beneath the fretwork. You could sit there while you put on your rubbers. The front hall was wide and very slippery. If you jumped from one Oriental rug to the next, you were likely to slide the entire length of the hall, gathering up all the rugs into a heap under the balcony of the stair case at the far end.

There was a gas log fireplace down at the end near the den

and the stairs. There were chairs set the whole length, and a couch across from the fireplace. The portrait over the couch was of Grandfather when he was much younger and wore a full beard. Grandmother had tried to get the painter, Mr. Adams, to come back and take off the beard because she said it wasn't like Grandfather any more, but the painter wouldn't do it. So Grandmother didn't like the picture any more, and wouldn't turn on the light over it.

Once when I was there Uncle Lloyd came in and began to tease Grandmother Kimbrough. She was running a doll carpet sweeper over a rug in the hall. She always used that after she had fixed flowers, to pick up fern leaves or petals that had dropped. She kicked out her foot at him a little, in front, saying,

"Stop it, Lloyd."

Quick as anything, he leaned down and caught her foot around the ankle. Then he made her hop all the way down the hall, from one rug to the other, while he whistled a tune. And she dragged the carpet sweeper behind her, laughing and scolding him, until he caught her up in his arms, at the end of the hall, and whirled her around and around, before he let her down at last. I lay on my stomach, on the couch in the hall, kicking my feet up and down to try to get my breath from laughing so hard. I nearly always thought of that when I came into the hall.

On the right of the hall was the parlor. The piano was there, and the pianola, too, that could be pushed up in front when you wanted to play it. In one corner bulged a gilt Vernis Martin cabinet. It had curios in it from the trips Grandfather and Grandmother had taken.

Folding doors opened into the library on the left of the hall. The library was one of my favorite places, with a curious piece of furniture in it. Back of this room was the dining room. And behind the parlor, on the other side, was Grand-father's little den. That was my other favorite place, except for the balcony on the stairs.

There was only room on the balcony for a little rug, and a bench that had a rose-colored damask seat. Once in a very great while, a string quartet squeezed into it and played with great restraint for a party. I am sure I was the only other person who ever entered it. I used to pretend the rose-colored damask seat was my throne, and my kingdom was down below me, with no one else knowing I was there at all.

Mother never let me take home any of the books from the library. She said it gave me something special to do there, so that I wasn't always under the feet of the grown-ups. I had other things to do in the house, too, but I *did* like the books. They had belonged to the boys. My favorites were the *Frank on a Gunboat* series—*Frank Before Vicksburg, Frank on the Lower Mississippi*—and I read them sitting on that curious piece of furniture. I do not know what it was called. It was neither chair nor sofa, but a little of both. The back of it was the wall itself, tufted in green velvet to a height of three or four feet. The seat which matched, was on rollers. When it was pushed against the velvet wall anyone would have thought the structure a tufted, green velvet chair, with a wide seat and a high back. But it wasn't.

There was an electric light overhead, in a jeweled shade with bead fringe. I liked it, so I always turned it on whether I needed a light or not. I sat cross-legged on the seat lean-ing against the back, which was really the wall. Then as I got more and more interested, I suppose I must have leaned back farther, because the seat would always begin to move out a little on the rollers. I could, of course, have pushed it back to the wall. That involved putting a marker in the book, and climbing down from the seat. Therefore, I always resisted the advance by bracing harder against the solid wall. No matter how inflexible the body, however, the force was always more irresistible.

The seat and I would stretch until I hung like a suspension bridge. My heels would be dug into the cushion to try to stem the traveling, my head bored into the tufted wall—the chasm below me widening, until finally, the middle section buckled up under the exhaustion of the extremities. All that was necessary then was to pick myself up, push the seat to its back once more, find my place in the book, and resume.

There were plenty of things to do upstairs; Mother needn't have limited me to the library for occupation. In the passage-way between Grandmother's and Grandfather's rooms, there was a drawer that pulled out and had a secret drawer behind it. The secret one was filled to the brim with sawdust. And the sawdust covered all of Grandmother's pins and rings. That kept them shiny, she said. I couldn't ask for a better occupation than poking about in the soft, grainy depths to fish out whatever Grandmother wanted to put on, blow on it to clear away the yellow particles that clung, dig it in again with my forefinger, if it were not the right one, and fish again.

A clothes chute was in that same passageway, too; not always restricted to clothes. I dropped in a good many other objects, with satisfaction, including myself one rainy day—though that frightened me into never repeating the performance.

Blowing down the speaking tube in Grandmother's bed-room was the best occupation of all, though it could not be overdone. The device was set in the wall with a mouthpiece like the one on the telephone, except that the opening was closed until you pushed down a little bar just alongside, in order to speak through it. First, however, you blew. At the other end, which was the kitchen, the blow resolved itself into a not unpleasant whistle. The recipient, who was Erna, would then step over to the tube, push down the bar, announce into her mouthpiece that she was listening, and put her ear to it for the message. The fun about it was that I could, once in awhile, blow into it, and when Erna had her ear safely wedged, send down a wail. She would answer, I could depend upon it, with a piercing scream, and the ejaculation,

"Lands, I'm on the cat again!"

Erna was six-feet-one, gaunt and spare of frame, and somewhat nervous. To adjust herself to the low position of the tube on the wall, she had to stoop considerably. The position was uncomfortable, and she was constantly shifting her feet about in an effort to better it. The cat could, therefore, easily have come under her vigorous footwork. And if I didn't overdo my performance, she was sure that it had.

Once when Grandmother was ill, and had a trained nurse, she asked the nurse to send a message down to Erna. The nurse was a stranger; the family had always had Mrs. Lothan, who nursed everybody in the town. The new nurse had never seen one of these speaking tubes before. Grandmother explained it to her,

"You have to whistle into it, to get Erna's attention, and then speak."

The nurse approached the instrument, pushed down the bar, as she had been directed, squared away, closed her eyes, and with grim concentration gave a spirited rendering, in a piercing whistle of *Yankee Doodle*. It almost frightened Erna into the hereafter.

After that I used to enjoy sending down some tune, myself.

The guest room I considered, without question, the most beautiful room in the world. It was papered in pale blue, had a white polar bear rug on the floor, curly maple furniture, and a gas fireplace with pale blue tiles.

Once Nordica came to Muncie to sing at Petty's rink and spent the night in that very guest room in the big house, or else that was part of my "pretend," until it became real. On the other hand, perhaps the hotel was full.

The roller skating part of Mr. Petty's rink had been covered over and filled with seats. I sat like one struck dumb; such songs as these had never entered my world. And I floated out upon them to a far different one. One song I remembered from that moment, always.

"Now sleeps the crimson petal, now the white;
Nor waves the cypress in the palace walk;
Nor winks the gold fin in the porphyry font:
The firefly wakens: waken thou with me."

The words had not the slightest meaning for me, but they had such beautiful sounds. And with Nordica herself sleeping in my Grandmother's guest room, they made a springboard from which to pretend. Every Sunday after dinner, when I was sent up to the guest room for my nap, I became Nordica. I lay on the bed which I embellished then with beautiful rich curtains that hung to the ground. It was early morning, and I was just awakening in that magnificent bed behind the close-drawn curtains. Outside in the sumptuous bedroom, I could hear people tip-toeing in, starting to speak and being hushed by the policeman on guard at the door. And then when there was no more sound of the crowd prying into my bedroom, I sat up wide awake, threw back the close-drawn curtains, opened my throat wide, and sang to the enraptured world gathered there: "Now sleeps the crimson petal, now the white." No wonder the big house was such a fascinating place in which to visit.

The people in it were interesting, too, and different from those at home. Grandfather was, of course, my idol. Grandmother Kimbrough and Great-grandmother Curry could be as much fun as people of my own age, both of them great teases and ready for a game. Great-grandmother Curry could move about only with a cane, so she sat still most of the time, but we played guessing games like "I have a secret hidden in the parlor. Guess where I put it?" She and Grandmother Kimbrough even had special words, which I never heard anywhere else. If I showed off a little, Grandmother Curry said quickly that I was a little "high tippy." If people were a little more fancy, she said they were "high tippy bob." And if they put on a good many airs they were "high tippy bob royal." If Grandmother Kimbrough didn't feel quite well, but not really ill, she said she was a little "dauncy." And if the cream were not quite sweet, but not yet turned sour, she told Erna that it was "blinky" and to use it for gravies and sauces.

Erna was a wonderful cook. Her cherry pies were the best in town, the boys said. And she could make Indiana succotash better than anyone else, too. Indiana succotash was special. It was made from the beans that are grown along the rows with the corn. The beans were cooked with bacon on the back of the stove for a long, long time. Then the corn was added.

There was almost always a cheese-cloth bag tied above the sink, where the scalded clabbered milk could ooze through and leave cottage cheese. And if there wasn't fresh bread baking, there were sure to be cakes and cookies. Sponge cake was Erna's specialty. She said herself she could live on buttermilk or cottage cheese and a piece of sponge cake, if it was light enough, so that you wouldn't know when you swallowed it.

Grandfather and I were in the den one late afternoon, about a week after the Thanksgiving dinner. He had stopped at our house, and brought me along with him; Mother said she would come to get me when it was time for supper. The air was crisp and had, he said, the smell of snow in it. As soon as we came into the den he lighted the gas fire. That was another good thing about the house. To light the fire you lifted one of the tiles on the hearth. Underneath was a ridged pipe sticking up; it was just like a secret. A key, which the rest of the time hung at one side of the fireplace, fitted over the ridges. Turning it turned on the gas. Then you put a match against a curly tan asbestos curtain, like the coat of a dog I once had, and the flames swished all the way up like water pushed by a broom.

Grandfather sat down in the revolving chair, in front of his desk that opened down from the wall. I climbed into my favorite seat, facing him. He was going to read aloud to me, and the best place for listening to that was in this heroic-size, black leather, overstuffed rocking chair. I could lie almost full length across the seat, or I could put my head on one enormous arm and my feet on the other. And I generally did all of these things in the course of the reading, not from boredom, but from sheer delight. We decided on my favorite book, too—*Leedle Yawcob Strauss*. This was a collection of poems in German-English dialect, and Grandfather read them with great flavor.

> "I haf von funny leedle poy,
>   Vot gomes schust to mine knee"

He closed the book, and I thought he was going to reach over his desk to his set of *McGuffey's Readers* on the bookshelf above. They were the books from which he had learned to read when he was a little boy. They were good stories, too. Just then Harris came into the den from the back hall. He had the wax taper in his hand, and we both watched him; we knew what he was going to do.

This time of day always meant for me, even when I was not there to see it, Harris lighting the light on the newel post. That marked for me, in Fall and Winter, like a clock striking, the time for supper, with Daddy coming home, shades to be drawn, and all of us closed up snugly inside our houses.

The lighter which he carried must have been about three feet long. It had a wooden handle, and a hollow metal shaft. Into this was inserted a long, white wax taper. There was a catch on the shaft with which you could push up the taper, and pull it back again. At the top of the metal shaft there was a slit. Harris held the lighter up by the wooden handle, until he could fit the slit into the bracket of the newel post globe high above his head. He turned the lighter in his hand, the bracket above him turned, and the gas came on with a little hiss. He lowered the lighter quickly, pushed up the wax taper, lighted it with a match, stretched it high again, touched it to the top of the glass globe, and the lamp on the newel post was lighted.

The globe itself was jeweled, encrusted with sharply faceted red and green glass, so that the light through it was not only colored but shifting and varied in shape.

Harris fitted the slit to the bracket once more, adjusted the flame to the right height, blew out the taper, and went out across the hall to the dining room and back into the kitchen.

The other lights in the house were electric, but this was the beacon for them all. The red and green prisms wavered across the darkness, warm and gay, and I watched them as I waited for Grandfather to go on reading.

"Emily, do you know about Harris?"

Grandfather's voice was an interruption to the direction my thoughts had taken. I settled back to meet it, but I could not think what he wanted me to say. Of course I knew Harris. He was there every day; he worked inside and outside the house; he did everything. He could even make wonderful candy—molasses drops—not just fudge. He was the best companion in the world, except sometimes when he was cross.

And when he was cross Grandmother would telephone our house and ask Mother to let me come up for a while.

"Lottie," she would say, "Harris is in one of his bad times. Could you let Emily come up?"

Mother would send me along to the big house, telling me to go see Harris. At those times I would find him very silent; other times he was full of conversation and stories. But I would play around, raking leaves, picking grapes, polishing the silver, whatever he was doing. And always, in a little while, he would begin to talk again. Before I left we were laughing and having fun, just like any other time. I told him more things than I told anyone else—even Zoe. I told him about the marks on Mr. Cassidy's fence; and once he went down the street with me to see them. I didn't know what to say to Grandfather when he asked me if I knew about Harris. Grandfather watched me a minute, and then nodded his head.

"I'm going to tell you about him."

It sounded like the beginning of a story, and I wiggled luxuriously into the back corner of the leather armchair. Grandfather leaned back, too, in his revolving chair until it squeaked and looked as if it were going to tip over backwards, though it never did. He rested his elbows on either arm of the chair, put his fingers together, looked across them at me, and began.

It was then that I learned—in the dusk with the flames shooting up the asbestos shield, and the jeweled light on the newel post beyond twinkling down the hall—that bad things went on in prison. That was why Grandfather had gone so often, not because he was sent there. But the relief of that knowledge was gravely tempered by the new things I learned.

The shoes that I wore were made by the prisoners in order to give them something to do. Grandfather did not try to tell me what it was to be without occupation, and to be enclosed within a small space. I am sure he felt I would have no idea of it, nor did he want me to. But I did have an idea —a clear idea. I knew my own restlessness, even in that wonderful, big, black leather armchair, and I knew that at any moment I could run from it, up on to the balcony beside the newel post, or out into the kitchen to Harris—and those men couldn't. I think I never again was entirely unaware of the privilege of free passage from place to place.

Grandfather was talking again about Harris. Harris, he said, was a "trusty," when Grandfather first met him. A trusty was a man who was a prisoner, but by reason of good behavior was allowed some freedom. Harris was permitted to work outside the actual prison, in the house of the Warden. The Warden was a friend of Grandfather's. Harris was still a young man—I knew that—but he had been in prison then for fifteen years. Grandfather leaned forward in the swivel chair until it banged to gravity again, and pointed his finger at me.

"*I* learned from him the deviltry of circumstantial evidence. Never forget those words, Emily, and never trust them the longest day you live."

He leaned back again.

"Repeat those words after me—circumstantial evidence."

I said them several times over, until he was satisfied.

Harris, he said, was what you called a victim of circumstantial evidence.

"That means that wrong was done to him, because of it."

And this was how it had happened:

Harris and two other boys, the oldest under twenty, more than fifteen years before this night when we sat in the den by the gas fire, had gone off on a bicycle trip. They were poor boys, but they did each own a bicycle. And they were taking a little holiday. Two of them worked on farms, the other in a store in the nearest town. They rode a considerable distance every day. They were young, healthy, and strong; they liked flying along the country roads, seeing how great a distance they could make before nightfall. They left their own State well behind them, and another one, too.

One evening, about six o'clock, far from home, they stopped in a village and bought some bread, cheese, and perhaps a few other things for their supper. Then they went on down the road, looking for a place to sleep. They came upon what seemed to them a deserted house with a barn not far away. They made no effort to go up to the house, but they leaned their bicycles against the barn, went in, found a hay mound, ate their supper sitting upon it, went out to the pump for a drink of water, washed their faces and hands, came back and slept in the sweet hay. The next morning they were up very early, and off again on their bicycles, loving, Grandfather said, the sun and the wind in their eyes and in their hair. They didn't have it very long.

At noon, going through a town, they were stopped by the sheriff and arrested. They were marched off to the jail with no explanation. That afternoon, handcuffed, they were put on a train and taken back to the village near which they had spent the preceding night. They still had no idea what had happened. But when they were brought into the local jail, a man jumped up and down excitedly, and said,

"That's them, that's them! I'd know them anywhere."

He was the owner of the little store where they had bought their bread and cheese and provisions the night before. But the house, which they had thought deserted, was occupied by an old man—a recluse, thought to be a miser—with money hidden somewhere. And that very night he had been murdered in his bed. There wasn't any trace of the murderer, except out in the barn some remnants of bread, cheese, maybe some apple cores. The storekeeper remembered selling them to three strange boys who had passed through the village the evening before—foreign to these parts and, therefore, suspicious.

The storekeeper, the mayor, and such other important citizens as the town boasted, together with the police force, were very smart about discovering in what direction the bicycle tracks led along the dusty road. Then they returned to the Council chamber over the fire house, dispatching a series of telegrams from the depot along the way, telling the police of nearby towns to be on the lookout for three dangerous characters wanted for murder. They included a description of each boy—supplied with pride by the man who had sold them the bread and cheese.

The upshot of the meeting over the fire house was that there was no need to call in any help from nearby counties; it was a local offense; it could be dealt with there; and the community patted itself on the back for a quick conviction. That would show the people round about how a wrong-doer was punished with swift vengeance. If there was any doubt in the mind of any of these representatives of the community as to the proper identity of the wrong-doers, he never mentioned it aloud.

The boys were put up for immediate trial. They had no money for legal advice, nor aid of any kind. They were orphans, I think, all of them. At any rate they had no families on whom they could call for help. They had to admit that they had slept in the barn adjoining the house where the old man was murdered. The fact that they had not one penny of the money on their person was considered more damaging to their case. It proved that they had hidden the booty and made a quick getaway, intending to come back sometime when the excitement had died down, and collect it all.

"It was such evidence as this," Grandfather's voice had grown deep and stern, "that convicted those three young lads to imprisonment for life. The only thing," and he said it bitterly, "that kept them from hanging was that they were under age."

For fifteen years before Grandfather met him, Harris had been serving his sentence. One of the others had died in prison; he didn't even know what had become of the third. The Warden himself was sick at heart over the case. The best, however, he had been able to do was to transfer Harris to his own house. That was not enough for Grandfather. He got Harris out of prison. It took him a long time, and it took me many years to learn all the details of what he had done to accomplish it. But Harris was released under personal parole to Grandfather.

That was why Harris was in Grandfather's house. That was why, too, I realized much later, he had his times when he was dark of mood with despair. Those were the days when Grandmother telephoned down the street to ask me to come. The reason Harris could tolerate me was that I did not remind him of the shame he carried. In his black moods he felt that the world was looking on him with suspicion. And I suppose it did. Even Grandmother, sympathetic as she was, had her moments of doubt, and Harris must have sensed them.

He had complete access to every tool outside of and in the house, and yet every Sunday, after the meat was carved, Grandmother would look down the length of the table and say,

"I'll take care of the carving knife, Father."

Sometimes he would protest a little, sometimes only sigh, but always he relinquished it to her down the table. She kept it beside her until the meal was over. Then she washed it, and locked it away herself, together with the sharp-pronged fork. I thought it was a general custom. I supposed that in every family in America the mother or grandmother washed and put away the carving knife and fork at the end of a meal.

In Indianapolis, every morning after breakfast, my Grandmother Wiles sent for a bowl of warm soapy water and had it placed on the table before her. Each time I visited there I watched her turn back the sleeves of her dressing sacque, shake her gold bracelets high up on her arm, and wash, piece by piece, the transparent breakfast china. No one else was allowed to touch it. I supposed this was much the same custom. It wasn't. All those years ago, back in the bleak, little farmhouse, the old hermit—the miser—had been killed with his own carving knife. Grandmother thought it was better for everybody else, and for Harris, to have the one at the big house out of the way.

In later years I learned why Harris left the big house. He left it at Grandfather's orders to take a job at a nearby plant. The parole had been extended, then, so that instead of being under daily personal observation by Grandfather it was commuted to reporting every three months, I think. The moment that was accomplished, Grandfather removed him from daily surveillance, put him out at the plant, and kept a check on his calendar of the days when Harris was due to report to his custodian. On those days the custodian—my Grandfather—made it his practice to go out to the plant, walk up and down the rows of workmen speaking to all of them, Harris included. It was the custodian, too, who persuaded him to leave this plant, and set himself up in business. Grandfather drove his automobile over to see him on the days when the parole report was to be made. And it was the custodian who went to the girl Harris wanted to marry, but was afraid to ask. Of course they were married, and they and their children became important citizens of their town.

I don't suppose that day in the big leather armchair in the den, across from the gas fire on the asbestos shield, that I understood half of what Grandfather was saying. But it was enough for me that something had happened to Harris that was wrong and cruel. It was enough, too, for me to learn about the place from which my prison shoes had come. In all of that misery it was comforting to know, at last, that Grandfather didn't have to go there.

I did sense, too, for the first time, and indelibly, that being punished was not so simple as Daddy's bedroom slipper or Mother's hand behind the glove counter—that sometimes even punishment was wrong when it was not properly administered. I felt that it was not going to alter the ministrations of Mother's hand, but I did sense that I was being told grown-up things, and learning about a different world from the one in which I was at least safe.

Grandfather had stopped speaking. I was quiet, too, putting together in my mind all of these things.

I heard Mother's voice in the front vestibule; she had just come to get me. I looked over my shoulder out the window; it was dark; the dusk had gone into night without my knowing it. I didn't want Mother to break into this. I wanted to keep it between Grandfather and me. I cast around in my mind for something to make the conversation go on. How, I asked Grandfather, had he gotten Harris here?

Grandfather, I think, recognized the ruse. He smiled at me a minute; he had been only very solemn up till then. He had gone, he said, many times, to see the Governor, who was his friend. The Governor had wanted, from the beginning, to allow him to do it, but there were difficulties which had to be gotten out of the way. It was against the regulations.

"Why," he broke off, "one time you went with me yourself. We drove down to Anderson to see the Governor. It was in the Summer time, and we went in the Haynes, just you and I. Remember what a good time we had?"

I remembered very vividly, indeed, the whole expedition. We were talking about it when Mother came to the door of the den. I knew I couldn't put off leaving, so I slid down from the black leather armchair and said good night.

As I was going out the door into the front hall, I turned around and looked back at Grandfather. I wouldn't forget, I told him. And I said again, to prove that I remembered it, "Circumstantial evidence." He held me a minute.

"Tell me the words again."

"Circumstantial evidence," I repeated, and went home with Mother, turning back at the front door for a last look at the friendly, winking colored light on the newel post that Harris lighted at dusk every day.

Chapter Thirteen

Mother always seemed to me to belong to the big house more than to our little house. Perhaps that was because most of the music was there, and most of all Mother belonged to music. She played only by ear, but with an unerring ear and so did Uncle Frank. Uncle Frank wrote music, too. He had wanted to be a composer, but Grandfather thought that wasn't a manly occupation, and put him into the Bridge Works instead. Uncle Frank always wrote all the music for the annual minstrel show at the Muncie Club. He and Mother always played together at the big house. She brought me into music almost as soon as I was able to sit up, and was unmercifully teased by the family about it. Once, at a Sunday dinner, Daddy revealed pitifully that she had telephoned him at the Bridge Works to come in as fast as he could, and had then hung up the telephone with no further explanation. He had pedaled home in an agony of sweat and anxiety, to find Mother sitting triumphantly at the piano. Their child was sitting on the floor at her feet.

"Now watch, Hal," she commanded, as he teetered into the house, his heart pounding and his legs shaking from the speed of his ride.

As he leaned against the portieres at the parlor door, she played a rousing march and then a waltz, and then a lullaby in 6/8 time, calling out, triumphantly, did he see, did he see that the baby was kicking her heels on the floor in perfect rhythm, changing the beat as her mother changed the selec-

tion she was playing. Wasn't it a wonderful surprise for him?
Daddy was not able, he insisted, to verify the child's performance. He was too confused from the ride. Mother would
invariably rally to the teasing this incident promoted, with
dark words of prophecy.

"Never mind," she would pronounce. "Many great musi-
cians have begun that way."

She could never, however, reveal her source for such fascinating information, nor state specific instances.

She herself liked to tell about the time Uncle Lloyd learned
a song from her. I was extremely young at the time—not even
old enough to drum out a beat, propped up on the floor by
an impatient mother. And I had colic. I had it, I was later
told accusingly, a good deal of the time. On this particular
night I had had it for a great many hours. Mother slipped
downstairs with me, in order not to disturb Daddy, whose
hours were so long and so hard at the Bridge Works. She
lighted the gas fire in the sitting room, pulled a chair close
up to it, and began rocking me, singing over and over an old
song. It was in December; the weather was bitterly cold. The
house cracked with it, and the sound frightened Mother a
little. She drew as close to the fire as she could, jumping, she
said, involuntarily when the floor creaked, or an icicle broke
outside the window. Then she began to feel the warmth of
the fire and to grow sleepy. Her vigil had been a long one,
but each time she started up gingerly, I wailed again, and
she would slip back into the rocking chair and resume her
singing. She began to be afraid that she would fall off to
sleep. Nervous, anyway, because of the sounds caused by
cold, she came almost to a sense of real panic that she would
slip into the fire with the baby in her arms.

There was a sharp tap on the window, and she jumped in
terror to her feet, the baby, of course, letting out an ear-
splitting protest. Uncle Lloyd was standing on the other side

of the window, and beckoned to her to let him in. She
wasn't sure that she was awake, or that he was real. And she
always remembered that, when she opened the door to him,
she almost doubted it again. He was in evening clothes—
white tie, tails, and an opera cape, which he took off from
around his shoulders and shook, because it was covered with
snow. He put it down with his high silk hat in the vestibule,
and tip-toed after Mother into the living room.

"From the big house, I could see the light down here," he
whispered, "just as I got up to my room. I came to see if
there were anything the matter."

He was home from Harvard for his Christmas holidays,
and had been to a party. Mother whispered back that there
was nothing the matter, except that I had had colic all night,
and she had been unable to put me down, lest my crying
wake Daddy, who was dead tired. Uncle Lloyd nodded.

"I'll stay here a little while," he said.

Mother went back to her rocking-chair by the fire, and
unconsciously began to sing again. She was reassured now,
protected from the unexpected snapping of the cold, and
from the terror of falling asleep. She rocked back and forth,
her head against the back of the chair, her eyes closed, singing over and over the same tune. The baby was quiet—not
asleep, but soothed.

Uncle Lloyd leaned over and tapped her on the shoulder.
He made a gesture for her to hand the baby over to him.
She demurred for a moment or two, but she was so weary
that her protest was half-hearted. She left him there, a young,
blond boy, rocking back and forth in front of the fire, the
baby in his arms. Sometime later—she had no idea when, because she had fallen into an exhausted sleep the moment she
dropped into bed—she felt a little tap on her shoulder.

"The baby's asleep," Uncle Lloyd whispered. "I've put her
down in her bed. Good night."

Uncle Lloyd leaned over and tapped her on the shoulder.

That was all of the story except that the following Spring when the Harvard Glee Club gave a concert in Indianapolis, one of the songs they sang was a song Lloyd Kimbrough had brought back after the Christmas holidays.

> "Bobby Shaftoe's gone to sea,
> Silver buckles on his knee;
> He'll come back and marry me,
> Pretty Bobby Shaftoe."

They sang it in parts and the audience loved it. But Lloyd had learned it more simply, late one cold December night, from Mother, wearily rocking her baby in front of the fire.

When Betty Ball and I started Sunday-school, our mothers took over the primary department at the Presbyterian Church. They brought to it imagination, and somewhat of a departure from the old way of teaching. They were accordingly reprimanded by the Elders. The word got around when Eleanor Spencer reported home to her parents that she had made a hot water bottle out of clay, for shepherds to carry in the field while they watched their flocks. Her family, interested in this piece of equipment for the Biblical characters, repeated it with some pleasure at Church. The Elders waited in a body for Mother and Mrs. Ball. Nor were they reassured that the object was simply a water bottle, and signified a detail of the long, lonely vigils out on the hillsides. They felt that whatever its purpose, its substance was secular, and they deplored it.

Mother and Mrs. Ball won out, however, routing the Elders and blazing a trail of activity and singing perhaps never before encountered under a Presbyterian roof.

We sang lustily, as we tramped around the room, dropping our pennies into the collection basket:

"Give," said the little stream. "Give, oh give, give,
    oh give;
"Give," said the little stream as it hurried down the
    hill.
"I'm small, I know, but wherever I go, the fields
    grow greener still.
  Singing, singing all the day
  Give away, give away.
  Singing, singing all· the day,
  Give, oh give away."

They could scarcely object to the "Flower Children" song:

"Our world is a lovely garden.
  God and our mother earth
  Care for the seeds and the brown mold
  Giving the flowers birth.
  Then grow, little children,
  God careth more for you.
  Turn your bright faces upward,
  Up toward the sky so blue,
  Up toward the sky so blue."

But they were dubious about our vigorous theatricals,
which accompanied the words. From seeds in the brown mold
to flowers in the garden, we gave a spirited performance.
Nor did we miss any of the opportunities in:

"Marching, marching we are marching, marching
  Mid gay flowers and Summer light.
  All the world seems filled with happy children.
  All the world seems dressed in colors bright."

At the close of the first year, we were actually so far reconciled with the Elders that our department was asked to par-
ticipate in a Sunday-school entertainment. I was even se-

lected to render a solo, Mother accompanying me on the
piano. I did not, however, sing a lugubrious hymn. The
choice was consistent with her determination to have the
Presbyterian repertoire cover a wider scope. She elected for
me to sing a little selection about sweet peas. I was exalted
by the prospect.

The moment of my individual performance arrived. One
of the mothers who was steering the program gave me a
little push from the wings. I advanced with the greatest satisfaction, to look down over the bank of ferns at the edge of
the platform at my mother. She was seated at the piano,
watching me with anxiety. I gave her a reassuring smile; she
began the introduction, and I started out upon:

"Sweet peas white, sweet peas pink."

A very curious physical phenomenon occurred. I seemed
suddenly to have a great urgency to swallow, and a total in-
ability to achieve it. Between the words "Sweet peas" and
"white," and the words "Sweet peas" and "pink," I struggled
to swallow a lump. A sweat came out on my forehead, and
in the palms of my hands. My eyebrows lifted in anxiety,
my eyes protruded. My chin stretched out in the strain, and
my neck bulged with the muscular effort I was making.
Eventually I did get the swallow down, and proceeded with
the next word. Mother was prepared for the second occurrence. The first had taken her by complete surprise into an
awful gap of silence. But the next time, between "Sweet peas,"
and "pink," she ranged up and down the keyboard in a series
of trills and arpeggios which would have astonished the composer of the simple little refrain. We continued to the end in
this rococo style.

When Miss Nanny Love asked if I might join the children's
chorus which she was organizing, Mother was dubious. The
memory of our Sweet Pea performance was still strong. Miss
Nanny won her over by saying that she thought she could

teach me to read music. There was no reason why a child of my age should not be able to read notes at sight.

That clinched it with Mother. Anything out of the ordinary in the way of reading must have held for her a strong appeal. She was, at the moment, teaching me the Greek alphabet and to read a few simple sentences in that tongue. Her theory was that I was bound to learn to read English, anyway. Before that time arrived, the sight of Greek characters would be no more mysterious to me than those of the English alphabet. Reading music would be another valuable experience. She enrolled me in Miss Nanny's class at once, and I loved it.

Miss Nanny did teach me to read music, too, which gratified Daddy enormously, and, paradoxically, piqued Mother a little, because she herself did not read it. Daddy was the one who could read music, and he got out songs for me to sing to his accompaniment. He scorned, however, the "Sweet Pea," "Golden Crimson Tulips" variety of selections. He chose a Columbia University songbook, which suited us both perfectly. I rendered with gusto "What If Tomorrow Bring Sorrow or Anything, other than Joy?" But our favorite was one which was accompanied only by mellow chords, the refrain progressing unaided. This was a source of inordinate satisfaction to me. I felt that I gave feeling to the words, too.

> "I need no stars in Heaven to guide me,
> I need no sun, no moon to shine,
> When I have thee, dear heart, beside me,
> When I know that thou art mine."

Mother was at the moment teaching me the prayer, and "The witch is dead, oh, the witch is dead," from *Hansel and Gretel.* But I preferred Columbia University selections.

In the Fall—this very Fall, when all the other things had happened—Miss Nanny Love decided to give a concert of her children's chorus in Indianapolis. She came to talk to Mother about it, and again Mother was very dubious indeed. She felt that certainly I could not be included in an enterprise so venturesome and which would not, moreover, get us home until long after my bedtime. Again, however, she was persuaded on the assurance that Miss Nanny needed her full chorus and the realization that I could spend the night with Grandmother and Grandfather Wiles. The concert would be in the afternoon.

I had a new dress for the occasion. Furthermore, it was the first dress in my life that could not be put in the wash. It was plaid silk, pink and blue, piped in pink velvet. It rustled when I walked. Mr. George McCullough, who owned the traction lines, loaned his private car on the Interurban, called the *Martha*. Besides the members of the chorus, most of the parents went over, too. Almost all of the Kimbroughs went along. Grandmother and Grandfather Wiles met us in Indianapolis.

When we got to the recital hall, I peeked out from the ante-room, and saw that we were to be on a real stage with a curtain across the front, and the audience down below. I felt that this was no more than our due, but I was pleased at such recognition. We left our coats and hats and leggings there in the ante-room, and marched on to the stage behind the closed curtain. Rows of chairs were placed in tiers, and I was in the center of the very first row, because I was the youngest and the smallest. The only quality that one could attribute to my voice was that of penetration.

The curtain rose, and I looked out upon a very large audience. To my even greater satisfaction, I found that a great portion of it was made up of strangers. I was in a real performance; it was just like Nordica. Miss Nanny came out upon the stage. She was just under six feet tall, and she was dressed in flowing Greek draperies. She bowed to the audi-

ence, turned around toward us, smacked her tuning fork
against the music stand, and gave us the note. We all hummed
it earnestly. She replaced the tuning fork on the music rack,
lifted up her baton, held it poised. We were ready to start
Handel's *Largo*.

At that very instant a little girl standing in the second row
immediately behind me quietly slipped between my neighbor and me, and stood in my place, pushing me back into
hers. The possibility of such an occurrence had never crossed
my mind, so that for an instant I was numbed. Miss Nanny,
evidently feeling that it was a situation with which she could
not deal at the moment, brought down the baton vigorously
on the first beat. I responded, my mouth wide open with
fervor on the first syllable of "Father," which is sustained
through something like eight counts. I sustained it, and took
advantage of the suspension to oust that interloper. I stepped
forward, and with rigid elbows flying behind me, jabbed her
back into her allotted place. Red-faced and triumphant, I
came to the last syllable of "Father," restored and on my
rightful spot. Mother said afterwards how ashamed she was.
Grandmother Wiles told her nonsense. The audience enjoyed
it as much as any part of the program which, she added, was
really very dull. On the contrary, it had seemed to me a very
spirited entertainment.

The music that I sang at the big house was not in the least
like any of the songs at kindergarten, Sunday-school, nor in
Miss Nanny's chorus. But I learned them at the same age or
even younger. That was because Mother and Uncle Frank
wanted someone to carry the air, while they improvised at
the piano. Uncle Frank always played bass, and Mother let
herself go on the upper part. They would play the same songs
over and over and over again, only stopping to throw a few
words to me over their shoulders:

"Again, Emily."

And I would roar out words and melody.

"If you ask me why I love you,
I will ask you if you know."

"Do not come too near. Maidens' wiles I fear.
So go your way, young maiden gay, and *pax vobiscum.*"

Always they would slide into other keys, throwing the new note at me impatiently. And I must pick it up, and go quickly on with the tune. If I missed they would both stop and whirl around in exasperation, demanding of me to *hear* it.

The singing at the big house always came about late on Sunday afternoons. After dinner I had to go upstairs for a nap. Grandfather and the boys always took naps, too, Grandfather in the den, the boys in their old rooms upstairs, the ones they had had before they were married; and Daddy generally took his on the couch in the hall. Mother and the girls talked together in the library. When I came down after my nap, I sometimes went calling with Mother and Daddy. Occasionally I went out with Grandmother and Grandfather. All of them paid calls, unless people came to the big house to call first. If they did I went out in the kitchen to play with Erna and Harris. But late in the afternoon, we started to sing. Aunt Huda was wonderful about words; she could remember all of them to every song. The rest of the family were always saying,

"Tell us the words to that again, Huda."

And she could start with the first word of the first verse, and go right through to the end. She was the one who taught the words to me, so that I didn't have to sing just syllables. Sometimes she and Daddy and Uncle Lloyd would be with me, gathered around the piano, all of them singing, and asking Mother and Uncle Frank for song after song. Grandmother and Grandfather would come across into the parlor from the library. The boys would pull up comfortable chairs for them, and one for Great-grandmother Curry, too, who loved to hear the music and would wave in perfect time her transparent white hand with the heavy blue veins on top. And they would sit there, Grandfather nodding his head, and tapping his foot to keep time, asking sometimes to have a song repeated and joining in with a big sustaining bass that rumbled along without words.

It was for Grandfather that we always ended with hymns. Just as it was time for Harris to light the newel post, we would begin to sing them. Mother and Uncle Frank would slide off the piano bench then, and Daddy would play from the music in the hymnals, so that everybody could read the words. But on Sundays Harris wasn't there to light the newel post lamp. He and Erna were both out from the time the dinner dishes were finished until late Sunday night. So somebody in the family lighted it, and everybody helped to get supper. When I was allowed to stay, and was not sent home to Zoe, I counted that day the widest good mark that I knew how to make on Mr. Cassidy's fence.

Grandmother, the daughters-in-law, and I would go into the kitchen a little before six. The kitchen was big, with windows on two sides. When the curtains at these were drawn and the stove lighted, it was a very pleasant place in which to be.

There was always a little uncertainty about cooking because natural gas was the fuel used. Natural gas was really the reason for the existence of the town. Its discovery had brought a big boom. Manufacturers came because production was cheaper. But in their exuberance over this natural resource, they set up sections of pipes at intervals around the town, and lighted them. These perpetual torches gave dramatic advertisement to the town. But they also diminished the supply alarmingly. Cooking was, therefore, apt to be uncertain in timing. You might have a good supply of gas, or the gas would be low, as people said, flickering down while dinner was cooking, until the process would be lengthened an hour or so. And many a cake fell.

So on Sunday nights we had a cold supper, not trusting the vagaries of the gas supply, since the boys would want to get home early because tomorrow was a working day. The girls raided the ice-box, bringing out what was left of the roast from dinner, pie, cake, pickles, relish, bread and butter, cottage cheese, buttermilk for Grandmother and Grandfather, sweet milk for me, coffee on the stove fixed by Mother, because she did it best. And always Mother's own little saucer of her favorite food, shouted at in derision by all the rest of the family, and eaten by Mother shamefacedly but defiantly. She declared always that she liked few things better than cold mashed potatoes. She did not scorn, however, the big dish of something which Erna always left to be heated up, baked beans, cheese and macaroni, or rice with green peppers and tomatoes.

When all the things were assembled, someone called the boys. They brought in the silver and a table-cloth from the dining room, and set the table in the middle of the kitchen, pulling out the leaves to make it big enough. They filled the water pitcher, too, and the one for milk, and waited on the table while the girls sat down—except that somebody was constantly jumping up to get something, and teasing the others and laughing. They had such a good time. They all laughed at one another so much that I thought I would make them laugh too.

I remembered a line I had read in a book called *Joan's Jolly Vacation*. I had thought it was so funny that I had giggled and giggled over it, and then I memorized it so that I could say it sometime at Sunday night supper, when every-

body else was making the others laugh. So I said, when someone asked me if I would like a piece of turkey,

"Shades of defunct lawn-mowers, I believe I will."

Nobody laughed at all; they just looked very surprised.
Somebody said, "Where on earth did she hear that?" And
Mother said, "Drink your milk. Remember about little girls
in grown-up's conversation."

It made me very sick at my stomach. I decided I didn't
have a very good idea about making people laugh, and didn't
try again.

Sometimes Uncle Frank and Aunt Helen would rush off
after just a bite, because he would be having a rehearsal of
some show for which he had written the music—the Country
Club, or the Muncie Club, or the Commercial Club. They
were always putting on something, and Uncle Frank wrote
the music, playing it with Mother beforehand.

After we had finished supper, we cleared the table and
washed the dishes. Grandmother said she didn't think it was
any fun for a hired girl to go out if she had to come back to
a pile of stacked dirty dishes. Two of the girls washed, one
in the kitchen and one in the pantry, and the boys dried.
They always shooed Grandmother and Grandfather out then,
made them wait in the library, and forbade them to do any
of the work.

When we joined them, we all went back into the parlor
again for a few more hymns before we started for home. And
that was the time that Grandfather, I know, liked best. He
would call me over to sit beside him; I didn't have to stand
by the piano then, to shout the tune. We sang *Holy, Holy,
Holy, Lord God Almighty,* and *Jerusalem the Golden*—they
were favorites—and *Abide with Me* for Great-grandmother
Curry; she liked that best. But nearly always we sang
Grandfather's favorite. It was about little children. He taught
that one to me, the first hymn I ever learned.

"For He cometh, for He cometh to make up His jewels,
All His jewels, precious jewels, His loved and His own,
Like the stars in the morning, His bright crown adorning,
They will shine in their beauty, bright gems for His crown."

His children were the jewels. And the second verse began "Little children, little children." We didn't sing another hymn after that one; it was always the last one, like dessert for Grandfather, saving the best for the end.

One evening, skipping along beside Mother in the cold Autumn dusk, I began to talk about Christmas. We had been to the big house; Grandfather had told me the story about Harris. I wanted to tell it to Mother, but I was afraid I would get it mixed up. I jumped over the cracks on the sidewalk, and from the sidewalk to the iron knobs in the stiff, dry grass that read "Water" and "Gas"—jumping on water was good luck, jumping on gas was very bad for you. If you got there by mistake, you had to go back and start all over again. Jumping made my breath come faster in white clouds of steam, because it was cold. The cold reminded me of Christmas.

I asked how long would it be before we had Christmas, and all the Christmas hymns at the big house, and the special part about "For He cometh, for He cometh." Mother took my hand, and slowed me down. Christmas, she said, was going to be different this year. How different, I demanded at once. What kind of difference? I did not see, I told her, how it could be different, because there wouldn't be time. The day was so filled up, there wasn't room for anything different. She laughed and swung my arm back and forth as we walked along. And as we walked in the crisp, sharp twilight, I reminded her of how Christmas would be.

I would wake in the morning, very, very early, but I would not be allowed to get up then. I looked questioningly up at my parent, and she nodded her head vigorously, putting to rout any faint hope that the difference this year might lie in that direction. Well, then, I resumed, with a sigh for that long wait, I would stay in bed until Zoe told me I could get up. Then I would go over to my fireplace and take down my stocking. All the time in bed, of course, I would have been trying to guess what the bulges in the stocking were. I would carry it upstairs to Mother's and Daddy's room, and open it up on their bed. I looked up at her again for confirmation.

We were crossing Vine Street under the arc light. She didn't look down at me, or nod; she looked straight ahead, and just squeezed my hand suddenly. But I was into Christmas morning, and I followed it eagerly. We would have breakfast, and I would play for a little while with my stocking presents. Then I would begin to ask if I could go up to the big house. I would be allowed to go ahead, too, by myself, because I would have errands to do for Grandmother Kimbrough.

The glass part of the front door at the big house would be almost covered with a holly wreath, tied with a shining, wide, red satin bow. The inside of the house would be different, too, because the folding doors into the library would be closed tight.

I would call, "Hoo-hoo!" and Grandmother would say,

"In the dining room, dear."

I wouldn't take off my coat and things, because of the errands to do. But I would go into the dining room, and see her and Erna unwinding from the big rollers, where they were always kept, the table-cloth and the centerpiece for dinner. Harris would be in the pantry polishing the cut glass with tissue paper. And Grandfather would be in the den at his desk, going over the signs to be put on the backs of the chairs in the library. I looked up at Mother anxiously; she squeezed my hand again. Grandmother would come back with me to the vestibule and give me some packages from the bench there. She would show me which were for the Riches, for Mrs. Little, for the Hagemans, the Franklins and the Vatets. She would tell me to deliver the ones on the other side of the street first, so that she could watch me cross. She would remind me to ask at the last place where I went on that side for someone please to watch me come back again across the street.

I would go with the presents to all of these houses and say, "Merry Christmas," but I would not stop to see their presents where there were children, because I had to hurry back in case the rest of the family had come.

They always took so long. But finally they would come—about half-past ten, sometimes nearly eleven—stopping in the vestibule to shake off the snow, calling out,

"Merry Christmas, Mother Kimbrough! Merry Christmas, Father Kimbrough! Merry Christmas, everybody!"

And each family would be pulling a great big sled, piled high with presents. The boys would carry the presents in and take them to the library door. They would knock on it and say,

"Presents, Harris."

Harris would be on guard there by this time, all of his work in the pantry finished. He would open the door a crack, not enough for me to see, even if I got down on my stomach and tried to look between his legs. He would put the packages on the chairs for which they were marked. Every chair had a name on a big sign tacked on the back. Grandfather had the signs made out at the Bridge Works, one for each of us. Grandmother and Grandfather Wiles would be up from Indianapolis, and Aunt Wilmina and Uncle Jervis would come over from Wilmington, Ohio. So there would be a great many people and lots of presents. And when all the people were there, and the presents were on the chairs, Grandfather would say,

"Lottie, I think we are ready."

And Mother (I looked up into her face again) would go to the piano, and play Grandfather's hymn, *For He cometh, For He cometh*. And Harris would fling open the folding doors into the library, and we would march in—all of us— singing Grandfather's hymn. And Harris and Erna would come from the kitchen and sing, too, with all their might. They would sing "in their beauty, bright gems for His crown." Somebody would call to Mother to come now, and get her presents, and she would hurry across the library. She would have to open the first present, because she was the first daughter-in-law. And she would squeal and dance over it, and be so funny. And everyone else would be laughing when they started to open theirs.

We were climbing our front steps; Mother stopped at the top.

"It will not be quite the same," she said, "but I think it will be the very nicest Christmas of all. And we *will* sing, I think, Grandfather's hymn."

Chapter Fourteen

Out at the playhouse we were making things again—stringing cranberries and popcorn, fashioning stars out of gold paper and chains of colored paper loops. I didn't care for it any more than I had cared for it at Miss Zenobia Stewart's kindergarten in the Universalist Church. But I began to accept it philosophically as an integral, if unpleasant, part of Christmas. I would have accepted almost anything, I think, so long as it did lead up to Christmas.

Sitting at the work table one morning, I decided, as I rubbed the paste on my fingers into dirty white crumbs, that Christmas was the best of all. Fourth of July was fun and beautiful to see, but scary. Hallowe'en was fun, too, but uncomfortable in a costume. Thanksgiving was good, but there wasn't really much to it when you got right down to what there was—the drumstick of the turkey, or, if you wanted, the wishbone. After that it was all over. Mr. Hinkley and the ice cream you couldn't really compare with any of those days; that was something extra and different. So leaving that out, Christmas was certainly the best.

Miss Richey said we could put away the tree decorations, and work on our Christmas presents. Next morning there would be a fresh batch of colored paper, cut out into strips, waiting to be pasted. But at least it was over for the day. I was the first one back at the table, my hands washed, my paper put away, waiting for Miss Richey to put in front of me the box which held my gifts in the making. The one for

244

Daddy was to be a bag of raffia to hold a ball of twine, for Mother a package of shaving paper with a cardboard cover hand-painted by me. Miss Richey had been trying to persuade me to reverse them, but I was adamant. I felt I knew, after all, what my own parents would like. My Father liked collecting string almost better than anything; he saved every piece of it that came into the house. I was never allowed to cut a knot, no matter how exciting the package that it tied. I had, therefore, supposed that string came only in small pieces to be rolled up and saved. When I had found out that you could get a whole ball of twine of the same kind and color, and make a mesh bag of raffia for it, with a string handle to hook on a nail on the wall, I knew that it would make the best present Daddy had ever had.

I was equally confident about the one for Mother. Except for music, the things that she liked the best of all were books and pictures. Miss Richey said that this book of papers was to wipe razors on, but I had seen Mother write on all kinds of paper. She would love the thinness of this. She could even put it over pictures and trace them for herself. The outside cover would be another picture which I would paint. Mother was teaching me about painters. She said that I would grow up to like pictures, she hoped, as much as she did. I felt confident, too, that I was carrying out her hopes for me, because I did already love one particular picture about as much as anything I had ever seen. I was going to try to repeat it on this shaving book.

The painting had come to Muncie in the Spring, with a collection. The collection was called "The Annual Exhibit of American Painters," and referred to as "The Carnegie Show."

This was the first time such an exhibition had come to Muncie, and the whole town turned out to see it. The Art League was running the show. Mother was the president of the Art League, and it was she who persuaded the schools to bring their classes to see the pictures, and the children to bring pennies to buy one to be hung in the Public Library. She gave a talk every day while the exhibit was going on, telling the children about the pictures and about the men who painted them. I was there every day, too, learning from her, she hoped, to identify painters—to distinguish Winslow Homer's "Ocean" from Childe Hassam's or Paul Dougherty's. For this reason, I was the gratified object of considerable attention on the part of the grown-up visitors. They said it was wonderful what taste Lottie was shaping in Emily.

They asked, therefore, what my favorite picture was. I had had no hesitation in selecting it. I chose it entirely by myself, and I was only too eager to show it to anyone who would allow me. It hung in a remote and dark corner, perhaps intentionally. I could bring people through the door, and around to it unexpectedly. I would say *"There,"* and wait for the gasp of pleasure which I was sure it would bring. Nearly everybody did gasp, too, immediately.

The focal point of the picture was a woman sitting at a very large piano. A little girl was standing close beside, leaning against her. There was music on the piano and the woman was playing. Close by, a tall lamp shed such a light that the mother and child had a sort of halo and cloud of rosy effulgence around them. The piano was close to long French windows. Through them you could also see the light from the lamp. It must have been a very powerful bulb. It shone on a snow-covered landscape turning it a brilliant pink—almost a cerise—a thrilling color, I thought.

The title of the picture was the best of all. My catalogue opened to it from constant pressure there. I would point out the printing with tremulous pride at such a beautiful idea. "Just a Song at Twilight," it was called. The people to whom I showed my favorite almost invariably asked if it were Mother's too, and I had to answer that I wasn't quite sure.

As far as my Christmas present was concerned I was confident that even if that had *not* been her favorite picture, she would certainly be more pleased with my reproduction of it than with a raffia bag to hold string.

I was making a horse and cart of wood for Grandmother Kimbrough. The horse was drawn on the wood; all I had to do was to color it. There were extra pieces to be pasted on the outline of the cart, which would make a real receptacle. This was for matches. You hung the whole thing on the wall, and it was called a plaque, Miss Richey said. Her ideas and mine did not seem to agree at all. She thought the cart of matches more suitable for Grandfather. But Grandmother, I pointed out to her patiently, was the one who liked horses.

For Grandfather, I was winding over a piece of cardboard a great deal of yarn of different colors. When it was finished it would make a ball. You snipped the ends so that the whole was very fluffy. There was a loop, also, by which you could hang this up. Miss Richey explained that this would be nice for a very small child who liked to look at bright colors. But I told her carefully that Grandfather liked bright colors very much, and would enjoy hanging this where he could look at it while he was shaving.

Grandmother Wiles was to have a receptacle for matches, too, to put on the mantel in the big bedroom in her house in Indianapolis, so that she would always have a match handy for lighting the gas log.

Grandfather Wiles was to have a calendar with a picture pasted on it. I would cut out and paste on the picture myself. Grandfather Wiles was very particular about what day it was, and what time. He liked everything to be on time and orderly. Grandmother Wiles wasn't interested in that at all, so of course his present would not have done for her. It would be exactly right for him.

Braiding the long strands of raffia for the twine holder by

backing away from the ends securely fastened to the work
table by a large black pin, I ruminated on my own aspira-
tions for Christmas: a baby doll with clothes that could be
taken off (I wanted no repetition of that dreadful Josephine);
an English pram for it, and a bicycle. If they were going to
fuss about my not being old enough for that, I would com-
promise on a new tricycle. The old one and I had come to a
parting of the ways against a tree trunk late in the Summer.
The machine, less hardy than I, had been twisted beyond
repair. It was a sissy tricycle, anyway, a girl's and not even
a boy's. It had two big wheels behind, with the seat between.
A little wheel was out in front, the steering bar running back
from that to the seat. I would have preferred a boy's bicycle,
with handlebars, and a rod in the back where an extra person could stand. But I was willing to be generous about any
vehicle provided. A persistent nagging worry interrupted my
happy reflections on Christmas bounty. I could not keep it
away for long these days. Mother had said that this Christmas would be different. Going home from the big house the
night Grandfather had told me about Harris, she had said
that this would be a different Christmas.

I finished one braid of raffia. Miss Richey took the pin out
of it, stuck it into some fresh strands, and I started a new
one. I wondered if Mother had meant there would be a surprise. I liked surprises, but if there was one thing I did *not*
like it was having something to which I was accustomed become different. Above all things, Christmas. So far, there had
been nothing out of the ordinary at home. We had begun
singing the Christmas songs in the evening before I went to
bed—*Holy Night,* and *We Three Kings,* and Mother's favorite of all—the Martin Luther one, she called it—*Away in a
Manger, No Crib for His Bed.* She loved that song as much
as Grandfather loved *For He Cometh, For He Cometh.*
She thought, she said, it was the loveliest hymn for children

that had ever been written, and we always sang both verses.

She was sewing, too, in the evenings—covering up her work when I came into the sitting room in my sleeping suit to say good night. So I was fairly sure of one item on my list —my baby doll—and she was making clothes for it.

I had been over to Mr. Cassidy's fence again and again, checking my recordings there. Everything pointed to a good episode ahead—that must be Christmas. And certainly it would not be a good episode if it were different.

Miss Richey told us it was time to go over to the stair landing in the house to rehearse for the Christmas entertainment. We put away our present-making and trooped across the porch into the house. Mrs. Ball leaned over the railing upstairs to ask how we were coming on. Miss Richey said she thought it was going to be a lovely party, but that we needed some extra rehearsals. She asked if Mrs. Ball would mind if we had one at the regular school hour, at nine o'clock, on the morning of the entertainment, the 21st of December. The grown-ups wouldn't arrive for the party until eleven. Mrs. Ball said certainly, that would be lovely.

We went over the play first. I was only one of the Wise Men, just the middle one, too. So I wasn't so interested in the play as in the songs. I was King Wenceslaus in one of those, and that seemed to me the high spot in the entertainment. I sang by myself. The page, who was the other person in it, sang, too—but after me. Mother would like the entertainment, I thought, especially the King Wenceslaus.

It was fun to do things for Mother; she got so excited about them, not just saying, "That's very nice, dear," the way some mothers did, but singing and whirling you around when something pleased her. She could get cross suddenly, too, which kept you on the lookout always. But she made you feel breathless all the time, as if something were going to happen any minute. And when you were with her, something could.

She had a special way of saying things, too. When we would come to this entertainment, on the 21st of December, I knew she would whisper to me before I left her to take my place with the other children,

"With your shield, or on it, Emily. Remember that."

She always said it when I was going to do anything special. It meant that she would rather have me not do it at all than to forget the words; but it was a different way of saying it than some mothers used, I was sure.

There were so many different things about Mother that it was hard to think how Christmas, as she had said it would be, *could* be more different than she was.

When I got home from school that day, I asked her again about the Christmas being different this year. Why had she said it would be? She was reading, all curled up on one end of the couch in the sitting room. I lay down on my stomach beside the fire; then I sat in the big green velvet armchair where Grandmother Wiles always rocked me, and then I went over on the couch with Mother while we talked.

She told me a great many things that day. She said I mustn't be disturbed about things being different. That we mustn't hold on to things just because we were used to them.

"Open your casements wide."

By that she meant, she explained, to pretend to open my windows, and look out to see what was all around; to let things from outside come in, and welcome them, no matter how strange they might seem. Then she laughed, and said,

"I was misquoting, you know. Don't ever do that."

I let that go.

When she was a little girl, she said, she lived in Indianapolis. I knew that. Then when she grew up and was married to Daddy, she came here to Muncie. And that was very different, very, very different. She had liked especially music, and books, and sports—sports meant playing games. I knew about those. I myself liked to play with the rosettes she had won as prizes in fencing. And Daddy had told me lots of times a story about it. I loved to hear it, although it was very scarey.

She would have lost her life, the story began, if she hadn't had strong arms from fencing and tennis. She had been spending the Christmas holiday with some cousins in Sioux City. She was about nineteen years old, then. A crowd of young people came to the station to see her off when she started home. They had stood laughing and chattering on the platform. It was bitterly cold, and icy underfoot, but they didn't mind it—stamping up and down to keep warm, and talking until the very last minute. Just as the conductor up ahead called "All aboard!" Mother jumped onto the lower step of the car, and the train pulled out. The door was locked. The porter stood inside, working and working to get it open, and making awful faces of fright. He ought to have pulled the emergency cord, but he didn't. He lost his head; he just stood there trembling at the mouth and making faces. The thing he was so frightened about happened almost at once. The train, pulling out of the station, went across a high bridge over the river. There wouldn't have been a chance of Mother's being saved if she had fallen. She didn't fall, although the step was so icy that she couldn't keep her feet on it. But her arms (especially her right one) were so strong from playing tennis and fencing that she held on across the bridge, swinging out over that terrible frozen river far, far below. Somebody did pull an emergency cord when they reached the other side of the bridge and the train stopped. Mother dropped to the ground completely unhurt, ran up to the door at the other end of the car, and climbed aboard safely.

I told her that I knew about that story and she smiled. She had been scared, she admitted, but it was exciting, too. Then, when she had come to Muncie, she went on, she found people knew a great deal about sewing and cooking and keeping house, and they liked those things. They didn't, many of them, like sports. She didn't know anything about their likes and she thought at first they would be very dull. "You see," she said, "they were different." But they weren't dull. It was fun to learn about sewing, cooking, and such things from Grandmother Kimbrough while she and Daddy lived in the big house before I was born. And then she found other people, too, who did like the things she liked. Together they began to read books they had always meant to read and had never gotten to. So they made a club, and called it "The Dante Class" because that was the name of the writer whose books they had read first.

And then they started a Conversation Club, where they met to discuss—and read papers the members wrote on—things that were interesting. And an Art League, where they learned and talked about pictures. I knew about all of those clubs; they often met at our house. One time Mother had gone to a party of "The Dante Class," dressed up in my father's dress suit, which seemed shameful to me. They had called a photograph of the party "The Houseboat on the Styx."

Now, she said, she wouldn't go back to the other time before she was married, in Indianapolis, for anything in the world. This was the place she loved, and this was the way she loved things to be. They were different. "So," she said, "if something would be different for me, I would be pleased about it, wouldn't I? And run to meet it, and not turn away from it?" I said solemnly, because she had become very grave, that I would promise her to go out and meet it. Only, I added, I should like to know what the special difference was to be.

She lay still a minute on the couch, looking across me into the fire. And then she said that perhaps she was wrong not to tell me. Parents weren't always right, she said. And she wished that there were some way for children to understand that parents were young, too, and often troubled. I didn't understand that, but she went on. So she and Daddy had decided *not* to tell me what the different thing was going to be, but let it be a surprise, because they were counting on how much I loved surprises.

I was satisfied. Certainly there were few things I liked better than a surprise—corn on the cob, maybe, and staying up after dark. They were the only things I could think of. I knew a surprise about her, too, I said, and I did hope I wasn't going to tell it. I was under a heavy strain, because Daddy had come into my room only the night before, when I was in bed, and told me a whopping surprise. He had made a secret with me that not another person knew except Zoe.

He wanted me to help him, he had said. I was the only person who could. It would be quite a responsibility. Did I think I could promise to do that, and keep it a secret? I put my right hand on my heart, my left hand up in the air, and nodded three times. Well, he said, he would tell me.

He had gone to Mr. Myers that very day. Mr. Myers owned the jewelry store in Muncie. Daddy asked if Mr. Myers would allow him to put in the electric lights for his new store—Daddy called it "do the wiring." And he had asked if in return he might have a piece of jewelry for Mother for Christmas. He explained that anyone would be paid for doing a job like that, but that he wanted a Christmas present for Mother instead. Running the Electric Light Plant, he said he had learned how to do wiring. He could do it evenings after he got through at the Plant. Mr. Myers said he would be glad to have Daddy do it. And he had let Daddy pick out right then the present he would work for and let him bring it home.

Daddy brought out a little dark red velvet box, and showed it to me very secretly—the lid snapped open on a spring. Inside, pinned to a white satin lining, was a gold pin in the shape of a star, but the star was made of pearls with a little diamond—Daddy said—at each tip. The diamonds glistened like icicles in the sun, and the pearls looked soft and smooth. I thought it was the most beautiful thing I had ever seen. Daddy said he thought it almost was for him, too. When he had closed the case he explained why I had to help with the secret—because Mother wasn't to worry about his coming home very late. I was to stay with her and ask her to sing songs with me or read to me; then she wouldn't notice that it was getting late and wouldn't be anxious. She would be occupied until supper time, and then Zoe would tell her that Daddy had telephoned that he would have to stay on at the Plant; they were having trouble with the generator. Would I do that? Of course I said I would.

Remembering it now, talking with Mother, I thought I could not keep from telling her, and that I should burst with the pleasure of not telling her. Bursting, too, to think that in just a little while, as soon as it was later in the afternoon, I would coax her to read and play music with me—knowing all the time that it was acting out a secret.

I did act it out on that evening and those that followed, and I kept it a secret. *Every* evening we read out of one of my favorite books, *The Rabbit's Ransom* or *Captain January*, skipping the ending which was disastrously sad. After the reading, Mother played the songs I knew. I learned others, too, from the *Father Goose Rhymes* book—that was the name of it, not *Mother Goose*. It had the wonderful acting and marching song in it:

> "Captain Bing was a pirate king,
> Who sailed the broad seas o'er."

And all the time I knew, and Mother didn't, that Daddy was putting in the electric lights at Mr. Myers' jewelry store.

Sometimes we walked, Mother and I, to the big house, where the bustle was already starting for Christmas. Grandmother always cleaned house from the attic to the cellar before every holiday, like Easter or Thanksgiving and especially Christmas. Those were extra and had nothing to do with the regular times of Spring and Fall house-cleaning. Chris was coming extra days to clean, and the house was shining. Grandfather said that when he put down his newspaper it smelled of Gold Dust by the time he picked it up. Erna was making mince-meat and fruit cake, and the smell from the kitchen was heavy.

One of the days when we went up to see them, Mother sat talking in the den with Grandfather and Great-grandmother Curry. Grandmother beckoned, and took me upstairs to the guest room. She asked if I would like to see a surprise, and could I keep it a secret. I felt that to know two surprises and to keep two secrets would tax me beyond my capacity. Yet to be trusted like this, twice, made me giddy with pride. I could only nod emphatically.

Grandmother pulled three dress boxes out from under the bed. I knew, she reminded me, that she always gave her daughters-in-law a joke present. This year she thought she had an especially good one, but I wasn't to tell anybody. Again I nodded.

She had heard Aunt Helen say that she would like an embroidered French shirtwaist for Christmas. That had given Grandmother the idea. So she had gotten these boxes from a pile she kept stored on the third floor, and had taken some frumpy lace curtains which she never liked, stuffed them with tissue paper, and puffed them all up in the box, so that they looked exactly like shirtwaists. Tucked into the front of each one, she showed me, was going to be an envelope with a check in it. That meant money. So Aunt Helen could pick out whatever shirtwaist she wanted, and the other daughters-in-law could buy whatever they liked. But they wouldn't see the check for a while, and would think that Grandmother had picked out these awful waists for them.

I thought it was the best surprise joke I had ever seen. When I came downstairs again to go home with Mother, I knew, I told myself, what being different was, because to know two things about Mother which she didn't know herself was certainly making me very different indeed.

The night before the school entertainment I thought I would never go to sleep. All the parents would be there. And, except for that moment of obscurity as the middle Wise Man, I would be doing a great deal in the entertainment. Furthermore, there would be real presents under the tree this year. The box for the poor children was separate and already prepared. The ones in view, though mysteriously wrapped, would all be for us children. So it was just like two Christmases. Zoe and I talked about it while I got ready for bed, and she agreed that it would be hard for me to sleep, but I must just try. I said that Mother and Daddy would certainly be excited about the presents I was making, and excited about the entertainment, too. She said they would, she knew, and left me with the dimmer glowing in the hall, to drift off in a haze of the sights and smell and jingle bell sounds of Christmas.

There were other sounds that woke me sometime in the night—quick footsteps as if someone were running, and people talking, and someone at the telephone. I called and called Zoe, but she didn't come. I thought of getting up to see what was the matter, but my room was very cold, my bed warm, and I only half awake. I listened to the sounds again, and then slid off once more to sleep.

The next morning I heard about the cause of the disturbance, but I had no chance to tell anyone about it until we reached the school. Daddy evidently told Miss Richey when she came for me, because she seemed to know about it when I started to tell her. When we came onto the landing, however, for our morning exercises, she said to Mrs. Ball, as soon as we had sung *Good morning to you,*

"Emily has something to tell you, I think, Mrs. Ball."

I was surprised and very pleased. This was a chance to do something, even before the regular entertainment—something all by myself—a story to tell, and I was bursting to tell it.

"Well," I began, looking around at all the other children to make sure that they were with me in my excitement, "I did have something happen this morning."

"Yes, dear," Mrs. Ball said, from over the balcony. She didn't sound very interested. I felt sure, however, that she would be when she really heard what it was.

"Well," I began again, "this morning I ate breakfast all by myself at the table, and"—I paused, because the real dénouement was coming—"I didn't have cream of wheat, I didn't have oatmeal; I had a whole cake of shredded wheat hot, and I crunched it in my hands myself."

There, it was out. The breath-taking event. I laughed to myself about Mother's surprise for me and things being different, and getting used to them.

I loved its being different; I didn't want it to go on the same way day after day, with a dish of cream of wheat or oatmeal set down in front of me, all fixed. One morning with butter on it, the next morning with cream. I didn't always want to sit at the table with Mother and Daddy. I liked sitting alone. Most of all I liked, and would remember always, I knew, the feel of the hot shredded wheat crunching under my hand. I looked around; my audience seemed not to be spellbound by the magic of this change. Mrs. Ball was turning to go away, after only a little smile. Miss Richey spoke again,

"Tell Mrs. Ball," she said, "why you had breakfast alone. What else happened this morning?"

"Oh," I said. If asked, I would oblige with the details. "I expect it was because I had a baby brother early this morning. And Zoe said everyone was busy."

Mrs. Ball stood stock still—looked over my head at Miss Richey.

"Lottie?" she asked. Miss Richey nodded, I guess.

"Was everything all right? It's very early."

"I know. Emily was to go to Indianapolis, of course."

Mrs. Ball repeated, "Is everything all right?"

"Wonderful," Miss Richey said.

They talked so fast over me I could hardly hear what they were saying, and I wasn't listening particularly. I was still thinking about the shredded wheat.

Suddenly what they were saying, and what I had said, did reach down to me. I had a baby brother. That was what was really different. It wasn't the breakfast food.

There would be someone else in the house all the time, doing things like me. And Mother had known there would be. But she had decided to make it a surprise.

Mrs. Ball and Miss Richey were talking across to each other over my head. Something about the first grandson in the family. I didn't bother to listen. There wouldn't ever again be just Mother and Daddy and Zoe and me. It wouldn't be just a different *Christmas*. It would always be different. Perhaps Mother wouldn't even come to the entertainment that morning—wouldn't *hear* me sing King Wenceslaus.

I was afraid that I was going to cry, right there on the landing with Mrs. Ball, Miss Richey and all the children looking.

I put my tongue between my teeth to hold back the crying. That is, I started to. Fortunately I remembered just in time *not* to put my tongue there. I remembered, too, exultantly, that *I* had something different to tell Mother, myself —something I knew was going to happen, but that would be a surprise to her. It was like her knowing about my brother and keeping it a surprise for me.

This very morning, on the way out to school, I had lost an upper middle front tooth. I had waggled it out while I was riding on the trolley, and had gotten blood on the floor but not on me. The week before, when it was first loose, Uncle Frank had told me that if, when it came out, I kept my tongue away from the hole, a miracle would happen. He said what the miracle would be, but I had kept it secret. I had never dreamed that anything so beautiful could happen to me, and I had made up my mind instantly, to guard my tongue day and night, in order to bring this about. A string tied around it at night, the end held in my hand, would protect the hole while I slept. And when this miracle appeared, it would stay forever, just like a baby brother.

I broke into Mrs. Ball's and Miss Richey's conversation. I urged the children to listen, too.

This was my moment. I would reveal my surprise, just like Mother.

"I'm going to have," I announced my triumph simply, "something more different than a baby brother. It will be"— I paused, choked up by the beauty of the vista—"a front tooth of solid gold."

Chapter Fifteen

The Christmas entertainment was over. Mother hadn't come. Neither, to my astonishment, had Daddy. When the entertainment began, and I realized that they weren't there, I felt suddenly as if I were in a strange place and didn't know anybody there. But afterwards, when the singing was over, all the parents crowded around me, so that I felt familiar again. They wanted to know about my baby brother and about Mother, but they had liked King Wenceslaus very much, too, they said; and I told them about my gold tooth. I decided not to keep it a secret any longer. Everyone was very interested. I decided to tell Mother, too, as soon as I got home, and not keep it from her.

Miss Richey dropped me at my house, earlier than usual, but she called me back to say again to be sure to give Mother her love, and to hug the baby for her. I said yes, I would, but I was in a hurry to get in. I ran up the front steps and pushed open the front door, which was heavy.

The whole family was in the sitting room—Grandfather, Grandmother, Aunt Helen, Uncle Frank, Aunt Huda, Uncle Lloyd, even Grandfather's brother, Uncle Jervis, and Aunt Wilmina from Wilmington, Ohio. I knew they would come over for Christmas, but I didn't expect them so soon. I was very excited. It was like a party, almost like Christmas itself, only it was at our house. They were all talking at once. It was so festive. I said:

"Hello, everybody. I'm home."

Nobody said anything to me. They went on talking. I waited a minute, but they didn't seem to see me. Once before it had been like that, the time Grandfather had bought his automobile, and I had followed Daddy and Mother up the street to see what was happening. They hadn't noticed me

"Hello, everybody, I'm home."

for a long time that evening. But there was certainly no automobile here. I decided to push through all of them, go to my own room, find Zoe, and get her to tell what Grandfather had bought now. I squeezed past Uncle Lloyd and Aunt Wilmina, who were talking together; edged around Uncle Lloyd and Grandmother, and was almost at the door to Grandmother Wiles' guest room, with my room beyond it, when Grandfather did notice me.

"Oh, Emily," he said, "I didn't see you. Mustn't go in there. Out of the way, dear, and be very quiet."

My Grandfather himself said that, and in a booming voice besides. He always talked with a booming sound, but he had never in my life said "Out of the way dear" to me. He went on talking, as if he hadn't seen me.

"*Little* Charles, little *Charles*. Charles, the second. Wonderful! Wonderful! Gives me a fine feeling, that does, Jervis."

Grandmother said,

"Hush, Charles. Not so loud. You'll disturb her. And you know she's going to call him Wiles. Wiles Kimbrough, to keep her family name."

"I am not for a moment," Grandfather told her, "questioning what Lottie is going to call him. I am only saying what *I* am going to call him. For me, he will be Charles, the second."

Aunt Huda asked him why he hadn't named one of his boys Charles, since it meant so much to him.

"Never thought of it," he told her. "Never knew it *would* mean so much to me."

The door from Grandmother Wiles' guest room opened. Grandmother Wiles herself stood there, with Grandfather Wiles and Daddy just behind her. I started to run to her and shriek. This *was* a surprise. But she looked as if she had been crying and that embarrassed me. I hung back. Grandfather went over to her and started to lead her, in a very courtly way, to the green velvet rocker, where she had always sat with me before this, to tell me stories. He was saying as they walked toward it,

"Mrs. Wiles, I was just saying that I have never felt so proud as I feel on this day, to have my first grandson, and to have him a second Charles will fill my cup. If you would permit me to share his name with you?"

Grandmother nodded her head graciously, and sat down in the green velvet chair.

"I should be happy to," she said, "and proud. Charles Wiles is, I think, a good combination."

That would be another surprise to tell Mother, except that surprises seemed to have lost their zest. Daddy had gone back into the guest room immediately. He didn't see me either.

I slipped out the side door. Once, long ago, last Spring, I had slipped out that door, and hidden behind the syringa bushes to see what was going on. But the syringa bushes were heavy now with snow, and I *knew* what was going on.

I wandered into the back yard. The hole was still there in the shingle on the house where they had cut out the picture of Mother, which the burglar had pasted there. I went over to my swing, brushed off the snow absent-mindedly, and began to swing back and forth, back and forth. I could, I supposed, go over to see Mitchell Woodbury, without even asking. Nobody would even pay any attention. But I didn't seem to want to much. I could probably lie down in the snow and make an angel and get wet, without anybody minding. But I didn't seem to want to. I dragged my feet on the ground and scraped off the snow. I had on my heavy arctics and they made wide tracks. I went on swinging, back and forth, back and forth, thinking about things that were different, and about surprises.

"Open your casement wide," Mother had said. And I thought about Christmas coming, and how the other Christmases had been as I swung back and forth, back and forth.

Zoe was calling me. I could hear her around on the front porch, and then from up the street past the Vatets'.

"Emily, Emileee!"

I didn't bother to answer her. I was thinking about the Bice.

The Bice lived somewhere outside of town in tents. They were gypsies, people said. How people knew that their name was Bice, or that Bice could be enough of a name for so many of them had always puzzled me. I never saw anyone speak to them. They came to town about once a week in a canvas-covered wagon, with swarms of children peeking around its flaps. A blind man always walked behind the wagon, holding on to it with one hand. Two or three dogs trotted along with him, too. All the Bice and the dogs were thin, with black hair and very, very dirty. I hadn't often seen any women with them. Once in a great while one would sit on the seat beside the driver, with a baby in her arms. I never saw any of them talk even to each other. I didn't know whether they could talk or not, and if they could, whether it would be the same language that we used. But I did know that they took children—sometimes babies, but not always. Lots of times, people said for a fact, they took children who wandered away from home.

I was wondering if the Bice would pick you up wherever you wandered or if it had to be in a special direction toward their tents. I didn't know where those were, but probably I could ask. When I had been displeased and unhappy at the Balls' about cleaning my rubbers, I had set out for home. I had always gone home when I didn't like it where I was. But I was at home and I didn't like it where I was. It was hard to think of where to go *from* there.

Something *Zoe* was saying caught my attention. She had

stopped calling my name. She must have gone around to the Woodburys' back door.

"Is Emily here? I can't find the child. Her mother is asking and asking for her."

I almost fell down I ran so fast. Up the back steps, through the kitchen, across the back hall where the telephone hung on the wall, and through my bathroom. The door of the bathroom closet was open. Just inside was the dirty clothes basket where I prayed. But I hadn't had time to pray about this. It had happened so suddenly, and just now they hadn't—all the family out in front—let me in to do any praying. I was at the door to my own room, looking in.

Mother was in my bed. It was higher than when I slept in it because there were several bricks under each leg. I looked and looked at them.

A minute before I had been scrambling to get to her. Now I didn't want to come any nearer. I didn't feel comfortable about looking at Mother. I didn't feel well acquainted with her, and it was not because she was lying in bed, though I wasn't used to that. Perhaps *she* was different, but I couldn't run to meet her until I was sure, and if she really *were* different, I didn't seem to want to. I kept on looking at the legs of the bed.

"Ommy," she said—that was my baby name, and hadn't been used for a long time—"the something different is over there by the fireplace. It's a baby brother. Go over and look."

She didn't say come to her. She knew I didn't want to. My heart choked me suddenly. I walked over to the fireplace. She kept on talking.

"They moved me down here this morning. It's handier for Mrs. Lothan to be near the kitchen. Will you sleep upstairs next door to Daddy to take care of him?"

I stood looking down at the baby in the crib. He didn't seem very much to look at. Smaller than I had thought he would be—not much bigger than my baby doll. He was pinker. He didn't have so much hair. He was more wrinkled. My doll had only two creases in its neck.

The crib had always been kept up at the big house. It was the one Daddy had slept in when he was a baby. Grandmother Kimbrough let me rock my dolls in it when I had them there on a visit. Now this baby was asleep in the crib.

Mother said, "Christmas is going to be just the same, Ommy, up at the big house. Only I have to stay here in bed for a little while."

She wouldn't be there to get her surprise make-believe shirtwaist from Grandmother. She wouldn't get her beautiful pin that was Daddy's surprise for her. He was still working for it every night, late, putting in the lights at Mr. Myers' store. And *my* book of shaving papers for her.

"Will you and Daddy bring me my presents from the big house, after you've had yours, and help me open them? And then everybody is coming back here to our own house for Christmas dinner. The very first time in your own house. But at the big house, sing loud *For He cometh, For He cometh*. Uncle Frank will play it on the piano. And Ommy —all His jewels, precious jewels, are the little children, you know, His loved and His own. We have a new one for Him."

The baby in the crib opened his eyes. They were blue. He jerked his hand up in the air. It was shut tight in a fist.

"Slip your finger down through his fist," Mother said.

I put my hand to my mouth and slowly pulled off my mitten between my teeth. My mittens were attached to a cord which went through the sleeves of my coat, so I let this one dangle. I slipped my first finger into his fist, and the baby held it as tight as I could squeeze hickory nuts in my hand to crack. I thought that perhaps, later, when he walked around with me, he would hold my hand like that, and I would say to people,

"This is my baby brother."

I looked quickly across at Mother for the first time. She was smiling at me, and I smiled back.

Mrs. Lothan came bustling into the room. She was the nurse. Everybody in Muncie always had her. She was tall and rather fat; "comfortable" people always said.

She told me I must run along. Zoe was looking everywhere for me, and Mother must rest. I was the only one except Daddy and Grandmother Wiles who had seen her. Nobody else was going to that day. I'd better run into the front room and tell all the family about the baby, because they wouldn't see him. She talked fast.

I went past Mother's bed, but I didn't go up to it. I didn't want to tell Mother about the Bice, and if I had gone over to her I would have had to. So I just kept on saying nothing and went out of the room to the front of the house.

The door to the bathroom closet was still open. I hurried in and closed the door behind me. Nobody saw me crawl way down into the dirty clothes basket to tell God and Jesus about the surprise for Them. I thought They would like it, but suddenly I was crying. I cried and cried and cried. I didn't know why.

Then I went out the back way again. Zoe wasn't anywhere around. I sat in my swing again. The tracks were still there from my arctics. I made them bigger and thought about how I would show my little brother to people, while he would be holding my finger tight. I swung back and forth, back and forth, holding my feet up in a little while, so that they wouldn't scrape any more. I swung very high and then I didn't try any more. I let the swing slow down by itself. I was thinking about all the family and my Grandfather in the sitting room in the house, and me out there by myself.

"Lettin' the old cat die," we call that kind of swinging in Indiana.

Books by Emily Kimbrough

EMILY KIMBROUGH, born in Muncie at the turn of the century, enjoyed literary success as a magazine writer and later as the author of best-selling novels such as *We Followed Our Hearts to Hollywood* and *Innocents from Indiana*. Her most successful novel was *Our Hearts Were Young and Gay*, written in collaboration with her girlhood friend Cornelia Otis Skinner.